WATER IN THE DESERT,
FIRE IN THE NIGHT

WATER IN THE DESERT, FIRE IN THE NIGHT

GETHAN DICK

First published in 2025 by Tramp Press
www.tramppress.com
Copyright © Gethan Dick, 2025

No part of this publication may be reproduced
in any form or by any means without the prior
written permission of the publisher.

All characters in this publication are fictitious,
and any resemblances to real persons, living or
dead, are purely coincidental.

All rights reserved.

A CIP record for this title is available
from the British Library.

1 3 5 7 9 8 6 4 2

Tramp Press gratefully acknowledges the
financial assistance of the Arts Council.

Trade Paperback ISBN 978-1-915290-16-8
eBook ISBN 978-1-915290-17-5

Thank you for supporting independent publishing.

Set in Perpetua by Marsha Swan
Printed by L&C Printing Group, Poland

Once, a long time ago, in London, I was coming up to the Elephant and Castle roundabout and it must've been a water main that had burst. It had come up through the tarmac, cracked it open, and cut a gully down the road. Underneath the tarmac, yellow clay banks, and through the bright, fast-running water you could see white quartz pebbles being washed clean, rattling as they went like in any stream bed. I'm not telling you this to say I saw it coming, but that tarmac was only ever just a skin. Underneath, it was always soil all the way down to the bedrock, and bedrock all the way down to the core. You've got to see that we're outweighed, outnumbered by all that.

And there were some times when I'd see it clear as day waiting to come back, the river at Bournevale, the smooth grey bark and black buds reflected in the water at Ashlake, the ring of stones in the grass at Wellfield, the hills dipping down along Valley, the water bubbling through the rocks at Springfield, the badgers at Brockwell, the heronry, or even, coming by there in the dark and suggestible, the hunter, at Herne Hill, the bulrushes and kingcups along the banks at the Effra, the cattle gathered around Stockwell, and on, and on.

And like I said, I'm not telling you this to say I saw it coming. After something happens everybody wants to say they told everyone it was going to, they saw it from way off, they know the moment they knew exactly when it was going to happen, they probably even know when they picked their pointy finger off that final pint and poked it at your face and told *you* it was going to happen. They're liars. No fucker saw this coming. I didn't see it coming even after it had happened. But it was coming, nonetheless.

And it's no help to try to sort cause from effect, to get caught in the loops of 'if this, if that', would things have been different or would it all have turned out the same but a year, a decade, a generation later? In the end, you are where you are. Because maybe it's like love: that there's a moment, a moment as small as when you're there trying to climb over some railings, and you're both laughing so hard you can't keep your eyes open, and something snags on one of the spikes and you're trying to say, 'Wait . . .' But the laughter's like a hammer in your belly and the words are underneath it and then there's a rip and a thud and the laughter's getting higher and higher pitched as your lungs empty out and it'll be bruises and mending but you're over. And then empty, ringing air as you both gasp for breath at the same time, then the laughter starts again. And it's not until years afterwards that you know that that was it: the moment after which no other future was possible.

Though obviously you don't know what that future's going to be. It's only by thinking very, very small that we carry on imagining we know what the future holds, and even then, life will get in the way. And like I said, almost all the things people reckon they say about the future, you only hear them after that future's already become the past. So, to be straight: I didn't see it coming, I don't know why it happened, and I don't know what's going to happen.

That makes me different to most of the people I've talked to about it, which, to be fair, is not that many. There was me and Sarah and Pressure Drop and Adi and, for a bit, Joy and Trevor, in the Arches – a set of converted railway arches on a cul-de-sac and an amazing place to hide. When we'd arrived in the dark the night before, I'd had no idea how amazing, beyond the heavy doors and a lot of very solid wall all around. The first night there we all huddled in Arch one, the United Kingdom of Divine Love Church. They had a carpet, along with cushions and blankets. We made nests and hid in them. Nobody wanted to stay up making guesses about the noises outside.

I must have slept. 'Must have' slept, as if there's some kind of shame in it, so, fine, I didn't 'must have' slept. I just slept. I was tired, it was night, I've always had a knack for it. No bed too uncomfortable, no bus too rattly, no house party too noisy. It's all changed now obviously, but back then I could've slept through the end of the world, and some would say that in fact, night after night, I did. People who can't sleep think people who can are thoughtless or simple or haven't understood the enormity of the situation. Actually, it's just like any other survival instinct – some people are better at it than others. Some are better at running, some at fighting, some can go for ages without food, some immediately cop off with the nearest alpha male, some sleep. And that first morning in the Arches it was pretty clear that only me and Pressure Drop had, and he'd been weed assisted.

It was quiet outside when I opened my eyes. I didn't move. The others were talking. There were shadows moving on the wall behind where the pulpit was – though there wasn't actually enough light to cast a shadow and 'pulpit' is too grand a word, 'lectern' maybe, or just one of those angled things that you sometimes saw at a restaurant with a menu taped to it. The others were trying to decide whether to look outside. They'd been trying to decide for a while.

Adi was saying, 'No, no, no, no, no – for a start, I opened this place up, and maybe it doesn't matter but that makes me responsible – not for you guys, but for what's in here, and I don't want that on my head right now.' He was always like that, proper, full of thoughts about how things ought to be done and how the things that had been done would be explained when the people in charge got back in charge. Now it just looks sweet and naïve, but back then Adi's uptightness seemed sensible and reassuring despite how young he was. 'Anyway, you don't even have any kind of logical or rational reason for opening up, do you? What's your reason for opening?'

'It's psychological.' That was Joy.

'That's not a reason.'

'Yes, it is. And you can't argue with psychology, if somebody needs something psychologically you can't argue with that.'

As well as being an idiot, Joy was super pretty and Trevor's girlfriend – all things that made it difficult to argue with her, but Adi wasn't giving up.

'Well if you can't argue with it, it's not just not a reason, it's not rational or logical either!'

'I think we will have to take the decision all together.'

That was Sarah – also difficult to argue with, because she was older and, it became apparent, only insisted on something when she totally knew she was right. I learned much later that she'd been taught to pick her battles by her father – a Black United States serviceman who came to build airbases in the Midlands and never went home to segregation after he discovered he could win a dancing competition with a local factory girl as his partner. Without knowing its pedigree I could hear the quiet, gentle ruthlessness in her voice. There was a collective rustle as she, Adi, Joy and Trevor all turned to look over at where me and Pressure Drop were still curled in our bundles. They couldn't believe we'd slept at all, let alone that we weren't awake yet.

There was something weird about the shadows on the far wall, they seemed to be moving too slowly or backwards or something that made no sense for shadows anyway. It was too dark for them to be there – any light that entered was coming in through a little bolt hole in the middle of the metal doors they were arguing about, piercing them so that a slim rod of sunlight hung dustily in the still, dark air above my head.

Joy said, 'Okay, but when they wake up, are we going to open them or not?'

Adi sighed. They were heavy steel doors, they'd creaked and clanged when he had let us in the night before. I couldn't clearly see the thick brick arches curving over our heads, but something in the way the acoustics flattened the echoes out of people's voices let you know that they weren't very high. I could see how Joy felt like she was trapped in a cave, but I was very glad they were there.

'First,' said Sarah, 'we should explore the inside – we need to see what we've got here. Then we'll know whether we ought to open up straight away.'

You could hear the relief in Adi's voice, 'Yes. Yes, that is a plan I like. Anyone else like that plan?'

Trevor backed him up, and Joy said, 'And then when we've done that, we'll open the doors, right?'

But Trevor was talking, 'Right, shall we wake the others then? Really we've got to make some progress, work out what our resources are, get organised, be ready for defence or attack, that's what the smart money's going to be doing right now.'

In an effort not to listen to Trevor's pep talk I started watching the shadows above the lectern again. They were still abnormal. Trevor was still talking about the importance of immediate action, so I interrupted him.

'The shadows,' I said, 'are not shadows. They're happening outside.'

As they all looked, my eyes pulled the forms into full focus. The colours were unavoidable once you saw them, bare branches waved against sky blue.

Trevor said, 'Nah, don't be …' but there they were, the houses brick red, the roofs slate grey, while a bird, probably a pigeon, flew by above them. You could see the bright splashes of daffodil yellow along the edges of people's gardens. So ordinary. So impossible.

Sarah started to cry, just a few big sobs and then she held her breath while she searched for a pack of tissues in her bag.

Joy said, 'I don't understand.'

'Camera obscura.' That was Pressure Drop, starting to slowly stretch his legs out from under his blankets, looking, as he stood up in the almost-dark, like he'd been assembled mostly from clothes hangers and the lint you find in the back of a tumble drier.

'I still don't understand,' said Joy.

'Well,' said Pressure Drop, 'it won't be the first time, or the last, and it won't change anything.'

'How long have you been awake and listening to everything?' Trevor sounded annoyed.

'That doesn't change anything either — you all agree with her that's crying, I agree with her, and she agrees with her,' gesturing to me, 'so let's find some breakfast. That trick of the light's not going anywhere.'

And so, in a slightly awkward silence, we did.

There was a small kitchen in the church with a Costco-scale supply of tea-break or coffee-morning supplies. There was no way of making tea or coffee but there was UHT milk and biscuits and, to especially Adi's delight, several crates of bottled water. He excitedly started doing calculations while we were looking through the packets to see if there was anything more exciting than chocolate digestives and, just when we'd turned up a packet of Jammie Dodgers, he happily told us we'd have a one-litre bottle each per day, and that we'd use a shared bottle for cooking each meal.

'Cooking?' asked Sarah.

Adi handed us our water rations. We finished the biscuits and milk we'd started, not really thinking we were paying attention to his calculations, but when we went off to explore we all carried our water bottles with us, as if we were hiking up a mountain or something.

So, in the Arches, this is what there was: six railway arches on a dead-end road, all with reinforced steel doors at the front, a window in the upper half and at the back a bricked-in passageway so you could get between them without going out. Arch one: the United Kingdom of Divine Love Church. Arch two: artists' studios above, and below a business called Culvers that made false teeth. Arch three: Peddler's Bicycle Repair. Arch four: House Clearance. Arch five: KLH Asian supermarket. Arch six: empty. Adi had the keys to everything: he kept a set of spares for the guy that ran the bike place. In time, we'd each find a corner that would become ours, but that morning we were all most excited about the supermarket, especially when Sarah pointed out we'd have to eat the fresh and frozen stuff before it went off.

We took baskets round the narrow aisles and filled them with everything we fancied that didn't need cooking. We brought it all up to the artists' studios where the sun was so bright that it felt like a block of yellow jelly the size of the room. We pulled a table covered in paint rings and unexpected burn marks into the middle of the space and started laying the food out. Enoki and oyster mushrooms, big pink prawns, bunches of all kinds of pak choi, pale wads of tofu, fat udon noodles, summer rolls, sweet chilli sauce, spicy seaweed, soy, wasabi, pickled ginger, cans of sugary fizzy drinks – passion fruit, guava, mango and lychee in their My Little Pony colours – bottles of beer even, still just cold enough to pool a little condensation around them on the table in shining rings.

We didn't talk while we ate. Everyone was too careful. We ate and passed things, and Pressure Drop opened the beers by holding them to the table edge and slamming his hand down on the lid, and every time he did it we all jumped a foot in the air. For dessert we ate little sesame seed-covered sweet pastry balls filled with coconut-flavoured bean paste, and when they were finished, Pressure Drop slammed open the last beer, stretched his legs so far out in front of him that they stuck out the other side of the table and said, 'And now we need to figure out where to drop a load.'

Joy looked at him blankly.

'There's toilets in every arch,' said Adi. 'We've already been using the one in the church.'

'That's fine for the simple, but we're going to need something more durable any minute now.'

And so the work of the afternoon began – the planning and construction of a place to shit. Obviously, I'm biased, but it was at around this point that I realised that Trevor was an idiot too.

I mean, I am also an idiot, though not the same kind as Trevor, and I'm probably actually a really dull person too. I look good on paper but there's very little substance – nobody realised it until I was at the end of my twenties, and even then it was only really me that realised it. It's entirely down to my parents. If I'd had different parents, I'd have ended up somewhere more likely, maybe a relatively competent but entirely uninspired town planner in a medium-sized dormitory town, or the logistics manager of a small refrigerated trucks business. As it is, that's not what happened. I grew up in Cuba – you see, already. My mum, Heike, was East German, and she went over there not long before the fall of the Soviet Union to work on a brewery that was being set up. When the Soviet Union fell, she stayed. And she met my father, Peter, a South London boy who'd slipped out of labouring through the grammar-school system and studied Spanish and ended up in Cuba because his dad had been in the local communist party and they'd raffled off a year's worth of Sunday dinners in his uncle's pub to send my dad to Cuba so that he could come back and give them hope, tell them about the tropical socialist paradise full of solidarity, equality, idealism and ice cream. They met in Camagüey, had me and named me Audaz, after a cooperative farm – the namers of which must have had hopes of nominative determinism that were roughly equal to my parents'.

When I was about six, Heike, who had become the fermentation wizard of the brewery, was moved onwards to the nation's first *prú* plant out east, near Santiago. *Prú* is the Cuban version of kombucha, the French brought it with them when they fled Haiti after the revolution. Closely guarded family rituals and secret ratios of Jamaica pepper, China root, *ubí* and *jaboncillo* finish up as the most perfect thing that you can imagine drinking on a hot afternoon. So my mum worked on setting up the *prú* oriental plant and for pin money she created Cuba's best yoghurt and innumerable pickled anomalies, among them Cuba's only sauerkraut and Cuba's most famous fermented hot chilli sauce. Basically, if there was a yeast or a strain of lactic bacteria in the mix, Heike was the boss of it. And my dad, at this point more than a decade into the fact-finding leg of his hope-bringing mission, translated. Bundles of paper would arrive in the post every week and he'd sit at his desk out under the mango tree with sweat dripping onto his typewriter, slowly clicking out the Spanish version of studies on animal husbandry of the buffalo in southern India or a sun-hungry letter from the South Wales Young Communists or the directions for use of a dry-grain feeder for up to forty chickens or twenty turkeys. And on the side, he would type up whatever official letters anyone in the area needed, as well as the labels for my mum's pickles, including the soon legendary *Salsa Piccante de Heike*, which she pasted onto bottles and jars on their umpteenth go-round with flour and water. And I went to school, down the dirt track with my white-socked classmates in the shadow of the tamarinds and tree-orchids, the hibiscus flowers flashing into colour as the sun came up and shone through them. We'd arrive on the tarmacked highway at the same time as the kids of the *Guahiros*, would ride up from farther out — saddle-less, three or five to a horse.

The horses were at the root of the legendary chilli sauce. Heike started growing the chillies because the smell of them acted like a kind of force field around the rest of her vegetable garden, dissuading anything passing from stopping to munch – or for that matter worm or nibble or egg – her rows of onions, beans, pumpkin, squash, courgette, sweet peppers, corn, melon, potatoes, cucumbers, tomatoes and anything else she'd spirited up tall, green and springing out of the red earth. But when the chillies themselves ripened she had to find a use for them and so she chopped them and mixed them with a handful of something and a couple of spoonfuls of something else and packed them down in salt and waited, and in time they became a fiery, fruity mix, mint and strawberry over a roaring sea of heat.

Word spread. By the time a few seasons had passed, whenever the guys from Santiago arrived to pick up their crates of refilled bottles they would bring a *Santería* delegation with them to bless the growing plants for the next harvest. I was never allowed to watch, but every time they came, a rooster went out to the vegetable garden with them and it never once came back. And the harvest never failed. And so I grew up, *la rubia*, the white-headed girl, speaking German and English and Spanish, eating papaya for breakfast and ice cream after school and *pan con minuta* with the fish-tail still sticking out of the roll on market days.

And then, when I was almost twelve, my dad's father got sick and it was decided that we'd go back to London.

It was a huge mistake, not for me, but for them. My father, though he was held together by the idea that he was carrying out his family duty, was ripped apart by the fact that he had, for fifteen or twenty years, lived something so strange and beautiful and magical that he would never be able to share it. Because how could you? You can't explain milk apples or coral reefs or falling in love in another tongue or it being dark but the air still being warm or the way a mosquito net around your bed makes all the world seem vague and distant when you wake.

My mother cried all the time when it came close to when we had to leave. She cried over papaya vines and sapote seeds, over mended mattresses and glasses made from lopped-off bottles, over rice and beans, over chickens and eggs, overall, overawed overtaken, overcome. I had no idea why she was crying – I couldn't imagine a world without those things. They tried to explain to me what Streatham was like, but they couldn't. No more than I will be able to one day, now that we're all in the living, breathing afterparty.

Everybody always wants to see a nice big death, a bloody and dramatic birth, but that's not this. This is the time of hoarding still, hidden piles of cans, bottles, bullets, packets. Things still work, and when they break you can still find another one – for a price. Which is just as well because either they're not made to be mended or no fucker knows how to repair them, not here anyway. Other places it must be different, places that weren't so far from a beginning when they hit this particular end, but here, until all the too much we had is used up, it'll be hinterland, until the last sole has worn through, the last bottle of whisky been drunk, the last knife been sharpened down to its stub, the last raincoat fallen to shreds, until then, hinterland. You can imagine, it's going to take some time.

People thought all the wrong things would protect them. You can't plan for the future anymore, you plan for something we thought was long past. This is like crossing the Styx in the Bronze Age – what you need is grave goods. A knife. A bowl.

A length of fabric. A fishing hook. A means of making fire. A piece of string. Gold.

Though the gold, that's not really planning for the past, that's me thinking about the future. Pressure Drop made the beads for me, back when we were in the Arches, but the gold was mine. Or, it was by then anyway. When Pressure Drop saw the gold, the first thing he did was shake his head and, his Dublin accent making his disappointment sound deeper, said slowly: 'That's the wrong kind of gold.' I thought he meant it was fake, or gold-plated or something. 'No,' he said, 'This is gold to be seen. Look at it, all filling up space with fancy twiddly bits. What you want is gold to be hidden. Put it away, I've got an idea.'

'What?'

'I don't know yet. I'll get back to you.'

We had settled into the Arches over a few days. Adi unlocked the doors linking the different arches together and left them that way. The church hall was the dormitory, the Asian supermarket was the larder, and the rest was where we mooched about. The artists' studios were the sitting and dining room – we'd moved stuff around so that the most comfortable chairs and most readable books were grouped together near the windows to soak up whatever warmth the sun brought. Sarah called that bit 'the parlour', and it was generally her spot, though everyone gravitated there at some point.

I split my time between there and house clearance – which Pressure Drop had nicknamed 'the glory hole' – mostly going through boxes of clothes and amusing myself with outlandish combinations or searching for books that I might actually enjoy. Peddler's was Adi's domain, and he went to work on fixing up a bike for himself. Trevor spent a fair amount of time in the glory hole with Joy in tow, hoping to find something supremely valuable probably. Joy sometimes played dress-up with me a bit, although she didn't like the way the clothes smelled. Pressure Drop floated – sometimes in the studios, sometimes on the mezzanine of Peddler's among the crates of greasy spare parts where there was a window he could open to smoke without anyone complaining. A couple of days after I'd shown him my treasure he came and found me in the glory hole – 'Come up to the studios and bring the gold,' he said.

Pressure Drop has a knack for saying words in a way that makes you actually know them. As if through years of practice he's discovered how to internalise a whole four-in-the-morning free association. The kind that goes, 'Where is the lighter? No, not that lighter, a lighter that works, hey, did you ever think how "light" is a word that means to leave and to arrive at the same time? Like, there's "light out for the territories" and "light here by me". It tells you that coming and going are actually the same thing, so if you're doing one then you must also be doing the other too, in fact, because of that, you never know whether you are coming or going because you're always doing both, you could just say "light" for both and then you're not giving the past or the future higher importance than the present, you're just there.'

Pressure Drop, at this point, instead of just handing you a lighter that worked and stumbling off to piss, would breathe the whole monologue deep down into his blood where it would lie dormant. Then, forevermore, if at any time he wanted to, he would be able to imbue the word 'light' with its total meaning and sonically stun the listener into blinking stillness with the truths and falsehoods of language and the momentary certainty that they'd never be able to speak again, because it was too strange, too beautiful and too terrifying that we are able to use words at all. I saw him do it with others, other words, other people. He got Sarah pretty good with 'understand' one time. I never asked him if it was something he did on purpose. It's not a question he'd ever give you a useful answer to. Anyway, the first time it happened to me it was with 'crucible'. When he said 'crucible' you could see it hanging in the air like the centre of a planetary model while cradles and melting pots, chalices and furnaces, all circled around it.

The day of the crucible was the happiest day I spent in the Arches. Me and Pressure Drop went down to Arch two and he collected a box of stuff he'd packed together from the countertop of the false-teeth place, and then up to the studios where he'd cleared a space by the window. When I asked him how he knew what he needed, he just said, 'If you think you can just pop into H Samuel and buy a pendant with the Lion of Judea on a Celtic cross then you have another think coming.' I looked to see if I could see it around his neck, but past the best dreads I've ever seen on a white man there was just his scrawny pale skin, some greying stubble and an Adam's apple so pointy it could've been a second nose. He saw me looking and said, 'It was a long while back.' Long while back or not, he still knew how to do the whole thing with a kind of sureness that made it look beyond practiced: directed, destined, ceremonial.

I stood there with the ends of my fingers stuck in yoghurt pots that he'd ripped off a carnival costume – clearly made to promote reduce-reuse-recycle – and filled with bright-pink glop that he'd mixed from powder from the false-teeth place. The pink glop smelled of toothpaste. He dragged a gas-canister blowtorch out from under a table stacked with half-finished stained-glass windows. When I pulled my fingers out of the then-set glop, he snapped a skinny stick of something into bits and stuck it in the holes and sprayed some stuff from the box into them and got me to stick my fingers in another set of glop-filled pots. I waited for it to set again. He brought some bricks over and lined them up on the ground beside some gloves that looked like industrial oven mitts. I stuck my fingers in a third set of pots, waiting again while he picked over the jewellery, going through it with pliers to take out any precious stones and leaving them like a pile of nail-gems in a jam-jar lid. And then, when my fingers were out of the final set of yoghurt pots he said it: 'Pass me the crucible.' And the shapes of all 'crucible' had ever meant and would ever mean spun in the air around us as I passed him the cast-iron pot that he'd taken from the supermarket.

We heaped the huge double handful of jewellery into it and he set the blowtorch on it. Bit by bit the delicate chain-links and filigrees flickered and folded in on themselves, like tiny sparklers collapsing into a pool of sun. Slowly, the whole lot disappeared down into less than a cupful of liquid rolling in the bottom of the pot. 'If you've got something to say, now would be the moment,' he said, putting down the blowtorch and pulling on the oven mitts. I couldn't think of anything. He picked up the pot and poured.

'Do not go near them until they're cooled,' he said, 'I knew a fella who melted his fingerprints off because he was in a hurry. Not that he minded losing them, in fairness. Go off to the glory hole and fetch the longest shoelace you can find.' So I got a torch and did. When I came back, he'd found a scalpel and rolled a joint. The pots were lined up with the sticks sticking out of them like mini lollies, and he was getting ready to cut them open. The pink colour made it seem like he was slicing fruit or flesh, opening up a wound to get a bullet out or pulling the stone from a peach. When he handed them to me they were still warm, like a pebble you've kept in your pocket, and not at all golden – dark and iridescent, like a mineral from outer space. They were amazing – totally my fingertips, the curved nail-ends of my index fingers and the squarer tops of my middle ones, the raggedy cuticles and the scratched-down nails. Seriously, the coolest fucking thing you ever saw.

Pressure Drop was smiling, smoking, happily slitting open the pots and tugging the sticks from the middles so there was a hole to thread the shoelace through. He saw the way I was looking at them as I threaded them on, caught my eye, raised his eyebrows. 'You wear that round your waist, you hear me?' he said, 'Your skin will rub them gold in no time. And if needs be they're a good size to swallow.' Which he was sort of right about. I did as he said, knotting the shoelace around my waist, and got on with how we kept busy in the Arches – planning to leave.

The first heady trip out was to pick up supplies from our own houses. We didn't need much, there was still water in the church and food in the supermarket, but there were things people wanted for a long stay. We argued about whether we'd take turns or whether we'd all go at once. Joy in particular was freaking out at the idea that whoever stayed would be locked in, because whoever went out would take the keys so that they'd be able to get back in without hammering on the doors. In the end, we agreed that we'd all go, and that we'd have half an hour to collect what we wanted.

The broken windows made our street look at if it'd had its teeth kicked in. We slunk down it in a quiet little huddle, each person peeling off uneasily, full of backward glances as they reached the house they'd lived in. I gave my own backward glances when we reached mine – being separated from the herd was scary. My house didn't feel like home anymore. Unlocking the front door it felt like I was about to rob the place. Rain had blown in through the smashed windows at the back, pooling on the bathroom floor and leaving my bedroom carpet squidgy. I rolled my duvet up and tied a belt around it, then showered – there was still water in the tank, even if it was cold. It was worth it, although every time I soaped a bit of myself I was worried that the water would run out before I had time to rinse it. I looked around my room. There wasn't much I wanted to take really. I lay down on my bed for a moment, wondering if it would be possible to bring the mattress, settled for a yoga mat, took a few more pairs of pants, some bits and pieces. At that point I wasn't feeling the pinch. Joy was another matter. Being stuck in the Arches was really getting to her, and going out – she came back from that first foray with a massive wheelie suitcase of clothes – didn't make it better, if anything she got worse.

The point at which she lost her shit altogether was when she got her period. She and Trevor fought and fought for days before, or she tried to fight and he would just walk towards the nearest one of us, using us as a human shield, because she wouldn't talk about whatever she wanted to fight about in front of us. She got worse and worse and then I found her in a ball with a pair of bloody knickers in her fist. She was just sobbing and then she started, 'I can't do it anymore. I want home. I want a shower, I want a tampon, I want a washing machine, I want a clean pair of knickers and a clean pair of trousers that are *my* knickers and trousers, I want it over.' I went and got Trevor, even though I actually had a mooncup in the bag I'd brought with me when we first arrived at the Arches. I'd packed that bag when I realised I couldn't barricade all the windows in my house – there just wasn't enough furniture. I wasn't planning to leave then, I still felt safe in that house. I had stockpiled dried grains and pulses from the wholefoods shop – guided by the spirit of my mother and my childhood memories – and felt relatively confident by then that the front-room fireplace was not totally defunct. And, in some way, I wanted to protect the house in the same way I felt it was protecting me. But I also wanted to be ready to leave if I had to.

Lots of people had gone already, leaving as soon as it began to feel like everyone was going to get sick sooner or later and a state of general slow breakdown set in. First some families disappeared: the ones with Range Rovers who, in more routine times, would drive back muddy on a Sunday night from wherever it was that they'd now decided to hole up. Then people with family in reachable distance. After the power cuts began, anyone who had somewhere better to go did. And with the deaths, soon enough there was only a handful of us left. You'd occasionally see a light or a movement in maybe one house in twenty on the street.

It happened over months, which is both quickly and slowly, depending on how you look at it in terms of total collapse. In the beginning, there was no huge drama. When there were huge dramas, like someone getting stabbed in the face in a row over stocking up on toilet roll or a family collapsing into triple-homicide under the strain of school closures and electricity rationing, they were reported as if they were tragedies rather than precursors. Curfews became ingrained. Public transport became history. Supermarkets became flashpoints. Temporary morgues became permanent.

Bit by bit, I lost contact with everyone. Mobile networks flickered on and off from hour to hour, then from day to day — you never knew if a message was sent, or received, or responded to. The idea of cycling across London to find out if a friend was even alive, let alone home, seemed more and more bonkers as time went on. It had become clear that there was no plan to get us out of the mess. Whenever word came through from on high it was just imploring everyone to be vaguely sensible.

So, sensibly, I packed that bag. I remember feeling really good about it, taking pride in thinking I knew what was useful. Like how, on the Sunday afternoon of a festival, I'd be the one who had the nail file in my penknife, the needle and thread in my wallet and the end of a roll of gaffer tape in my bag. I packed all that. Plus: clean pants, my favourite sports bra, warm socks, paracetamol, lip-balm, a thermal t-shirt, sunglasses, hoodie, leggings, raincoat, flip-flops, mooncup, and a massive load of gold wrapped in a blue plastic bag, you know, all the usual stuff you'd bring if you didn't know where or how long it would be for.

But obviously I didn't offer the mooncup to Joy — it wasn't something I felt like sharing, and I felt pretty sure that sharing it wouldn't have solved anything anyway. And it came out of Joy getting her period that I found out what Sarah's work was, because I came back and talked to Sarah about Joy and said in a light way that I'd not wanted to lend her the cup and as things sometimes do when you start talking about your vagina one thing led to another and I told her that I had a copper coil.

'I can take that out for you,' she said. At that point, the idea of being fully protected from pregnancy seemed like a pretty smart idea, something I was feeling fairly smug about in fact, so I thought she was mental, and it must've showed. 'How long have you had it, and how long do they last, five, six years?

What do you think the odds are of you meeting somebody else in that time who knows how to take it out?'

'You're a doctor?'

'Midwife — retired midwife.'

It's not what I would've guessed, but it made total sense. She had the feel that women of a certain age who've done proper jobs have, you see it in ex-teachers, ex-librarians, ex-nurses: the ability to be sure they've made the world better, even though everyone who was actually in charge acted like what they were doing was not very important.

Trevor was like her in that respect, I mean in that he thought he'd been doing important work, not that his work actually was important, it was some kind of recruitment management or something. He actually thought that the fact that all the people with bullshit jobs like his had had to stop doing them was one of the reasons everything had gone downhill, and once we'd explored the Arches a bit he got it into his head that he was going to kick us into shape.

He called a meeting and got us all to sit down to describe what our abilities were to see how they could best be used. It was hilarious, like some kind of management consultancy team-building exercise crossed with a job interview. We had to say what three types of animal we thought we were most like and tell a joke, and then we had to present ourselves and describe our 'skill set' with our strengths and weaknesses. He had it all planned. In the absence of a photocopier he'd even got Joy to help him write out the questionnaire sheets that he wanted us all to fill out. He'd gone round the studio finding enough pens for us all and even found a stack of *Asterix* books that he'd set up as clipboards for us, which meant that throughout the whole session you couldn't concentrate on what he was saying because obviously it was boring bullshit but also because you were using almost all your conscious mind to resist the urge to discover what happened in *Asterix and Cleopatra*, as if that one would be something other than Romans being beaten up and a banquet. It didn't go exactly as he'd expected. Pressure Drop refused to describe himself as an animal because he said it was dehumanising. Adi ended up taking an insanely long time to explain to Joy that studying Materials Technology didn't necessarily mean making cloth. I tried to go along with it as seriously as I could, because I could see that Trevor was getting more and more frustrated that the team he was trying to build to take on the smart money was actually just an utter shit-show composed of halfwit oddballs. I explained my animal choices (crow, butterfly and octopus, since you ask) and then went through the things I felt I could do better than most people. This was the question to which Pressure Drop had answered, 'Smoke,' causing Trevor to clear his throat in a way that sounded like a door hinge, to which Pressure Drop clarified, 'Smoke weed.'

I answered that I could speak German and Spanish. Trevor nodded sagely, obviously happy that somebody had answered something that would, in a sensible world, actually be considered a skill. He then made a little speech about the difference between skills and abilities, 'skills' being things you'd learned that might or might not be useful – 'No offence Audaz, but I don't think any of us is going to be heading off on holiday anytime soon' – and 'abilities' being capacities that we might or might not have developed – 'Like, I have a very high base-level of fitness. Even if I don't do much exercise, as soon as I start doing any kind of fitness challenge, I'm at a much higher level than my mates very quickly.'

And then he asked me what my abilities were. I was pretty tempted to do a Pressure Drop on him and say being able to spot the group of people most likely to be going on somewhere else when a venue was closing, but I told them I was good at remembering stuff. People usually talk about photographic memory but mine has always been more of a tape recorder. Song lyrics. The stops on the number 35. *Los héroes y mártires de la revolución*. It's all just sound running down the dorsal pathway, in through the back of my skull and then it rolls around in there, curled on spools of mental magnetic tape, waiting to be rewound to the heads. Not that I tried to explain any of that to them, I just said I was good at remembering stuff.

And suddenly Sarah was interviewing me: what kind of stuff was I good at remembering? How did I remember it? How much could I trust what I remembered? Trevor was a bit confused to have lost his spot as ringmaster, but by the time he'd worked out how to take back control, Sarah had finished. He moved on and soon she was almost having a panic attack at the idea of having to tell a joke and letting us know that she knew how to deliver babies, which he said didn't look like it was going to be useful immediately, and moved on to Joy, who picked a unicorn as one of her animals and listed attractiveness as an ability. And then Trevor told us about himself, how his skills were planning and evaluating, and his abilities were physical strength and natural leadership. Anyone who tells you they are a natural leader is a natural dickhead.

So after that little session, Sarah said we needed to talk, and that's when she told me about her plan. Essentially, there was a town in the mountains in the south of France called Digne-les-Bains where she had spent chunks of time since the seventies and it was, if you listened to Sarah, like a kind of epicentre of practical possibilities for the new world of disorder. It had rivers and geothermal springs, so clean hot and cold water all year round, it had mountains and forests with mushrooms and deer and wild boar and dogwood and chestnuts and plums and it had valleys and plateaus with apples and pears and walnuts and olives and wheat. It had people who knew how to work the land and how to hunt. It had clean air and sunlight. She was going there to set up a midwifery school, and she wanted me to be her first apprentice. The way she spoke about it, the place, the expansiveness of her plan, it was like a film trailer, something like a cross between *The Sound of Music* and *My Side of the Mountain*.

In my mind's eye I could see snowy peaks and blue skies and the leaves turning golden and the shoots coming up green, the blood of the kills and the juice of the berries, waterfalls thundering into pools. 'Bread,' she said, 'I promise you, there will be bread. You think that's not important now, but give it a month or three months and bread will mean something completely different. There will be bread. And there will be bread next year, and the year after, and the year after that. And besides, you've never really done anything with your life, have you? I bet that apart from what you happened upon by accident, you've never really learned how to do anything. You've probably been telling yourself that you'll soon get around to it, or that by now it's too late, switching between them day by day, and both of them are just a reason not to. I'd say now is probably your moment, your chance to do something really, truly exceptional and safeguard generations of women by remembering a whole lot of useful information, and using it, and passing it on.'

It was harsh, but fair. After just a few days stuck in the Arches she pretty much had me already with the talk of the

Edenic many-horizoned Digne-les-Bains, but really it was the offer I'd been waiting for all my life. Save the world in a feminist way using a hitherto untapped superpower that had, up until this point, only been useful as a sort of party trick? Swap being able to recite 'Alphabet Aerobics' or remembering a thirty-strong drinks order on cue for saving lives? What half-arsed, shoddy, burnt-out-without-ever-really-having-lit-the-wick wouldn't want that chance? Obviously I said yes.

 I tried to act all serious about it, you know, like it was a solemn moment from a kung-fu movie where the sensei agrees to take on the young ninja, but Sarah, as soon as she realised she had me hooked, just said, 'Good, it'll be mostly homework for now, you can start with this.' She handed me a fat, battered paperback titled *Spiritual Midwifery*. The cover had a repeated pattern that looked like peacock feathers but was actually little inky sitting Buddhas with green robes, blue haloes and flaming aureoles and tiny little third eyes. I flipped the pages, past diagrams and black and white photos of fat-faced babies and men and women with long hair, to where it fell open at a fold-out in the middle. It was, in full glorious technicolour, an eastern-mystical style painting of a woman giving birth – the sort of image that would have a lasting effect on you if you stumbled across it at an impressionable age. Like the way that bit in *The Female Eunuch* about tasting your own menstrual blood comes back to you every time you have your period, until finally you actually do it and then you realise that it changes nothing and that you and everybody else still have just as long a way to go, baby.

 So, this painting has a weirdness that just keeps you looking at it. In a room draped in Indian bedspreads a woman is giving birth, assisted by three women, one of whom is pregnant herself, and a man. Everyone has haloes, especially the baby, and everyone is white and has long flowing locks, except the baby who is three-quarters of the way out, bald and purplish-blue. The women are wearing floaty paisley tops and jeans with rainbow turn-ups and the man has a peasant blouse and enormous hands, one of which cradles the birthing woman's head and the other of which rests on her stomach. On a dresser behind the women is a pile of neatly folded blankets and a kettle. Outside the window, a voyeuristic squirrel looks on from his perch on a flowering tree-branch. The birthing woman stares into space, eyes wide, lips parted in orgasmic wonder. The man is looking at her, two of the other women are looking at the baby and the pregnant woman is looking at the man.

In biro, somebody has drawn a thought bubble above the head of the pregnant woman and written in it, 'Well, I hope by the time I have my baby the feminist revolution will have happened and Sarah will be able to do this without the whiteface and the fake beard!' When you look at the picture again it really, I mean really, looks like the artist has painted them all as women and then somebody said, 'No no, the one in charge is meant to be a man. Don't worry, just give her a beard and make her hands bigger and nobody will notice.' Nothing explains the Peeping Tom squirrel though.

Sarah said, 'It's a bit seventies, I was never one for natural childbirth at all costs, but it's all that's going to be available for the moment so you might as well start there. How long do you think it'll take you to get through this and actually learn something from it?'

It was a proper book, a couple of centimetres thick. I said I wasn't sure, but at least enough time to read it to myself out loud.

'Well, best get going straight away then – you don't know how long you're going to have it for.'

After that Sarah started spending about an hour every day checking what I'd read and asking what I'd learned from it. She insisted that we both wash our hands at the start of each session. Honestly, it was a total pain in the arse to wash your hands in the Arches, and it used up the water supply, but there was no arguing with her.

She said, 'The first rule of childbirth is: wash your hands. When women first started giving birth in hospitals nobody knew about germs, and doctors went from examining corpses to delivering babies without washing their hands in between. Proportionally, more women died after giving birth in those hospitals than would've died if they'd been left to do it on a mountainside alone. So wash your hands. Properly. With soap. No matter what the situation. Correct hand-washing is now a matter of life or death.' She insisted on proper hand-washing in the most medieval of conditions.

She was super clean, Sarah. Each morning she'd disappear off to the back passage, as Pressure Drop had christened it, with a mug of water, a toothbrush, a flannel and a jar of cocoa butter, and she'd come back looking like she'd had a shower. And while the rest of us all developed a certain funk over the weeks that followed, she never did. One thing is for sure, next time there is an apocalypse I will not be packing leggings. They seem like a brilliant practical, lightweight idea but they start to smell of piss really quickly and they are much more annoying to wash and dry than knickers. I found an old, like really old, fifties maybe, pair of men's woollen pinstripe trousers in the glory hole and switched to them. They never stink of piss and they've only been washed about twice in almost a year, and they're warm.

Capsule wardrobes for the end of days is something I reckon I could write a feature on by now, and art-direct the photo shoot probably. We had a few laughs, me and Joy, playing dress-up in the glory hole, despite her complaining that the clothes smelled like cat pee and old people. A couple of times we even gave the rest of the gang a laugh, showing up at the end of the afternoon in cocktail dresses or enormous suits padded out with cushions or stupid-looking hats. The difference was, though, I was actually looking for things to add to my wardrobe, whereas she would never have considered wearing any of that stuff as clothes rather than jokes.

It's petty of me, but when I was sure that Joy and Trevor were not going to come with us to France – she refused point blank to consider cycling and he tried to make it look like he was being each-to-their-own about it but he basically thought we were off our boxes – I was delighted. Pressure Drop and Adi were up for it though: Pressure Drop because it was clearly His will that he'd found himself holed up with somebody who was planning to head south, and Adi I think mainly because the idea of it gave shape to things.

Sometime after the thought of cycling to Digne had taken root, Adi got the rest of us together to tell us that we should make a list of some small essentials that we wanted to bring with us, outside of the allocation he'd already calculated for clothes and sleeping bags and water and stuff, and that whatever we listed shouldn't weigh more than two kilos. The plan was that when we had the lists we'd work out what needed to be done to go about getting what was on them. Joy and Trevor didn't play. Planning for a future where you couldn't own more than you could carry was not one of their life goals. They headed off into the glory hole while we settled around the table in the studios. Adi gave us each a biro and a piece of paper and sat down with us to write his list – though he was not writing his list for the first time.

Sarah's list was stationery and pharmacy: a five-year diary, a textbook, a self-winding watch, nail clippers, nail file, needles, thread, medical alcohol, magnifying mirror, tweezers, two kinds of doctor's scissors, a nit comb, a baby sling and teabags – which she'd probably have considered pharmacy for herself. Up to that point, I don't think Pressure Drop or Adi had really thought about Sarah's plan, beyond that for Adi it gave him a goal and for Pressure Drop it gave him a staging post on the way to Zion, but the five-year diary on her list got them. Her projection into the future shook them by the shoulders. Not that they didn't believe in it before, it just hadn't occurred to them as a real thing, a future you would actually see the present bleeding into.

My list was all stuff from home, and even if somebody had been through my house by then, I didn't think they were the kind of things that would get taken: a cigar box full of tiny envelopes, carefully handmade and labelled by my mother and filled with seeds, spores and starters; a pumice stone (go ahead and laugh, I know whereof I speak); a black and white photograph of me and my parents, taken by a pinhole photographer in Havana before we left Cuba, so it's in negative, bright-white palm trees against a dark sky behind us, my dad's beard pale and our teeth black; a pair of kitchen scissors. Adi was dead against the kitchen scissors, adamant that anything you needed a scissors for could be cut with a Stanley knife – we had a similar argument about cable ties versus gaffer tape a little later in the packing, with the same result: he took one, I took the other.

Pressure Drop's list: pillow. When Adi heard Pressure Drop's list he just started laughing and walked off shaking his head to make some further tiny but important alteration to the bikes, muttering that we were all flipping crazy. Pressure Drop grinned, looking like it wasn't the first time he'd been called flipping crazy and he hoped it wouldn't be the last.

Sarah smiled back, stood, and said, '"If a man carry treasure in bullion, or in a wedge of gold, and have none coined into current monies, his treasure will not defray him as he travels. Tribulation is treasure in the nature of it, but it is not current money in the use of it, except we get nearer and nearer our home, heaven, by it."'

Pressure Drop went large-eyed at her, like he was soaking it in through them, then said, 'You should bring that book too.'

'I've got some of it anyway.' She tapped her forehead and smiled again.

After Adi's list-instigation we spent quite a bit of time in the glory hole, picking through crates of other people's pasts to salvage things for our future. It was hard not to be struck by the slow way things decay even when they're packed away carefully – supple plastic becoming brittle, fabrics quietly generating their own dust, sticky films appearing on rubber, metal oxidising. It was also hard not to be struck by the sheer amount of useless crap there was in there. It was much easier to find something that gave you momentary amusement – a pair of massive bottle-end glasses, a commemorative candelabra and a stuffed squirrel anybody? – than something that you had any inclination to carry with you. For every penknife or warm cardigan there seemed to be at least a dozen hi-fi systems or jugs or discoloured polycotton shirts or beer-branded ashtrays or pairs of velour slippers. In a way, seeing how unnecessary it all was made the packing for the journey easier. As did the realisation that in fact, the whole world is glory hole now.

The next trip out was in search of a watch for Sarah. While Trevor had no interest in any other part of the planning for the journey, the watch excited him – he knew exactly where to go. With the *A–Z* that Sarah had brought from her house, he and Adi worked out the way to a road in Kensington that was lined with fancy-ass watch shops. It was just going to be the two of them; Trevor had a motorbike and Adi would go with him. Adi was stoked, he loved motorbikes. They put hammers in a rucksack and went out to where the bike was parked. That time, we locked them out and agreed to keep watch for their return. They came back a few hours later, Adi grey and sweating with terror and Trevor high as a kite, and tipped dozens of watches out of the rucksack onto the table, Trevor immediately swearing at himself for possibly having scratched them.

Trevor told it more like a daring but ultimately foiled heist rather than the pant-shitter Adi had experienced – Adi said later that he'd been terrified from the moment the deafening engine turned. When they'd got to the street with the shops, breaking the windows with their hammers took them much longer than expected because the glass didn't smash – it shattered but stayed stuck together. You had to keep hammering and clawing until you'd punched a hole big enough to get through, which made another fuck-load of noise, and then what was left of the window was impossible to see through so you couldn't see what was going on outside when you had climbed in. Trevor had wanted to break into three shops, but when he was hammering the second window – by then Adi wouldn't do anything except keep watch – a group of men with their faces covered came round the corner yelling at them. Trevor dropped the hammer, nearly landing it on Adi's foot. Adi grabbed it – he was worried about fingerprints, bless him – and they sprinted for the motorbike. Then they got lost on the way home, and every thundering metre the engine took them, Adi was bricking it that it would be their last.

Sarah picked through the pile of watches as if they were tomatoes at the market, with Trevor acting as salesman. He wanted to show them all to us, 'Look at that, look at that,' he'd say, delightedly picking up another and detailing its specifications and how many tens of thousands of pounds it was worth. When Sarah finally made her choice, something small and round-faced with a brown leather strap, he said it was only worth about six thousand pounds. He seemed both disappointed at her lack of ambition and pleased that she hadn't chosen one of the prize models.

The pile of watches stayed on the table like a centrepiece, but it didn't have time to gather much dust. When Joy and Trevor announced they were leaving, Trevor began a carefully structured negotiation about their right to take the watches with them, seeing as he'd gone and fetched them and if he and Joy left they'd no longer be a drain on the food and water in the Arches. The negotiation fell flat when he realised that we didn't give a fuck about the watches as long as Sarah could keep the one she'd picked out. They packed them into Joy's wheelie suitcase as part of their departure flurry, which involved a certain amount of backhanded well-wishing from Joy and a final inventory from Trevor. I was so relieved they were gone. I mean, in many ways they were not such bad people, and they were excited to be heading off to live their dream of looted department stores, but fuck me, I didn't make it through global plague and the total disintegration of society to spend the rest of my life silently rolling my eyes at neo-liberal cock-knockers.

Adi needed a job once they'd left as he was no longer the buffer between the two of them and the three of us, so he threw himself completely into organising our departure. He was obsessed with weight: he'd found a scales in the glory hole and he knew the weight of every piece of kit we had. Where possible, he'd actually written the weight on the object in permanent marker. Pressure Drop encouraged him in the preparations, saying that as soon as Trevor found somebody who wanted something that was locked up with us, he'd be back. So Adi wrote and rewrote lists, measured legs, adjusted bikes, packed and repacked and weighed bags and sent me and Sarah into the glory hole to search it for his magical essentials and then, after a streak of a good few days of us not finding things he'd been hoping for, he announced that what was needed was a trip to Decathlon in Surrey Quays. Seriously, few things had ever sounded more ridiculous to me as a means of survival – were we going to eat a cut-price snowboarding helmet? – but I was really curious to go out. He tested and retested our two bikes, worrying about the amount of noise my freewheel made after his motorbike trauma. Then we put the hammers, a kitchen knife, a puncture-repair kit, two bottles of water and a packet of chocolate digestives in a bag and snuck out in the early morning. We were all jitters – the first bridge we went under had some pigeons waking up on a ledge and they scared the living shit out of us. But as we carried on, we got into a rhythm. The city had that same emptiness that it always had at that time anyway, the deserted streets that you'd see from the wrong end of the morning on your way home from a house party.

We planned the route before – and by 'we' I mean Adi. He had this conviction that if he planned stuff it would all go well. I've never believed much in planning – practice yes, but not planning. Adi took us by the small roads. Up and down to Tulse Hill, round behind Brockwell, off and over the back of Ruskin, tall streets that would soon be snowed under with cherry-blossom and magnolia flowers just like they were every year. Zigzagging to avoid Camberwell, dodging across to get north of Peckham before we reached it and looping little green space after little green space as we wove through on the flat between Peckham and the Old Kent Road. Crossing the Old Kent Road was a sudden exposure, we hunched small over the handlebars and shot ourselves across the immense gulf of the six lanes as quickly as we could. We slipped between sixties blocks to the Meadows – where I once watched a huge meteor shower and wondered if that's what London would look like under attack, void and grey and the sky streaked with light – and curved round the back of Millwall, then through more sixties blocks until we arrived at the vast expanse of the Surrey Quays car park. Even though we'd seen nobody the whole way there, by then it was completely light and we were already a little freaked from crossing the bigger roads to get there, so the car park was fucking terrifying. It was almost completely empty, and we were the only things moving for miles around. The tall office and apartment blocks here and there around the edges made us feel certain we were being watched from on high. We tried to stay by the hedges, but it was more to make us feel better rather than any actual use – they only came up to our waists. By the time we'd crossed the blank desert and had the canal basin on one side of us, we were so hyped we didn't know whether to run or to hide. The water spread out below us and the high glass walls of the shopping centre reflecting everything around made it feel like we were just targets. We sprinted through and then stopped as soon as we were out of sight. We put our heads around the corner and saw the doors of Decathlon, the answer to all our prayers. We hid between some big wheelie bins for a bit to try to calm down. Adi said we should try to eat some biscuits, that the sugar would help. My mouth was so dry from the fear that they were impossibly gritty and I started coughing and then I got the giggles at the idea that we'd managed to get all the way there safely and then I was going to choke to death on biscuit crumbs.

We managed to drink some water and I got myself together, and we went towards the doors. They'd already been smashed, but there was nobody else around and there was still a lot of stuff in the place. In hindsight this was surprising, because I was a moron to have thought that Decathlon was not the key to survival. In fact, during the course of our journey the sheer quantity of Decathlon kit doing the rounds convinced me that if everyone in Europe had died and the continent got repopulated in thousands of years' time by people from, say, the Andaman Islands, their archeologists would probably think that 'Decathlon' was the name of our great leader and that 'Kalenji', 'Nabaiji', 'Quechua', 'Kipsta', 'Arpenaz', 'Artengo', 'Olaian', and all the rest were the royal sons and daughters.

So, in whispers, Adi and I made our supplications to the illustrious of the realm. We padded quietly up and down the aisles, Adi ticking things off on his list and discussing – just discussing with himself really, I had no opinion – the few substitutions he was having to make. We came round into the hiking and hillwalking aisle, and Adi was looking for a particular kind or size of tent. He stepped over a fallen mannequin to read the labels better, and I was thinking how it was unusual, but, you know, progressive, for Decathlon to use a mannequin of an overweight person when I realised it wasn't one. Adi was so absorbed in the slight differences between the tents that he didn't even notice me hissing, 'The fuck, Adi, that's not a fucking mannequin.'

He looked at me.

'Adi, get the fuck over here.' He stepped back, almost treading on the man. At that point my mind was yelling questions at me. Pretending? Asleep? Dead? Sick? Murdered? Murderer? The man was face down and his hoodie covered his head.

Adi grabbed my arm. 'Audaz, that's not a mannequin!'

'I know, Adi, I fucking know!'

'Is he dead?'

'How the fuck do I know!'

'Take his pulse.'

'No way, I'm not fucking touching him.'

You could see his hand poking out of his sleeve, pale and plastic-looking. There was what looked like bruising or pencil shading all around where it touched the floor, which I later learned was where his blood had pooled within his flesh.

'It's easy, you just …'

I interrupted him, 'Adi, choose the fucking tents and let's get the fuck out, yeah?'

We backed away from the man.

'We should at least check if he's breathing,' Adi said, but we kept backing away without doing it. I didn't know which kind of people we were, whether we were the people who should check if somebody was okay and try to help them, or whether we were the people who, in doing so, would end up dead. The answer, all things considered, is probably both kinds.

We stood like mannequins ourselves, straining our ears to try to hear anything that might let us know if we were about to be next. I know now that he could've been dead for days before you'd really smell anything, but back then I had no idea,

I thought people were more like supermarket chicken fillets and imagined that the absence of stink meant he'd been killed just a few minutes earlier. I was also sure that he was going to do like in a film, jolt back into life and swipe at our ankles. I could hear Adi shallow breathing beside me, which inspired me to try to get my own breath under control. When I had, I whispered, 'Adi,' and nudged him gently in the ribs, 'get the tents.' We were both fixed to the spot. I nudged him again and he managed to move. He approached the tents, keeping the man in his sights, edging past him, and quietly took two. He edged back to me. Looking over our shoulders, we tiptoed out of that aisle. The fact that the man hadn't attacked us in death made it possible to breathe a little more deeply and, as quickly as possible, we collected the last few things on his list, loaded it all into rucksacks and got out.

It wasn't just that it was horrific to see a dead body, although it was, every bit as shocking as when you see the emergency services dealing with some horrible mangled accident, worse, in fact, because at least in those cases you could tell yourself that people who knew what to do were on the case. It was more that seeing him made me wonder about the others.

When we were unlocking the bikes, I asked Adi what he thought the population density of London was, because I was sure it was the kind of thing he'd know. He did – about five-and-a-half-thousand people per square kilometre. So on the ride back I did mental arithmetic: if the population density of London was about five-and-a-half-thousand people per square kilometre and half of them were dead, that was two-thousand-seven-hundred-and-fifty dead bodies per square kilometre; if three-quarters of them were dead that was three-thousand-three-hundred-and-seventy-five dead bodies per square kilometre; if seven-eighths of them were dead that was four-thousand-eight-hundred-and-something dead bodies per square kilometre; if fifteen-sixteenths of them were dead that was over five thousand dead bodies per square kilometre. And that's not even counting the pets. I couldn't work out how many square metres each dead body had to itself, but whatever the sums were, the whole city was a giant morgue. I felt like all those bodies were rammed up against me, as if I was pushing them out of my way with every move, squeezing past them, breathing them in. We didn't see any others on our way home. A few live ones, none close. They mostly seemed as wary as we were. A small huddle on the steps of a church watched us ride by, a couple with their heads down walked quickly away from us and a guy on a street corner shouted at us in a way that sounded confused or mad or maybe desperate. We didn't try to interact with anyone, pedaling harder without even trying to understand whatever glances or yells came our way. We were sweatier and sweatier the closer we got to the Arches, because the bags were heavy, but also nerves at the thought of being seen going in. I stank of stress when we arrived. Pressure Drop and Sarah were hungry for news of the outside world, but all I had for them was intrusive thoughts about being surrounded by death.

The idea of everyone rotting all around us gave me the creeps, and to try to crush the creeps I imagined my mother talking about it. She managed to put things into a different kind of scale. Both socialism and microbiology had taught her that nothing would ever work as long as we imagined we were individuals — everything was about cooperation. A bunch of stuff she'd believed on a deep hunch since the seventies, and which for years had sounded like total nonsense, had now filtered its way from scientific studies and peer-reviewed papers, through the fringe and finally out into the mainstream. Not only was she not surprised that most of your serotonin is produced by bacteria in your intestine, or that faecal transplants reduced the risk of cancer or that vaginal seeding helped babies' brains develop, she was amazed that people needed to conduct studies to discover things that she accepted as self-evident truths. She believed in the gut-brain axis and prebiotics before anyone thought they existed, and nothing ever grossed her out. In the upstairs bathroom, between the shower and the water heater, she kept what she called *la biblioteca de matrices*: shelves full of various jars of gently bubbling glop – mothers, starters, matrixes. I saw her lift out with bare hands and sniff and even taste things that anyone else would've flushed in disgust. Whenever she was enforcing the household no-food-waste rule and encouraging me to eat a piece of blue bread or pink cheese she'd say, 'It's not to be afraid of,' with great seriousness – as if worrying that my refusal would offend the organisms that, to my mind, shouldn't have been living on my lunch. She'd often add, 'You know, most of the cells in your body are not even human.' For her, all life was one disgusting and beautiful moving part and humans were neither singular nor distinct but a series of interlinked ecosystems, our bodies just landscapes of fertile valleys and arid plains, scattered villages and megapolises, full of all kinds of denizens. Dead bodies were still populous chemical replicas of the Archean oceans – they just had a different balance of inhabitants.

It's only now, with everything unravelled and rewound all around me, that I can really see why my mother never recovered from leaving Cuba. When she was there, she was exceptional, outstanding, an incredible woman who not only understood the inner workings of yeasts and bacteria, but could also make a home. And there, making a home meant everything – and I don't mean it meant everything to her, lots of other things were important to her too, I mean it meant everything as in knowing how to do absolutely everything. It meant she could send her daughter out to school with her hair tightly plaited and her shirt shining white, she could grow the potatoes that fed the family with enough left over for scraps for the chickens that laid the eggs that fed the family with enough left over to trade for milk that she made into yoghurt that fed the family with enough left over to trade with the man who ran the ice-cream cart whose brother worked in a place that made tiles which she stacked carefully in piles under the bed, carefully calculated until one day there were enough. And then the same all over again but this time for cement and then one weekend she turned me and my dad out of the house on the Saturday morning and told us not to bother her. And with a little precisely directed help from us she moved all the furniture into the garden and told us we might as well scrub it all down if we wanted to be good for something, and she got down and mixed tile cement and laid a tiled floor through the whole house – kitchen, bedrooms, hallway, sitting room, veranda. My father and I set the house up underneath the mango tree beside his study.

That evening we sat around the kitchen table, still under the mango tree, and my mother rubbed her knees and the neighbours came over with the meal that my mother had prepared and put into pots and asked them to cook for her because we couldn't go into the house. That night the strangeness was beautiful, going to sleep in my bed with the net around it out in the garden, hearing the voices of the neighbours and my parents who were sitting on the rocking chairs laughing and gossiping.

And the next day she got up and went through and put the grout between the tiles and we slept in the garden again. And on Monday morning she sent me off to school with my plaits as tight and my shirt as white as ever, and she went to work. That afternoon when I got home my dad was working under the mango tree as usual, all the rest of the house still set up around him. I don't know if she'd told him not to or if he just didn't dare take the risk, but he hadn't moved a thing. She'd bought *congrí* on her way home – I thought that was incredibly exciting, even though it was just the same rice and beans as ever I had never seen her buy them already cooked before – and when we'd eaten it she and my dad moved everything back into the house. And from that day on, nobody for miles around ever walked onto her veranda with their shoes on, not because it would make the floor dirty, but because the dust from their soles would've been a disrespect to the energy and capability and ingenuity of the woman who had put it there. My dad was incredibly proud of her, and as a child I was pretty certain that basically everyone in the town, the region, the province, probably everyone in Cuba, knew that my mother was a fine woman and able to do anything. And that counted for a lot, really a lot, it counted for everything.

And then she moved to London and it all counted for nothing. Nobody cared that she could grow everything that you could buy in the supermarket, and if something needed to be fixed it was considered weird that she would do it. Our neighbours in Streatham once called the police because she was up on the roof putting a piece of leading back in place after a storm. She never recovered from the feeling that the world had completely lost its sense of what counted. In Cuba she knew, and it was clear to absolutely everybody, that making a home that was clean and safe and happy was vital work. She never got used to that sureness being walked all over and crushed down by capitalists, by globalists, even by feminists sometimes. So she did her best to recreate Cuba in a Victorian redbrick in Streatham.

I say she, but they did it together, her and my father. That house was its own little self-sustaining island of two. My father set up his mango-tree study in the front room, typewriter and all, and gave himself the slow-burn mission of compiling the complete works of José Martí and translating the whole lot into English. He unpicked and reworked his translations constantly and he was always a little anxious that somebody would suddenly decide they wanted to publish it before he was ready. This was not really a risk: he occasionally – very occasionally, not even once a year – got some kind of love from a university or some other institution for his work, but that, along with Heike's encouragement and his own belief in the importance of the task, was enough for him. He never finished it.

Heike never had a job herself, but she was busy all the time. She inherited my granddad's allotment when we arrived, and anyone who had words against her getting it in September had shut their mouth by April when the growth began – she dug so much love and care into that stretch of ground that it denied her nothing. She was an active member of the local wholefood co-op where her German-ness was respected. Although she never entirely got her head around the cost of things, she had a kind of practical faith that the higher the nutritional value of a food the more expensive it should be, which meant that she managed not to be bothered by the fact that dried beans were more expensive by the kilo than supermarket cake. She volunteered at a local charity shop, where her running battles over what was or wasn't too worn out to be sold became the stuff of legend all the way to regional management and the stuff of wardrobe back at ours, right down to her once 'mending' the worn-out grips on the soles of a pair of trainers with a hot poker and a Stanley knife. And she ran the house on a shoestring – a shoestring neatly spliced back together and with a twist of Sellotape around one end because the aglet has fallen off.

She never really made any friends in London. Every now and then she would get a little pally with a woman from the allotments or the co-op or the charity shop, but she would always end up coming back from a cup of tea at their house shaking her head and saying, 'Ach, plastic clothes pegs,' or, 'Ach, dreamcatchers,' or, 'Ach, air freshener,' or, 'Ach, Jesus,' or some other such damning indictment, which meant that she would never, ever be friends with such a person. If she'd been born a generation later she could've had her following. Even as a mortified teenager I knew that it wasn't just right the way we lived, it was cool. And it made an amazing backdrop, because it was beautiful through and through: her rows of jars of many-coloured pickles and preserves; her allotment overflowing with everything worth growing; the cover of a thousand mends that she crocheted for the sofa that was in the house when we arrived, and was still in it twenty-odd years later when I left.

When I went back there to pick up the bits and pieces I planned on taking with me, I didn't at all manage to register the enormity of it, no more than I had when we left Cuba. Unlike my mother, I only understand that something will be left behind forever after the fact.

When we left the Arches I was just full of excitement at getting out, we all were, it carried us all the way to Fairlight. Leaving Fairlight was fine too, striking out on our adventure-mission, although when we left Fort Mahon I was leaden and tired at first — maybe that's the difference between leaving and being left. Later, when we left the *Château*, everyone was jangling with rage and relief. But the whole way we were dragged and propelled into every departure by Sarah's dream. She didn't talk much about her plans. Say something once, why say it again. She talked about it that time in the Arches when Pressure Drop and Adi agreed we'd all travel together, and she talked about it again one time, after we'd crossed over to France but before the *Château*. We were in the flatlands still, where cathedrals appeared out of the yellow-green wheatfields like galleons and then were left astern as we pushed on across the plains.

That night we had found a great place to sleep, a garden with not just a brick-built barbecue but a wildly exploding weed-threaded vegetable garden, tangles of peas and beans run through with bindweed, courgettes gone marrow among the dandelions. We'd grilled slices the size of saucers and eaten them alongside huge plates of rice cooked with gone-to-seed onions and wrinkly tomatoes and handfuls of parsley on top and we'd filled bags for the next days too. We were even planning to dig up some potatoes before we left in the morning. So we were full, and we'd had a good day's ride. We were sitting at the patio table, the pot and plates washed and drying on the windowsill. Above us, swifts banked and dove. Bit by bit, the dusk seeped into the sky and their skywriting was written over by the scribbling, ragged-handkerchief flight of bats. The embers of the fire became slowly more visible as the dusk fell. I was sitting with my hands on my belly and Sarah nodded towards it and said, 'We'll be there in time.'

'You're so sure of the place,' I said, 'you don't worry that it won't work out?'

Sarah rummaged in the top pocket of her rucksack and pulled out a postcard. It showed generic-looking fields of lavender and the bell tower of a church.

She turned it over to read the back of it to us: '*Cours, camarade, le vieux monde est derriere toi. Jean-Luc*'. She gently uncrumpled its corners, her shoulders soft as she said, 'It arrived after deliveries had basically stopped – I can only think that somebody in some sorting office must have realised it was important and taken it upon themselves to make sure it reached me. We always wrote to each other. He wouldn't have written if he didn't know they'd be there when I came.'

She looked up at us, suddenly self-conscious and left exposed by the flimsiness of the cryptic postcard-compass that was guiding us all on our journey. 'It means to come,' she said, a little insistently. She quickly tucked the postcard back into the rucksack pocket, took a small, tight breath in and shrugged, saying, 'If not there, elsewhere. The knowledge I have, even what you have, is too important. It's the birthright of your daughters, their daughters, anybody's daughter, anybody's son for that matter. One way or another, I'm making sure it survives. I'm going to make a place where, years and years from now, in every village from Nice to Lyon, from Marseille to Turin, there will be at least one woman who's come to give birth with us, and when another woman in that village is ready to give birth, the others will say, "Go and ask her, she gave birth with the *sage-femme*." And when they do ask her, she'll have something useful to tell them. It's my job, and it will be your job, to make sure she does.'

So I worked at it, in quiet daylight moments all through the journey. I read, reread and learned by heart the whole of *Spiritual Midwifery*, pushing past Ina May's use of 'lady' instead of 'woman' and her weird nicknames for the vulva and perineum and letting paragraph after paragraph consolidate in my mind. It became my only defence against the earworms: every now and then, particularly on a long uphill drag, I'd get a fragment of a song stuck in my head, like a splinter off the previous world working its way into my flesh. In other times, when my memory got hung up on a song, I'd always just listened to it, but now the only way I could get rid of them before they drove me mad was to recite whole chunks of the book aloud to myself as I rode. Sometimes Sarah would be nearby and she'd interject with additions or disagreements, but mostly the words just mingled with my feet turning the pedals and my hands tugging on the hoods as I pushed forwards towards whatever was ahead.

We were somewhere after the village with the bones and starting to come towards serious-looking mountains when we began hearing the wolves. It scared us half to death. The first night we heard them we were camped in a tiny nursery school in a little village. We'd pushed all the miniature chairs and tables to the edges of the classroom to make space. The laminated magnets for the days of the week and the weather were still on the blackboards and on some of the hooks there were still coats and schoolbags, as if some kids had left in a hurry. The toilets were so small they looked like they were for dolls.

I used to be able to think it was just as well it hit little kids and old people so hard, that it was a kindness. Can you imagine if something happened that spared the kids and there'd just be millions of little ones, hungry and cold and alone, dying scared and slowly? At the beginning of the chaos there were all kinds of stories, first of people killing their pets, then of them killing their kids. Whole families gassing themselves, parents drowning their children as they slept or putting them to bed in chest freezers and switching them on and closing the lids in the night. There were tutorials. I can't think about it anymore.

It's so fucking pathetic, the way we're made. We think we are able to imagine what it's like to be somebody else, to go through something that somebody else is going through, but we aren't. Nothing touches us really until it becomes something that's happening to us. If you were really able to imagine the horrors that people go through in their lives you would never be able to move again. Even just one of those people who killed their own child, try really going there. The softness of their skin as you pull the covers from around them and smooth their hair away from their face, the cosy weight of them as you pick them up, their breath in your ear, holding their head tucked in against your neck as you carry them into the bathroom, the little arm that flops as you shift their position to lower them into the bath; you can't do it. You just cannot imagine the pain and sadness and desperation. And all that, I used to just be able to not think about it at all, like, I could just think, 'Oh, that's awful,' and it wouldn't feel at all like I was going to fall through a hole in the world, like if my mind came any closer to the thought it would be like acid, dissolving away everything inside me. And that is just because now I am a tiny bit closer to knowing what it would be like to have to do something like that.

We think we can feel something for other people, but we have no idea how little we really feel. We are hard-hearted motherfuckers. We allow ourselves to imagine that we are just talking about cartoon characters or clay figurines or apples. That way we can just say it is lucky so many of them died from the illness or were killed kindly by somebody who loved them because otherwise they – I say 'they' but don't think of anything that's really a 'them', don't think of them crawling, toddling, don't think of them trying to reach a door handle to leave a house that has nothing in it but their dead family, don't think of them curled in a corner, hungry and cold and afraid and nobody ever coming to look after them ever again. In fact, don't even get as far as saying 'they'. Just say 'because otherwise'. Leave it at that.

But before, like I said, it wouldn't have touched me any more than the thought of wolves. The thought of wolves when they're happening somewhere where you can't hear them yourself is kind of interesting. The thought of wolves when you can hear them is fucking terrifying. You recognise it immediately, and not just because you've heard it in films and stuff, the noise makes you feel something is coming to get you the same way that a cloud passing quickly in front of the sun makes you think a pterodactyl is swooping down to eat you. It's like you don't hear it in your ears at all, you hear it in your spine, and then in the roots of your hairs, and then in your bowels.

It woke us all up immediately. We tried to tell each other that we were just being dramatic and it was probably just dogs, but that lasted about thirty seconds, and then I said that we had to go and check that all the doors and windows were closed. It was like a dream, all the out-of-scale furniture with just enough moonlight to see by. We crept along the corridors and through the classrooms, pushing gently at each window and expecting at every second the horror-movie moment where slavering jaws spring at you out of the dark outside. Every time they were so loud that we were sure they were in the playground they'd then get louder again.

All the doors and windows were closed. We went back to our sleeping bags. Schools are a good place to camp if you're able to get in and are not looking for food. They generally don't have anything rotting in them, the toilets are in a separate bit of the building and the playground makes it feel like you have space to see somebody coming. But none of that helped with the wolves. There was no way we were going back to sleep. Sarah went and searched the staffroom in the dark until she found two blocks of cooking chocolate in the back of a cupboard and we sat and ate that until we felt a bit sick from the mix of adrenaline and sugar, and then we got the giggles from Pressure Drop going on about a time when he'd been so frightened that he'd actually pissed himself. We all agreed that the next day we weren't going anywhere and finally fell asleep in the early morning.

A downside of schools is that they often do not have anywhere to dig a shit-hole, but this one had big wooden planters along one of the walls of the playground, which still had the straggled ends of dozens of dried-up collapsed sunflowers in them. Plants just get on with things really. There did not seem to be any signs of wolves in the playground, but back then we didn't really know what signs of wolves would be; we were probably looking for half-eaten grandmothers and discarded sheep's clothing. Finding neither of those things, we took turns in the planters, Pressure Drop complimenting the efforts of whichever teacher had planted the sunflowers – he was, still is, convinced that only good people are able to have a relationship with plants. In that, he's more generous than my mother was, but she had wildly high standards. I know I was a huge disappointment to her, though she partly blamed that on decadent capitalism. She thought that if I'd grown up in Cuba in a school full of kids striving to climb the next rung of the ladder – from labourer to mechanic, mechanic to lawyer, lawyer to president – I would've set my sights on biochemist or diplomat or at least doctor, instead of skidding around the edges of the music industry as a fixer and minder and finally, at the age of almost thirty, essentially losing my job to Google Translate and becoming a part-time teaching assistant. She was right that the lack of motivation from my peer group didn't help – the school I went to was much worse than what I'd have got in Cuba.

In the secondary school I would've gone to in Cuba you could be suspended if you were caught chewing bubblegum while in your school uniform. When we arrived in Streatham I went straight into a South-London comprehensive, which my dad's idealism and my mother's lack of understanding of the total fucked-ness of the place conspired to keep me in for six years. In my time there I learned not just how to chew bubblegum while wearing a school uniform, but also how to roll a joint inside a pencil case and how to put a condom on using my mouth, so I clearly mastered some setting-specific life skills that I wouldn't have had the chance to develop if we'd stayed in a tourist-free town somewhere between Bayamo and Santiago.

And they were actually useful skills to have. They kept me right in the middle – not straight, not off the rails. My parents didn't believe in me having money though – you could take them away from their socialist paradise, but you couldn't stop them believing that having a fiver in your pocket corrupted you quicker than radioactive isotopes. So I never had a penny, which really just pushed me back to Cuban styles – swaps, exchanges, skills for stuff, make do and mend. I did a lot of Spanish and German homework in exchange for crisps and Chupa Chups, and if anybody asked why I always needed subbing in the chicken shop I'd just shrug and say, 'My parents are communists.' It was basically accepted – you didn't eat pork because your parents were Muslim, you didn't blaspheme because your parents were Christian, you didn't have money because your parents were communists. End of story. And so, take that perennially skint me with questionable skills, add an ability to adapt Cuban ass-shaking to drum'n'bass, an unending supply of awesome vintage clothes from helping out with donations in the charity shop and a knack for the non sequitur as put-down, give that person long, blade-straight hair with the tropical-sun bleach still growing out at the tips like a dip-dye, a chest so flat that even the walls were jealous and you have me: ready to leave school with three good A-levels, one in art and the other two in Spanish and German – both languages I'd been fluent in since learning to speak.

I had no plans to go to university. I wanted to get into venues for free and go to festivals all summer. I made myself useful. I got to know a bunch of people who ran club nights and organised festivals and I made sure they all knew I was fluent in three languages, and sooner or later I was writing emails for them to techno DJs and Reggaeton artists, and then I was translating contracts and checking riders, and it wasn't long until I was meeting people at airports and helping them sort out their accommodation and their lost jacket and their forgotten pill prescriptions and whatever other pills they needed for their gig too. That work barely pays, so I honed excellent blagging and gatecrashing skills, and stuck to the idea that if you got in when you shouldn't have, you had a duty to make yourself the most fun, most charming, most bring-the-good-vibes person in the place. While my mother was convinced that the only way to live your life was to use your capacities to improve the world for the greater good of all mankind, I was convinced that I should be using mine to have a good time. There's a lot of people, or there were anyway, who go on about how going out all night and taking drugs and having casual sex is a rubbish thing to do that leaves you feeling empty and sad, but I think that's just people who aren't very good at it, the same way anyone in a job they're bad at will feel miserable. I was great at it. My parents just let me get on with it – if I'm honest that was probably because they had no clue what I was up to. Maybe in some way my mother saw and admired the ingenuity that went into keeping it all in the air on no money, and my dad was able to enjoy the idea that each next generation would do something that seemed totally ridiculous to the one before – it's what he'd done – but also they genuinely just had no idea.

I was often jealous of Pressure Drop and his weed. The pillow that had constituted his list of what he wanted to bring with him on the journey was actually just like a thin shell of 'pillow' that was entirely filled with weed, kilos of it crushed down, plenty more than the two kilos that Adi's calculations allowed for, and every now and then he'd decant a couple of handfuls of walking-around-weed into a leather pouch. Weed is easy, but it was never really my thing, I always preferred the credit I got for rolling a really good joint to actually smoking one. Smoking is gross and the happy, gentle, uselessness always bored me, which, pretty handily, made me think that drugs weren't really for me until I was older. The chances of me ever coming across the kind of drugs I liked again are so slim that they'll have to live on in memory. The first time I ever took anything worth taking was when a friend slipped me a wrap at a party saying, 'Take this.' I thought they meant all of it. I'll never forget the way the whole room started to shake, the edges of everything, including me, fizzing and vibrating. That was on the Friday night, and on the Monday morning, when I'd just about got it back together enough to go home and was cycling past one of those galvanised-railing fences along the railway lines, the way the sun slanted and strobed through the gaps flipped me right back up again. I couldn't get my teeth unclenched until Tuesday. But the thing is, if that's what you want you've got to have something planned that's up to what you're going to take. You can smoke a joint and go sit in the pub and chat to randoms, but if you want to get completely out of your head that scenario is going to be rubbish. So I didn't do it every week, but when I did I really loved it: festivals or big weekends and just blazing through them like a comet, trailing glitter and sweat and mint wrappers in my wake. And all that will literally never ever happen again. Over. Gone. Done. You just have to let it go and marvel at how spoilt we were that we could bring so much of our energy and resources to bear on making a space and a time where it was beautiful to spend seventy-two hours flying.

The thing about living in the moment, is that you can't plan for it, and I think that's the difference between planning and preparation: planning is imagining your future, preparation is trusting your past. And not just your past, but all the pasts that are spiralled up in your DNA. For example, on the journey to the coast we could smell something was wrong far quicker than we could see it. Without ever having experienced anything like it we could recognise the stink of a house with bodies in it – you know it in your guts, you recoil from it before you even know what you're doing. As soon as we were out of the mishmash of London we avoided houses before we even got near enough to know they stank. Just days into the journey our precortical reptile brains were veering us away before we got close enough to know why.

That didn't happen with Laura's, although it certainly stank – like really vile vomit, the way bile smells when you're heaving up teaspoons of the stuff having voided the rest of your stomach, but with an undertone of crispy socks. Really disgusting, but not a smell that spins your internal compass and points you off in a different direction entirely. It got worse and worse as we rode down the road. We couldn't see a thing, the trees and bushes closed us in, even reaching up and meeting over our heads so that we were in a sort of storybook tunnel of dappled, stinking shade. Eventually the smell slowed us, stopped us.

'What do you think it is?' asked Adi, and Pressure Drop said, 'The devil's fucking knob-cheese I reckon.'

Sarah always tried not to react when he said stuff like that, you could see a lifetime of teaching herself to pretend she hadn't heard in the muscles around her mouth, but you could also often see in the corners of her eyes that she found it funny. It made me think that she'd grown up in a shit area. It's the sort of thing that becomes super-important, not to use or listen to bad language, because that's how parents help society decide which kids are going to be stuck there and which kids are going to get out. You still saw it in the primary schools I worked in, the first-generation immigrants' kids, polite as all hell with every kind of dog-whistle parenting, matching hairties and ironed sweatshirts and a new schoolbag in September, while the middle-class kids would show up with holes in the knees of their trousers and the plaits from the day before. Every little thing counts when you haven't many things, and not swearing is one of those things. Although really, growing up mixed-race somewhere in the Midlands in the middle of the twentieth century wouldn't have left her much room to put a foot wrong no matter how much her parents had earned, and I can't imagine that her Southern Baptist father went in much for cussing. Whatever the reason, Sarah, even though she sometimes wanted to laugh at what she still called 'colourful language', didn't.

We carried on because that's what the road did, and quickly we heard sounds of life – a woman's voice singing. It's all just a mishmash of instinct and conditioning but there are sounds that instantly make you wary and sounds that convince you very quickly that it'll all be fine, and singing is an 'all fine' one. Especially when you manage to filter through the strangeness of the fact that you're cycling through eerie quiet and gross smells from London to a town you've never heard of in the south of France, where you will become an apprentice midwife and pass on the knowledge of our forebears so that women can continue to get babies out through their vaginas, and somewhere on this journey in the midst of the stink of the devil's knob-cheese a woman is belting out a really quite convincing rendition of 'Disco 2000' and every now and then a bunch of cows join in as backing vocals. So despite the stink, we turned in through the gate we'd just arrived at, got off our bikes and wheeled them towards the singing. We reached a gate into a muddy yard and there was a tiny person in the middle of a herd of little brown-and-white cows and even littler calves, sitting on an upside-down bucket and milking into another.

It seemed rude to interrupt, so we waited 'til the crescendo, the, 'Ooh oh-oh-oh ooh ooh ooh, oh-oh-oh ooh ooh oooh', where the cows seemed to sing along again, and then we called out to her. She jumped and spun round to face us, kicking over the bucket of milk as she did so, its whiteness pouring all over the mud and cow shit like the total illustration of what it was no use crying over. She looked at us and we did our best to look non-threatening – honestly, if we'd wanted to look threatening I don't know how we would have done it.

'Sorry about the milk,' said Sarah.

'Oh, that's all right,' said Laura, 'It's what I was going to do anyway, just not there. You're lucky, you've arrived just as I'm finishing. Wait there, I'll be back in a minute.'

She turned back to the cow which, having started when she jumped at our arrival, hadn't moved since, and finished milking it straight onto the ground. Then she slapped its arse and it walked off. She opened the gate on the far side of the yard and all the cows moved towards it, jostling like commuters trying to get in through the doors of a bus.

Laura closed the gate after them and came towards us, brushing her hands on her trousers. 'Come into the house,' she said, 'I don't really live in there anymore, but we can go and sit round the table. Do you want some milk?' I really didn't after seeing it all mixing with the dirt, but we followed her.

Laura was a geologist. Her parents had run the farm – her dad really. She'd come back to help out when things got difficult. They'd died and left her with the herd of thirty cows. Her father had never liked milking, but they'd been dairy farmers for generations, so he spent his life breeding a herd that only needed milking once a day and didn't need milking all winter until they calved in the spring. So Laura was left with them, and she milked all the cows to get rid of the extra after the calves had fed, threw the milk in the bottom of the slatted shed – hence the stink, thirty cows for weeks and weeks is a lot of off milk – and mostly lived on porridge because there was plenty of milk and also there was a huge supply of oats that'd been left for weaning the calves, but this year they wouldn't be weaned.

We were all excited by the new company and it's hard to tell when you meet under such extreme circumstances, but I think we actually would've got on in normal life. We ended up staying for a few days, and me and Sarah and Adi learned how to milk cows. Pressure Drop said he wouldn't touch those rubbery teats for love nor money and that any job that meant you had to work on a Sunday was an unnatural perversion. When Sarah pointed out that doctors and parents had to work on a Sunday he said that was because those weren't jobs, they were vocations, and that the fact that you had to look after animals every day was proof that you shouldn't eat any part of them. He made his porridge with water.

Laura had, realistically, gone kind of mental – though 'kind of mental' is a relative concept. I suppose you could equally say, Laura had adapted in a specific way to an extreme living situation, wearing all her thermals under bloodstained overalls and sleeping in with the cows. Like, if you have been isolated on a farm with no company except for cows for months and in that time you've had to singlehandedly deliver almost twenty calves using only the garbled dregs of what you remember your dad doing when you were a kid as your reference material and then every day you have to milk out the ones who are producing more milk than their calves need, which is all of them because for hundreds of years they've been bred to produce more milk than their calf needs, but you can't milk them too much because if you leave a bit in the udders that's what'll trigger them to produce a bit less in the long term, and it takes about fifteen minutes per cow so that's seven-and-a-half hours a day and that only leaves you on average four-and-a-half hours of proper daylight to organise keeping yourself warm and dry and fed and the rest you try to sleep, you would go kind of mental.

When she talked about the calving – not sleeping for days and blood on all her clothes and no time to wash anything and no hot water to wash any of it anyway – it seemed like she was talking about war. I mean, obviously she was just talking about birth, but we used to talk a lot less about birth than about war, and to see so much more stuff about war than about birth, so that's where all our blood and exhaustion references are. Like, if you think of the number of people you know. Knew. Whatever, anyway, if you think of the number of people who've given birth compared to the number of people who've gone to war, and then think of the amount of telly there used to be about birth compared to war, the coverage is pretty disproportionate. Maybe by the end of my life that'll be the other way round. Not with telly obviously, just with telling. Live in hope.

When Laura found out what Sarah's job was she wanted to get a load of it off her chest about the conveyor-belt feeling of dealing with the whole herd. Sarah said she reckoned she wouldn't have been much help with cows but you could see all the same that she got why it had blown Laura away. Pressure Drop stuck to his line that it was all the result of a perversion of the natural order of things, and Laura basically agreed with him – she said after the cows ran dry she was going vegan, that pulling the calves out of their mothers had been so intense and weird and blood-soaked that she thought she'd never want to eat meat again and that she was sick of the sight of milk. Adi wanted to bring a cow and calf with us, he said they'd come in handy.

Adi had been the most excited about discovering the farm. You could see his need to put all the pieces in place kicking in. He still believed that things were going to go back to normal. As if there was back. As if there was normal. There's only forward, and you can only go forward from where you are, however wrecked that place is. I knew that back then, I knew it even before, I was never one for thinking about things after they'd happened, but I understand it differently now. Not just understand it, I am it. But Adi believed that one day the clock would run backwards and it would once again be the time of beer in taps and burgers in freezers and bread in packets and milk in cartons. He was so held by the solidity of how things had been that he thought all this was temporary, a hiatus, a parenthesis, a blip, that sooner or later there'd be that bit where you wake up and it was all just a dream.

That's why he was brilliant for organising the journey: he believed in it from beginning to end because he believed in its end. Bringing the cow was the most, maybe the only, completely illogical thing I ever saw him argue for. You could see it was just stronger than him, this idea that he'd be preserving some sacred tie with the past and that all he'd have to do was invent a machine that made cornflakes and everything would go back to how it was before. We didn't need to argue him out of it, he did it himself. But you could really see the fight going on inside him.

I didn't want the cow. Apart from it was just mad and would've made the journey too slow, I found the milking pretty weird. I mean, the actions and that are okay, there's a certain satisfaction in getting the right kind of pressure in the right place and the jet zinging out into the bucket, but as soon as I'd remember that I was doing it to another creature and not some kind of arcade game, the velvety feel of the teats would start to freak me out and I'd have to take some deep breaths to keep myself on the job. I think I'd find it even harder now, the whole idea of taking the milk. At least there it was after the calves had fed, though they watched us like they knew we were pouring away something that was meant to be theirs, that was blood and bone of their mother and was meant to become blood and bone of them – sunlight to grass to milk to flesh. Sarah says that in France they say, '*un enfant une dent*' because for every child you'd lose a tooth as you bled away the calcium in your milk, and that the breastmilk of women in refugee camps has basically the same nutritional content as that of the mothers who eat the best diet in the world. Breastfeeding is the body strip-mining itself. Just mother becoming child. Nature's great recycling act. Laura really didn't want us to go and be left alone with the cows. Not just because she was lonely and tired, but you could see that she saw it ahead of her, that she was heading towards the moment when they wouldn't need her anymore. The calves would be ready, the milk would have stopped and she'd just have to open all the gates to all the fields and let them get on with it.

She didn't want to come with us, she thought we were out of our heads to think we were heading to the south of France – though, bizarrely, she'd actually been to Digne on a field trip when she was at university – and she thought Pressure Drop's idea that he was going to carry on to become part of the founding of a new world in the mountains of Zion in Ethiopia was off the scale loopy. That was fine by him. A large measure of what he considered the truth and sense of an idea seemed to come from how crazy the rest of the world thought it was. That, as he'd say, was just Babylon trying to turn you from the path. One time Sarah asked him what he'd been before he was a Rastafarian, I suppose wondering if he'd been Catholic. He told her that when he was a teenager he'd been a nihilist, but that in the end believing in nothing took so much effort that it had to be a fight against the way He made us.

When the time came for us to continue towards Digne, or Zion, Adi took the map out. Laura quickly interrupted his serious speech — about the possibility of the map falling into other people's hands and them then knowing that there was something worth finding where the marking was — and snatched the pencil out of his hand to mark the spot where we were. And we said goodbye and were back on the bikes, back on our way.

We came through Fairlight in the middle of the morning. It was one of those grey days, low cloud and not quite raining but you could feel that it might. We wanted to stop early rather than get soaked, and we'd reached the coast so we were unsure what our next move was supposed to be. Not that Fairlight felt like the coast. It's an odd place, you don't realise it's on the sea because it has its back to it. You can see why, when the town's falling off a cliff. You can hear the sea, and when you come to the ends of certain roads there it is below all of a sudden, opalescent and choppy, but instead of any of the seasidey stuff you associate with the south coast, the piers, the proms, the sticky-floored arcades, the little marinas, it's more like as if a suburb of Guildford has accidentally been picked up and dropped on the edge of the land. So riding along between trees and green fields, and then meeting a tall man in yellow oilskins with a bundle of shining fish dangling from one hand, was like seeing a mirage dreamt up by people who'd headed for the coast in search of somebody with a boat. Martin once said that people had forgotten more than they ever knew about fishing, but by that morning's showing he was remembering it pretty well. So he stopped walking towards us, and we slowed and stood down astride the bikes and we looked each other over. Sarah did the talking.

I don't believe in love at first sight, but actually whether you believe in something or not has nothing to do with whether it exists. I miss him so fucking much. I've missed him all along, but more than ever now.

Anyway, Sarah came straight out and asked if he'd been fishing from a boat and said that we were looking for somebody to take us across the Channel, and that we didn't have much to exchange but that maybe we could work something out. And he looked us over some more and I could feel it all starting in my stomach, my cheeks getting hot, everything just like when you're thirteen and you deliberately forget your pencil case so that you can ask the boy beside you to borrow a pen and maybe touch his fingers when he hands it to you. That feeling of being totally transparent or naked, like you've cracked open your own ribs and everyone can see your heart beating faster and faster.

Martin nodded and said, 'You'd better come over to the house and meet Julie.' And my heart just stopped and I thought I was going to be sick. Seriously, I was on the point of saying that no thanks it was fine we'd just carry on, but obviously I couldn't have done that in any way that wouldn't have looked completely insane to the others.

So we followed him down a footpath that ran along the edge of a golf course that had become a meadow, Sarah just behind him, then Adi, then Pressure Drop, then me, all the while telling myself that this was idiotic, that it was not possible to fall in love with the back of somebody's head, even less so when they were wearing a woolly hat, that I was just excited that we'd reached the coast, that I was hungry and could see the fish, that anyway there was this Julie in the picture and with all that tumbling around in my head I didn't even manage to listen to anything they were talking about. We arrived at the house and by the time I'd shut the gate behind us she was there in the open doorway with one hand on the door jamb and the other on her rounded belly, looking like an ancient symbol of a household god, protecting every threshold that counts.

So at that point, obviously, Sarah knew that Martin would be taking us across and she turned around to beam at all of us, this huge smile of pride and the rightness of everything and Pressure Drop was nodding gently back to her. I could hear Martin saying, 'This is where our parents lived,' and then I could see it, their same black hair and same pale-blue eyes and same broad knuckles and my heart went up out through the top of my head, soaring up into the damp grey sky like violins in the throat and soda bubbles in the back of the neck. And like I said, I don't believe in all that stuff, in thunderbolts and the one and a moment when everything falls into place, and in fact fuck's sake look at where we are now and what happened in between, so 'falling into place' my arse. But the whole day I was basically dumbstruck.

Sarah and Julie immediately made a deal — we would stay until after the birth and then Martin would take us across in a fishing boat. And as soon as the deal was struck, Julie started organising us. In the house, she was the boss. She had us moving things around to sort out where we'd sleep, sending Martin up to the loft to find bedding and sheets and Adi out to the shed to make space for the bikes and setting me and Sarah to turn the rooms she'd given us into bedrooms. The house was big enough to handle it, and Martin and Julie had already unsentimentally set about making it even roomier, dumping all their mum's knick-knacks from the shelves, stripping everything electrical from the kitchen and anywhere else in the house, throwing out loads of the clothes from the bedroom cupboards — though keeping their mum's fur coat and all their dad's knitted sweaters. Martin had his childhood bedroom; Julie, who needed the space to move about at night, had their parents' room; Sarah had Julie's old room, to be nearby and have a proper bed; Pressure Drop and Adi had the dining room, their beds made up underneath the table for space; and I had the sofa in the front room. Adi tried to tell Julie that we should just use our sleeping bags, but she refused to hear of it, saying that we'd be staying there at least a month and that halfway across France we'd be thankful for having spent the Fairlight weeks between cotton sheets. We were too early on in the journey for me to know how right she was.

It was an adult version of building a den behind the sofa. Standing lamps became tent poles, glass-fronted dressers became clothes cupboards, tablecloths became bedspreads. Sarah was all for the houses within houses, she later said that it was important for Julie to be doing it, that it would make the birth easier if she felt she'd prepared the world for the child that was coming into it, but having shared various bed spaces with Sarah for months on end I reckon she was just really relieved she'd be able to stick her feet out from under the covers when she got too hot at night.

At lunchtime Martin grilled the fish on the barbecue. They were beautiful, like shining slices of horizon, the sea meeting the sky slowly being brought down to earth by the flames. When is that going to happen again, that I can eat a mackerel?

Once, in the Arches, when the supplies of stuff from the Asian supermarket that could be eaten without cooking were starting to make meals more and more like nutritional Tetris, there was a conversation about food. I was craving vegetables and without really thinking about it admitted fantasising about lettuce and apples and raspberries and broccoli. Sarah said toast and marmite. Pressure Drop wanted oranges. Joy said that when we got out she and Trevor were going to raid a department store, a really posh one, and get all dressed up in anything they wanted and have a huge meal with champagne and foie gras and caviar and chocolate. Adi said that he just wanted a fish-finger sandwich on white bread with butter, and Sarah just looked at him so sadly and said, 'Oh love.'

'What?' said Adi. 'It's hardly foie gras and champagne.'

'Adi, there's been no electricity at all for over two weeks – even if you found somewhere with some kind of super-insulated freezers everything will have defrosted by now.'

'Yeah, not straight away, but when things get sorted out.'

Joy was nodding. Sarah looked over at Pressure Drop for support.

Pressure Drop and Sarah were, at first glance, pretty unlikely allies, her with her Ecco trainers and grey cardigan and him with his huge Doc Martens and swinging dreads, but they had more in common than any of us realised back then. And she got her support.

'Look lads,' he started, 'I'm not sure you understand what's actually happened here, but this is the big one. This is fire in Babylon; sword, famine and wild beasts have been riding among us for some time now and not as something far away. How can you live in a city where a child stabs another child to death every couple of weeks and not see the sword? How can you live in a city where one child in five is going out to school without having had any breakfast and not see famine? How can you live in a city where foxes steal babies from their beds and the politicians fuck pigs and not see the wild beasts? Plague is the last horseman. It's not like you weren't fucking warned. The book on this was written a couple of thousand years ago and there's millions of copies of it anywhere you look. The last horseman is riding among you and everything that's been built by Babylon, everything, all their edifices, life lived not as intended, will crumble, if it hasn't already. So go ahead and paint your nails because there must be enough Jezebel colours left in this land to poison a river, but accept the reality of the fucking situation. You can sit around and wait to see the sun turn black and the moon turn red and the stars fall to earth and the sky be rolled away like a sheet of parchment as the bullocks and the unicorns arrive, or you can choose to see what's been unveiled: that it's the moment of the last fucking battle. We need to find the ground on which Armageddon will be fought and you need to choose your side. There will be no more fish fingers. There will be no more white sliced bread. There will be no more butter. All these and all other abominations will be purged from the face of the earth.'

Adi took advantage of the fact that Pressure Drop had to breathe to say, 'I think it's a bit strong to call a fish-finger sandwich an abomination.' But he probably shouldn't have.

Pressure Drop rolled his shoulders back and pulled his chest up, full of air again – that man could breathe, trained to hold it down better that a yogic master – and opened up again.

'And that is because you have been sleepwalking into this your whole life. That is because you have no real understanding of what it does to the earth, which was made in perfect harmony, to drag every fucking fish from the sea, even from the darkest depths where the light of the sun has never touched, to fill the soil and the air and the water with poison and have the barefaced nerve to tell the people that you're doing it to make things grow, to make animals your slaves and say that's the natural way of things, and all this, all this has been there right in front of you but you have looked at it with the eyes of a child, and we have to grow up now, kiddos, we are through the glass, darkly, and that is how you're going to have to see things. Which side are you on, boys, because Noah was given the rainbow sign, no more water, the fire next time, and the fire is fucking coming.'

Pressure Drop looked at Sarah. 'Right?'

'Well,' said Sarah, 'I probably would have said something more like: given the situation outside it's great that you're looking forward to foie gras because it comes in tins, but you are probably never going to eat another banana as long as you live.'

And so I ate the mackerel thinking about that. Thinking about the fishes of the sea re-multiplying. Thinking of the bananas and mangoes and avocados and papayas ripening happily in their own countries without the danger of being bundled onto boats and eaten under a cold grey sky. Thinking of Cuba and how far across the ocean it was. Thinking of the journey ahead, of some place in the middle of France where we would say to each other, 'Do you remember the mackerel?' and in that moment the fish took on their true size as nature's incredible bounty, taken from it by skill and cunning. And they were amazing: the silvery-blue skin all black and blistered and the oil seeping out onto our fingers. There were two each. We gave thanks by stripping every scrap of flesh from their bones so that the remains burned in the fire like a handful of twigs. When Adi said to Pressure Drop that he thought he was a vegan, Pressure Drop just said that you didn't have to fish on a Sunday.

Pressure Drop played no part in the organisation of the house on any day of the week, never mind Sundays. At first, he set himself up in a chair on the patio out in the back garden and just sat there smoking for three or four days. If Martin came and asked him to help with something he'd help, and sometimes Julie would come and sit across the table from him and have a cup of tea, but mostly he just sat there, smoking and watching. He said he was reading the questions – that that was the most important part of any test, to get the questions right, not the answers. That was typical Pressure Drop, but we soon developed a habit of offhandedly asking his opinion before launching into a new task because otherwise you'd get halfway through and he'd suggest to you that you do things in the way you'd only just realised that you ought to have done them, having spent the last half-hour or half-day or half-week doing them the opposite way. Very annoying, but he was so often right that you couldn't have a go at him.

After about a week he brought a package full of seeds over from the garden shed where it'd stayed bundled in the panniers of his bike. He spread everything out on the table on sheets of newspaper, having made Adi go round all the houses on the street to look for a newspaper he would even lay them out on because he said he didn't want them poisoned by bad vibes. He made careful selections, half a dozen of this, three or four of that, and potted them up, labelling them carefully – back wall, middle row, outside edge, stuff like that.

Sarah started working with Julie, and I sat in. It was half a kind of weird internal yoga and half biology class. We'd go up to the loft where we'd cleared enough floor space for us all to lie down and Sarah would talk us through stuff. At first it seemed like it would be impossible to actually follow what she was saying as an instruction: 'Now the wall of your vagina closest to your spine is like a beach and the wave of movement comes up it towards your cervix and then dissipates around the entrance to your womb.' And then we would all stick our fingers up each other's fannies to check what was actually happening. It was brilliant. You'd be amazed how little it's possible to know about a part of your own body. Or maybe you wouldn't. I was; this whole part of myself that I'd been working with for over half my life, and I'd even intimately encountered other people's, without ever really thinking about how it was doing what it did. And it became clear to me that Sarah's plan had to work out, because at those moments she was truly awesome. Despite whatever she absorbed from the nuns in convent school in the sixties — never feeling the cold and never getting stinky mainly, better life skills to learn in secondary school than mine in fairness — she had an ability that seemed to come from beyond her which allowed her to teach women to know and be unafraid of knowing and believing in their own bodies.

You could see it with Julie, every session we'd come back downstairs to the kitchen and even though by then she was walking like a penguin and her back was killing her in the night she'd have this sort of grace, like a physical certainty that what she was doing was important and that she was doing it well.

I'd have some of that as well, and maybe all the fanny gymnastics were also a part of what made the sex with Martin so amazing, but it was definitely also just written in the stars. The first couple of days we just circled each other, barely speaking. There was nothing to take the edge off, no way of not seeing it for what it was and no way into it that wasn't total. It was an intense situation, for all it had going for it — six people who don't really know each other, except for the two who are brother and sister, which in itself has its own tensions, in a house in a village that's falling into the sea, preparing for the birth of a baby after the world has ended.

Everybody had and probably still has a different idea of what had actually happened. Pressure Drop thought it was the end of Babylon and the rise of Zion. Sarah thought it was the ecosystem shrugging its shoulders. Adi thought it was normality taking a gap year. Julie thought it was proof that her baby was the most important one that had ever or would ever be born (in this, at least, she was right, just like every other woman who thinks that) and Martin thought it was *Swallows and Amazons*, but with the potential for knife fights.

The thing that was difficult was that there was no such thing as a bigger picture, like, for years before everything crumbled, people had been going on about how we'd lost the overview, that it had all become more and more fragmented, but fragmentation is our natural state. It is very recent in human history that we have any idea of overview — until stuff like newspapers and reading became really common, overview was just what the oldest person in your village remembered and what the farthest-travelled person discovered.

There was no sense that what was happening to you was linked to what was happening on the other side of the world — apparently it was only when they invented the telegraph that people realised that weather wasn't just a local phenomenon, born of the conditions of sun and soil at that exact spot, but that in fact fronts moved across the country, dropping the same heavy rains or blowing the same strong winds. Though Martin would probably say that whoever thought it was telegraph operators on the plains of America that decoded the weather should speak to a tenth-century Faroese sailor.

Anyway, so we lost the overview. First we lost it a bit and people tribalised. The rich blamed the left, the left blamed the right, the right blamed the others, America blamed China,

China blamed Europe, Europe blamed Russia, the godly blamed the godless, the godless blamed the godly, and so on and so on. But when things really went to bits we completely lost the overview. We didn't even know who was blaming who anymore. It is hard to remember now what it felt like to think we knew what was happening: that a nation had chosen this or that, that a building we'd never seen had been blown up, that somebody we'd never met had died. It's hard to understand why we thought any of it was important.

There were always so many people saying it was all lies anyway, I don't know how anyone reporting on stuff managed to keep themselves motivated – except the ones who were lying, who must've just been excited at how well their lies were working. But then when the communications started going down, and when the electricity didn't come back on, there was no more overview. Your understanding of the world shrank down to what you were actually living, along with the bits and pieces that you could glean from the other alive people that you came across.

It was hardest for Adi. Pressure Drop was secure in the idea that this was the final promise coming to pass, and Sarah had her mission, but Adi was totally waiting for word of what was 'actually happening'. He couldn't believe that we were the main act. I suppose the opposite of that is what's kept me going. Even when it was absolutely clear that I wasn't the main act I was always somehow convinced that I was, so I just carried on like that. I suppose I miss the audience, but hey, here you are.

So, basically, six people is not enough overview. It wasn't enough in the Arches and it wasn't enough in Fairlight. It had been a few weeks. The weather was getting better, we had the house in good order, the long drop was dug, the seedlings were nearly ready to be planted out, and there was, as Pressure Drop said, a grand stretch in the evenings. I don't really know whose idea the bonfire was, but as soon as it came out we were all for it. We knew there were other people in the village, or around it, but we'd never really seen them. We didn't realise we needed to – it was still early days.

I went into town with Adi and we painted 'Bonfire at the Beacon, first sunny day in May' on a wall near the supermarket and took one of the shopping trollies. For the next while, every now and then I'd get ready to head up to the Beacon, filling the trolley with flammable stuff ditched from the house that we reckoned was too toxic for the barbecue, like the creosoted fences we'd ripped down from between the gardens, and anything we found along the way that looked burnable. We didn't take things from inside houses, but we took garden chairs and bits of trellis and branches and whatever was going. We had an axe with us, and we smashed things up as we went. By the time we'd got a decent pile together up on the hill it looked like something a furniture-eating monster had shat out.

The best – and worst – thing about making the bonfire was that it was often me and Martin who dragged the trolley up there together. It was ridiculous, the whole thing: t-shirts getting sweaty, arms squishing together as we adjusted our grip on the handle which got slippery, the comic interludes as we ineptly chopped or smashed stuff up, the giddy careen back down to the house, laughing and breathless. It got to a point where it felt like when we arrived back at the house all pink and damp the others wouldn't look at us because we looked so much like we'd been fucking.

And that was on top of the fishing. The day after we arrived, Martin said that it'd be great if one of us could help with the fishing. It'd be easier and much safer with two, and quicker, which was important now that we'd need three times as many fish. Adi volunteered straight away. I didn't have the nerve to. The pair of them came back with a catch, but Adi looked pretty glum and Martin said that with the way Adi threw up, with him on board they'd lose more food than they came back with. Adi looked all sheepish at me and said, 'Sorry Audaz, it's going to have to be you.' And I tried not to let the cartwheels I was turning inside my head show on my face.

Here's a thing – somewhere along the line we got this idea that romance comes before intimacy, but maybe it's better the other way around. The fishing was in no way romantic, but everything about it was intimate. The first few times, high tide was in the early morning. Martin would come and wake me up, quietly so as not to wake the rest of the house, and we'd make a thermos of sugary tea – unconsciously wondering how many kettle-boils the gas canister had left in it – and a stack of crackers with peanut butter, whispering in the half-light. Then we'd go and put our oilskins on in the big front porch, where what had once been a suntrap conservatory had become part potting shed, part drying room for fishing gear. Obviously we were already wearing our clothes at that point, but there was something in the getting dressed together that made it feel like we'd just got out of the same bed. And those early mornings were fucking beautiful: the sun coming up through the mist and the ground soaked in dew, and the birdsong. Everything was dripping, cuckoo spit on the sticky burs, spiderwebs full of droplets, and the glowing green of the translucent new growth of the leaves and weeds.

We'd go along the path where we'd first met and then cut down to the cove, the brand-new meadows of the golf course, juicy and full, giving way to gorse and scrub towards the top of the cliffs and the rattling of the sea on the shingle getting louder and louder as we went down to meet it under the huge flocks of gulls gliding purposefully down the coast. Martin's fishing boat then was just a little dinghy with an outboard – he said he'd get another before we needed to cross, anyway, he only had enough fuel left for another twelve or fifteen fishing trips. He'd strap the jerrycan of fuel at the back while I packed the tea and stuff into a compartment at the front. Martin used all the real names for bits of boats, but even after I'd absorbed them, just thinking about saying, 'I've stowed it in the bow,' rather than, 'I've put it in the front bit,' made me feel like too much of a total dickhead to ever use them. We'd tug the lifejackets from under the seats, drag the boat down to the water's edge, gripping and grabbing, shoulders straining while the sea shushed us, and push off with the oars. Martin would row us out, with me taking the odd turn.

Actually I take it back, the fishing was totally romantic. I suppose it felt like there was something generally romantic about the very early morning. Now when I'm up in the small hours walking the floor with the bundle all I want is to crawl back into the warm cave I've left under the duvet before every whisper of the heat of my body has left it, but it wasn't always like that. When I used to meet the early morning from being still up, it always seemed as if seeing that pale-grey sky with the edges of things becoming softer in the daylight than they were under the streetlights was an achievement, an award that I'd won on the merit of my own unstoppableness. Then the other times I'd seen them was when I was getting up crazy early for something exciting – to catch a plane or a train or, in the new order of things, a fish. Whatever it was, it used to feel special to be up and about while everyone else was still asleep.

It was like that when we left the Arches. We'd got everything packed up the day before and the bikes were loaded and waiting downstairs. Pressure Drop had got us to name them, he said that you should name anything that you were going to trust as a companion, so there they were: Sputnik, Buck, Louise-Michel and Ninja. 'Sputnik' was mine, named after a petrol station we always used to pass on the way to Santiago, a pink steel-frame racer with pale-blue bar tape on the drops, as happy and sleek as I ever could have hoped for. 'Buck' was Pressure Drop's, a solid grey hybrid, the kind you used to see a million of whenever you turned your head during rush hour. He'd customised it with red, gold and green insulation tape – I never found out why it was called Buck. I asked him once, but he just said, 'It's a long story,' and cracked himself up laughing. 'Louise-Michel' was Sarah's, named after a French anarchist, which seemed weird to me at the time but later made perfect sense, a Dutch-style bike in navy blue with a low, curved crossbar, a kickstand that made a noise like a mantrap when you raised it and a wicker basket with leather straps and buckles. Adi had wanted to take the basket off and put a waterproof handlebar bag on the front, but Sarah wouldn't let him. 'Ninja' was Adi's, a black and lime-green mountain bike, named after the motorbike he'd always wanted.

So, panniers on, they stood, waiting for the stable door to be opened. Adi had put an amazing amount of love into getting them ready. It was another of those things where you could see that he had half an eye on how impressed people would be when things went back to normal. He took photos of them on his phone, which he kept charged with a little fold-up solar panel he'd brought with him, waiting for everything to come back online. He'd done the same with the kit we were bringing, laying each of our selections out neatly and climbing onto a chair to take a high-angle photo down onto it before we packed everything up and strapped it to the bikes.

I get him doing it – look at me now with this, desperately trying to hold onto a story while my mind goes fuzzy and grey around it – but it felt weird seeing him take pictures, like somebody who has a vintage car and then gets all the vintage clothes and vintage picnic basket to go with it, but you know they have to go and buy their picnic in the supermarket like everybody else.

It was great seeing the bikes ready, I was so excited to leave. We'd been cooped up in the Arches about eight weeks by then, and though the view was limited, through the windows of the artists' studios we'd been able to see winter slowly being pushed out of the way by spring – the tops of trees above the roofs becoming fuzzed then filled with green, solid grey skies replaced by blue ones with piles of dark and light clouds dragging squally rain behind them, the sunsets getting later. I slept badly the night before, worrying we wouldn't wake early enough and worrying that something would happen, that Trevor and Joy would come back with Team Smart Money and ransack us for the stock of bottled water that remained, or that some new and unusual chaos would make us scared to go out.

There was never any sense to which nights were noisy and which were not. Pressure Drop was sure it was the moon, but it never seemed that way to me, plus if it was the moon then we weren't actually there long enough to be sure that's really what it was. There wasn't, as far as I could see, any pattern to when it would happen. Just some nights the noise would start, far away and then moving like a monster through the city, engines and gunshots, crashes and explosions, roars and screams. The sounds would get closer and closer and then move on farther away. It was honestly really fucking scary, and it made me horrified at the thought of what might be happening in places where a lot of people had guns. And once we'd headed out of London, I understood even less why it would happen – like, we were now so few that I couldn't see what there wouldn't be enough of. Except crisps, obviously, which even I wouldn't shoot somebody over.

We never got a death count, because by the time people stopped dying nobody was counting anymore, but on our street there were sixty-four houses, all of them three-bedrooms, so let's say an average of four people per house, that's over two hundred and fifty people. And, okay, a bunch of people left, let's say half the street – though there's no real reason to think that a higher proportion of them survived – but when the explosion scared us out our front doors there were only six of us left. We never discovered what the explosion was, but it was big and it was nearby. I can't believe it was a bomb, maybe something at a petrol station or a gasworks. I don't know enough about explosions to have any clue really. Adi said it must have been close, because the houses lost their windows, but in the dark there was no glow of flames or rising column of smoke lit from below, just the sound of car alarms going off all over the place from the shockwave. I don't know how close you have to be to an explosion to have your windows blown in. If I'm lucky I will never find out I suppose. Anyway, it scared us all out and we gravitated to the centre of the street, pulled by the torch that Adi was holding.

The dark of the city is so different to the dark of the land. In Cuba when it was dark it was totally dark. Our house was outside the edge of the village and sometimes I'd walk back with my parents from people's houses, late at night, after spending hours stalking lizards and stealing ice cubes with the other kids while the adults sat rocking on a veranda and talked and laughed, and after you'd moved away from the little halo of the bulb or the oil lantern it was like swimming out to sea, just surrounded by nothingness. We'd know we were on the road because you could hear it under your feet. They'd walk with me between them, one hand each, my father's feet slapping on the cracked tarmac, my mother's swishing and crunching on the dry grass, me in the middle, rattling and padding on the loose gravel and soft dust of the hard shoulder in between. You were properly in the dark, moving within it, it was a warm soft thing that you could press your face into, like foam or fabric, solid with the sound of cicadas and frogs. Even in the house it spilled in through the windows, flooding under the furniture, silting in the corners of rooms, clogging up the gaps under doors.

It was a dark that you breathed into you, that slid solidly from your lungs to your blood and rolled, like tiny heavy marbles, to the back of your head, where the weight of it drew you down into it. It is dark like that here too, though here I feel like I see the moon and stars more. The stars are like a duvet or candyfloss, thick and full, the expanse of them seems three-dimensional in its denseness, then speckled with impossibly bright ones that glitter red and green.

Jean-Luc says that because we are in the mountains we are closer to space. I find it hard to believe that a few hundred metres vertically could make a difference when they are so far away that we had to invent light years to talk about the distance without filling pages with zeros, but Jean-Luc says a lot of things that you think couldn't be true but are. And he knows the place.

Jean-Luc grew up in Digne. He went to Paris to study, just in time for '68. Then, after the dust had settled and his studies were finished, he slowly made his way back home, but the long way, via the weavers of Senegal, the indigo pits of Mali and the Berber spinners of the Atlas mountains, bringing with him bundles of dried plants and fabric and alongside him was Françoise Bensaïd, who he'd met in Oran when they were both looking for a way to get to France. They arrived in Marseille and hitched back up the river valley. They arrived not long after his father's funeral. His father was a proper paysan — some olive trees, some vines, a small field of wheat that was more trouble than it was worth — and his mother had sheep. His father died in a freak accident, struck by lighting in the forest. The blow had left a red welt in the pattern of a tree from the back of his neck all the way down to his waist. He'd had his shotgun and a pitchfork — the neighbours said he must've been after rabbits, that he had the pitchfork because he dug traps for them. But Jean-Luc knew it wasn't that. His father collected truffles from the forest and sold them to a restaurateur from Lyon. He kept it all completely secret, his neighbours thought the restaurateur was somebody his dad had met in the army — which was true — who showed up every now and then unexpectedly — which was not true at all, in fact Jean-Luc would be sent down to the phone box in town to call him when his father had enough truffles in hand. As a kid Jean-Luc had no idea either — he'd just be given the coin and told to go and invite the guy to come and eat with them and to say to come at four, or at seven, or whatever. He always wondered why, when he showed up a few days later, the guy never came at the time he was told to, but it was just a code to let him know how many truffles there were, so that he knew how much money to bring.

Whenever his dad went looking for truffles he'd take his shotgun with him so it'd look like he was going hunting, but the pitchfork wasn't for digging them up. His father had been told by a priest one time that the ancient Greeks thought that mushrooms were the result of the earth being struck by lightning. This was supposed to be proof of the nullity of all pre-Christian thought, but that's not how Jean-Luc's dad took it. He watched the autumn thunderstorms move across the southern slopes of the mountains, noting down in a little waiter's notepad where the lightning bolts landed. Then, when he'd finished the olive harvest, he'd head out across the hills with the dog and his shotgun and a little trowel at the bottom of his bag. The word in town was that he was a terrible shot and his wife a terrible scold, because he'd be gone for days and come back with nothing more than a couple of rabbits and a quiet smile.

A dozen truffles was worth a month's wages back then, and Jean-Luc's dad had only ever had a month's wages from the army. For a family pulling a living from the soil there was a lot of money at stake. One year Jean-Luc's dad decided that it was worth helping the lightning's decision-making process. He knew the lightning would be drawn to a metal rod, but he also knew that if he started leaving strange bits of metal out in the forest, sooner or later somebody would know that it was him, and in a place like Digne the problem isn't even that people find out the answer – the fact that they've started asking questions is enough to send everything skywards. So he'd go out on days when he thought storms were coming, with pickaxes and shovels and suchlike, and hang them up in trees he thought were good, and then after the storms had passed he'd go back out and fetch them. And it worked, and he kept noting everything down in the little leather-bound book. That year, Jean-Luc's dad got him to start using the twenty-four hour clock when he invited the restaurateur – the first time he told him to come at '*seize heures*' the guy corrected him back to four o'clock, but Jean-Luc's dad had been clear – '*C'est le monde moderne maintenant,*' he'd said, '*tu lui dis bien seize heures.*'

And so it was that Jean-Luc's dad was eventually struck by lightning climbing up an oak tree in a rainstorm to strap a pitchfork to its branches with its points to the sky, to draw the force of the sky down into the force of the earth so that he could turn the force of the earth into the force of the human mind, because when one night Jean-Luc admitted to his father that he wanted to go and study in Paris and then see the world his father got a mouse-proof tin full of ten franc notes out from under the kitchen dresser and showed him that the truffles would pay for it.

As soon as things had calmed down after his arrival, Jean-Luc headed out to get the pickaxe and the spade that his mother had told him were still out there. There was no sense in getting caught out after all that time. And the thing is, Jean-Luc swears that it's true, that truffles explode outwards from a tree hit by lightning, that the seed of them in the soil is waiting to be called into being by a shock from above, and to prove it he has his father's notebook and the years he spent pretending to be a terrible shot himself and walking the hills. Pressure Drop says you don't need truth when you have reality, so, fine, mushrooms are the result of the earth being hit by lightning. And when Jean-Luc says that a few hundred vertical metres can make a difference to a star, you tend to believe him.

Anyway, the stars that Jean-Luc says we're closer to here are impressive, and the dark is empty in a way that stretches as far as you can't see. It is the opposite of the dark, thick with strange noises that echoed around us, on the night we first took refuge in the Arches. We were all scared to our doorways by the explosion and left our houses behind us, drawn by Adi's torch, which made our faces appear around him like mushrooms. He was jangling a chunky bunch of keys nervously in one hand. He looked from it to us and said, 'I know somewhere nearby that's safe. I'm going there now. If anybody wants to come, get your stuff and meet at the end of the road in ten minutes. Bring whatever bottled water you have.'

We all recognised each other: people you'd seen getting in and out of cars or on their way back from the shop with the milk or asking you to sign a petition about the binmen, but nobody I felt I'd ever actually spoken to. So we looked at each other and nodded and half-ran half-stumbled back to our houses to grab what we could, and came back with whatever pre-filled rucksacks and shopping bags of random shit we had. Adi got us all to turn our torches off and we went, tripping and breathing too loud, down the cul-de-sac to the Arches.

And the Arches is where we had stayed, barring a handful of heart-thumping forays into the outside world, until the moment, months later, when we finally set off in the very early morning to begin our journey from there to Digne-les-Bains.

All the prep that Adi had done to ready our steeds in his hours in the Peddler's workshop was visible in that moment, their paintwork spick and span, their panniers perfectly adjusted. They champed at their chains in the main hallway as he unlocked the heavy doors and they creaked open one last time. We wheeled them out and Adi locked up behind us, careful as always. We whispered to each other, everyone checking that everyone else hadn't forgotten anything, then we set off, excited and apprehensive and already slightly nostalgic for the safety and simplicity of the Arches. The grey light and the dry, slightly sick feeling that not enough sleep gives you lifted as we got moving. We were slow, unused to the weight of the panniers and the top-heaviness of the sleeping rolls strapped to the carriers. But we were leaving. Adi said he knew the way out of London, and we followed him. The idea was to be out of it before it was fully light, on the grounds that baddies sleep late. The city started to spool past us.

The rhythm of cycling is like dancing, it falls into four-four time and rolls round and round again as you push forward, the uphills bringing the tempo down. When I crashed out of the music industry's fringes and was working in schools, some kids painted as if they were running, filling the pages with one chosen colour, with no thought but racing to the end of it. Rowing is like swimming crossed with sawing wood, there's a part of it that's all about making it smooth and letting your breath push into the movement at the right moment, and a part of it that's about trusting the apparatus to do its job without forcing it. I got better at it over time. It's fucking tiring though, and no matter how I worked at it I was never going to have arms and shoulders like Martin. You can go on about equality as much as you like but almost all men are stronger than almost all women. I could row you quite a long way in the flat calm, but if I wanted the boat held steady in waves or brought safely through a gap in the rocks, I would definitely hand over the oars. You have to be realistic, and you have to learn to take pride in and give importance to stuff that didn't matter before.

Some notions are only as useful as the situation that gives rise to them. It turns out that, in some not insignificant ways, trying to stay alive in the absence of pre-existing structures of care and mutual aid is not really a situation that is conducive to men and women taking on non-stereotypical gender roles. Sarah took it hard too, maybe harder than me. She'd come up through the bit where women were meant to manage to do all the boring unpaid stuff that society would collapse without as well as burn their bra, sexually liberate themselves, learn to use a hand drill and hold down a career. Pressure Drop was the opposite – he saw the whole thing as a re-establishment of the original order, that women would be respected and venerated for their ability to bring forth children and nourish their family and men would be respected and venerated for their ability to be strong and plant weed in the correct place to ensure a bountiful harvest.

They never really had an argument about it – the closest they came was one time in Fairlight, not long after the Beacon, when we were all sitting around on the patio after dinner and Pressure Drop was saying that Rastafarianism was the natural religion of all oppressed peoples and that every people was oppressed by their rulers and therefore Rastafarianism was the natural religion of all people. Then Sarah said that all religions were oppressive and that a religion that thought that 'sanitary towel' was the worst possible insult was no better than any other, and certainly no better for women. Pressure Drop went into a long speech about how respectful Rastafariansm was of women and Sarah asked him why they weren't allowed in the gatherings then. The rest of us just watched the ping-pong: Pressure Drop saying that the problem wasn't that society told women they had to cook and clean, the problem was that it told them that cooking and cleaning was worthless; Sarah saying that even when women abandoned the cooking and cleaning and did exactly the same jobs as men they were still paid less for it.

I don't know about Rastafarianism being feminism's next wave, but the nicest, most good-humoured and easiest to brush off chat-ups I ever had always came from old boys with dreads. That might've been because it reminded me of arriving in Santiago on market days with my mother, but it was also that you could feel immediately the moment that they realised that you weren't going to get off with them – there would be a subtle but definite change of gear in the chat, but they would keep talking to you, as if the chat-up was the excuse for a conversation rather than the other way around. And it is also true that once control of the food supply had become a high magic rather than a daily chore it didn't seem to bother Sarah that in Fairlight it was always her and me and Julie who made dinner, apart from grilling fish on the barbecue, which is another total cliché.

Here it is Françoise and whoever helps her, but it is Françoise in charge, and the fact that a real hot meal is something that we are all so utterly grateful for changes everything – even if Françoise was less witchy we would still be spellbound by steam above a plate. Though those are also the kinds of things that Charles would have been delighted to hear at the *Château*. You can't always pick who'd agree with you.

We heard the *Château* before we saw it, which was unusual enough. People had stopped broadcasting their presence. I sometimes wonder how many people we didn't meet on our journey, how many just looked through the corner of a window or avoided the smoke they saw rising. More than we met, probably. It's so hard to have any sense of how things actually are. But the ones who want to be met are all taking a risk so something in them – naivety, Toxoplasma gondii, a Type A personality, who knows – is pushing them out into the open. In the case of Charles and the henchmen it was a risk they took because they were sure they'd come out on top. Which in many ways, even with us, they did. When we got near we were all uneasy at the sound of so many people at once, though it didn't really sound scary, just chaotic. There'd been nothing like that since the Beacon.

The Beacon Bonfire started slowly. Maybe in the last few days before some other people had added to the pile, but we weren't sure and we had no idea if anybody would actually show up. We went up there in the late afternoon with some meagre supplies – a couple of thermoses of tea, a bottle of cheap whisky and some packets of biscuits and peanuts – and lit it. Everyone wanted to light it, except maybe Sarah, or maybe she was just better than the rest of us at pretending that she didn't want to, and in the end, after we'd gone round a few times trying to be that impossible mixture of honest and polite, Pressure Drop said that we should take a box of matches each and we'd all light it at the same time. And Adi asked where he thought he was going to get that many boxes of matches from, said that there was no way he was walking all the way back down the hill for them, and Pressure Drop rooted under the bottle of whisky in the bag he'd been carrying and pulled out a bundle of old newspapers and a handful of boxes of matches, wedged between his knuckles as if they were dominos.

Julie started laughing, 'Right Pressure Drop, get that crystal ball back out and tell me if this is going to be a boy or a girl then.'

'I can't do that here,' said Pressure Drop, 'It'll have to wait 'til tomorrow when we're back home.'

We each took our box of matches and a couple of scrunched up sheets of newspaper and got in around the teetering pile of broken chipboard and dead branches and lit it. It took quickly – we'd brought a load of cardboard and shoved big torn chunks in around the base, but still I was surprised. Almost immediately there were flames rattling against the wood and a thick column of smoke elbowing its way up into the blue sky.

Once it was lit there wasn't much to do except wait. Pressure Drop stashed the boxes of matches back in his bag while Sarah, Julie and Adi pulled a plank and a couple of upturned drawers out of the woodpile, made a bench, sat down and opened a thermos. Seeing the three of them sitting there I suddenly realised how young Adi was. Slow learner that I am, I'd only been around him all day every day for about two months by then, but seeing him sitting next to Julie, who I knew was about the same age as me, I could see that he was at least ten, maybe more, years younger than us. He was only about twenty, if that. I suppose I'd been kidding myself for quite a long time that I was only about twenty myself.

While I was feeling old and slightly sorry for myself, people started to trickle up the hill. They arrived on their own, or maybe in pairs, hanging back at first, near enough to see us but far enough to run if they didn't like what they saw, then coming forward. Most of them arrived carrying something, a bottle or a bag, or dragging something to be burnt. Martin and Julie were clearly on nodding terms with some of them. Slowly, a ring of people gathered around the bonfire. It's good for drawing people in, a fire, and if you don't know what to do you can always poke at it. It was all very civilised at that point, the atmosphere was how I'd imagine a council meeting that'd been called to discuss something sombre.

People said hello to each other, introduced themselves, began a little small talk about where they lived, who they'd lost and how they were getting along. It's not that everyone had lost someone; everyone had lost almost everyone. They'd lost the people they were already sure were dead and they'd also lost the people they had no way of being sure if they were still alive. As they made their way in dribs and drabs up the path and shifted around the fire to create spaces, you could feel the dead among us, like phantom limbs, words that don't finish your sentence, the arm that isn't around your waist when you walk towards a group of people you don't know, the sideways glance that is not there to meet yours, so that yours just tumbles out of your eyes into nothingness. It was hard not to guess at the shapes that should've taken up the empty air around people.

Anyone who walked up the hill with somebody, you could see it made them feel awkward, guilty that some already-existing bond had survived – usually they'd quickly excuse it, 'We live on the same street, we didn't really know each other before ...'

There must be quite a lot of people I knew still out there, doing things that sound like lines from unwritten songs, stalking the aisles of supermarkets with a spoon in one hand and a hammer in the other, burning the furniture in the fireplace of a house that isn't theirs, stealing warm socks from the dead and the gone. By now they'll have started banding together, but at the time of the Beacon Bonfire everyone seemed still stuck in their singular state of shock, living on what they'd stocked up. But maybe that's just who came, maybe people who'd already grouped up didn't need to – though we had and we did.

From those who showed up, it looked like you were most likely to survive if you were between the ages of twenty and fifty. There were more men than women – again, later experience suggests that that was more who came than who existed. Maybe there was some genetic factor, because a few of the people who walked up together turned out to be siblings, but it wasn't that simple, because a lot of people who'd survived had children who'd died. There were no children at all until a woman turned up with a tiny baby. She looked rough as hell, gel nails grown halfway out and chopped off unevenly so they looked like stubby claws and hair that had clearly been fending for itself for some time. She stared and stared at Julie. In fact, most people did, goggle-eyed at the thought of bringing children into the world, or at the thought of the children they'd had that'd left it. Nobody really knew what to say to her, not even the woman with the baby who sat down on the bench beside her but had to be dragged into talking by Sarah. You could see she was trying to guard her words – now I have much more of an idea why.

She'd given birth before the lights went out for good, alone in a hospital full of tears and quiet panic, with nurses and doctors who kept rushing off to try to stop somebody else dying. Sarah could see she was in a bad way, her skin looked dusty with tiredness, and she'd just fade off in the middle of sentences and sit there staring into the fire. She wouldn't let Sarah hold the baby so that she could drink some tea because she said she'd only have to take the baby back after. Julie tried to persuade her to move into one of the houses near us, but she wouldn't, her husband had been working in Scotland and she was convinced he'd be home any day now and that she had to be there when he arrived.

'It could be today,' she said, 'I should be getting home now. Besides,' she said to Julie, 'you're doing all right, and you still think that you're about to reach the finish line. Maybe when you've realised it's the start line we can talk. Right now, there's nothing you can do.' And she put the baby back in the buggy and went, following it slowly down the hill with just enough of a grip on its handle to stop it getting away from her. She wouldn't even say where she lived. I felt shaken and sorry for her, but it was just that she'd realised you can't warn someone about having a baby – it's always either too early or too late.

So nobody knew what to say to Julie, just what not to say to her – not to talk about grief or death or loss or fear, which in a way left them with nothing. When the evening started to come, she and Sarah headed home. By then there were about thirty people around the fire. Pressure Drop had rolled a series of heroic-looking spliffs and sent them off through the crowd and Adi, to his confusion, had found himself not exactly cornered by, but definitely in the sights of, two women. I had been doing some sterling work on the whisky we'd brought with us when Martin, having had conversations with the people he knew well enough to have a conversation with, gravitated back to beside me and reached over to be handed the bottle. I stood as near to him as I dared, letting myself come as close to leaning into him as I could without actually doing it. Somebody had brought a guitar with them and Pressure Drop had improvised a drum with an upturned bit of cupboard and they were playing Oasis songs. I don't think Pressure Drop was much of an Oasis fan, but he was a great percussionist. He'd never talked about being a musician, but he'd clearly spent more time than most in the drumming circle.

So that was the set-up, and as sure as humans have been getting drunk since before they were even humans you could see that the evening was about to go that way. I love that point, where you can see that a party is starting to feed off its own energy, where the disinhibition takes over and people start to sing along or laugh louder than they should, where the unfolding chaos gives anyone who wants it the space to dance or tell outlandish tales or happily shrink down their notion of personal space until they're shouting in each other's ears and hanging onto each other's arms. And there it was in the flickering firelight, and it was beautiful to see. The sun went down, paint flakes and bark peeled back from the wood in the fire and whirled through the updrafts as glowing confetti and a group of three or four men roamed the edge of the woods in the half-dark with an axe, happily arguing about which tree they should attempt to chop down to have something more to burn.

There are moments in our lives that when they're happening it feels like we were born to live them. It's like you feel it from your throat to your pelvis, as if inside you was stacked a set of thick metal disks and slowly they twist on their axis until they're all aligned and there is an unbroken line running down the front of them and then that line splits open and you, your best, shining, most powerful self pours out. I know some people experience this at moments that are meant to be important, like, they save somebody from drowning or they meet their biological mother for the first time, but not me – I am basically a dickhead, so for me it was the Beacon Bonfire.

Ultimately, you don't charmingly gatecrash many festivals without, at some point, getting together a party piece, something that you can pull out when the beat of the generators doesn't keep you dancing anymore and somebody takes out a musical instrument. When the guitar guy managed to get his guitar back – he'd handed it to somebody who knew only the chorus and none of the chords to several U2 songs – I was ready. I slipped away from Martin's arm, fished the torch out of the rucksack by my feet, and headed over.

'Hey,' I said, 'I've got one, G, D and C and then the chorus is G, D and A minor.' I'm not musical like that, I can't play a note, but I'd learned long ago that those are the chords. Guitar-guy nodded, like, obviously he knows those chords.

'R.E.M.' I say, '"End of the World", Nah nah naaah, nah nah naaah, nah nah na na.'

His eyebrows went up. 'You sure? You actually know the verses as well?'

If you want to be able to do something when you're anywhere along the spectrum between half-cut and out of your head then you've really got to play to your strengths, and I can't really sing but I can remember the words better than anyone, better, probably, than the people who wrote them in the first place, so that song is like my perfect fit.

I looked at him, grinned, nodded, held the torch up as a microphone and gave him my most cocksure, 'Oh yeah,' loosening up my shoulders and adding, 'We start with the chorus though, that'll give Pressure Drop a chance to get the drums going, okay?'

'Okay,' he said, 'There's no way you'll be worse than the last guy anyway. You point to me when I'm supposed to shout "Leonard Bernstein" okay?'

Martin, who, he told me a few days later, thought at first that I needed the torch to go off into the bushes and be sick, was looking at me, smiling, like, ready to laugh if it was funny, but also just happy, proud. I could feel the heat of the whisky in my blood rising up into my cheeks to meet the heat of the fire and guitar-guy went, 'One two three four', which, seriously, is there any song worth singing when you're drunk that isn't improved by somebody going, 'One two three four' at the start? And the heavy disks spun in my chest and my belly and all lined up perfectly, and the line of light split them open down the front of me, and we began.

Pressure Drop, warned by the 'One two three four', was soon driving it forward on the upturned cupboard drum. We went through the chorus once more, louder, everyone was looking, even the axe gang were coming back over to see, loping unsteadily through the tall grass, black and tawny gold in the firelight. I had them all.

For me, the words are just waiting to appear in my mouth, like watching a cartoon or video game where the character puts their foot out in thin air and a stepping stone or a cloud appears beneath it, but I know from the outside it looks like a feat of great skill. I'm not saying it's the best possible use to which I could've put enormous natural memory talent, impressing the shit out of late-night drunk people, but it works every time, and it's always made me – and usually them – very, very happy.

By the time you're through the first chorus and are piling into the second verse even the guitarist, likely a person who has learned and sung many songs themselves over the years, will be impressed, and when the moment finally comes to shout, 'Leonard Bernstein!' they're all on your side, they'll hold up the last rounds on the chorus, and you get real cheers at the end.

But maybe every time I'd ever sung that song before was just practice, because to sing it then, in that night so full of darkness out beyond the fire, with the beating hearts of the people around me echoing in the emptiness left by the dozens that each of them had lost, with them shouting along, tears on their cheeks and hope in their throats, that was something I was born to do. And Martin saw it.

I couldn't have had better applause if I was headlining the Pyramid Stage. I walked the few steps back over to Martin, smiling and shaking my head to the calls of, 'Encore!' He had a massive stupid grin on his face, and when I got back to my spot beside him he put his arm around my shoulders and squeezed me in close, saying, 'Fucking great, Audaz, that was fucking great.' And he kept his arm there.

One of the axe gang reckoned he was going to sing next, but it was another case of chorus-only knowledge – it's a very common pitfall in the guitar-campfire situation. But his ineptitude spurred others into action and soon one of the women who'd set their sights on Adi was happily, tunelessly and unseasonably belting out 'All I Want for Christmas Is You'.

Me and Martin stood there passing the bottle between us and him occasionally intercepting the spliffs that were still circling through the crowd and a few times somebody who knew him wandered up to slap him on the back or pat him on the arm and compliment him on the bonfire, and he'd offer them a swig from the bottle and say, 'Thanks, you know, it was a group effort really, Audaz did a lot of the work, dragged stuff up here and painted the sign and all.'

And they'd nod me an acknowledgement and say something like, 'Yeah, nice work on the song,' and every time I felt like the queen – that in that instant Martin was as close to the chief of the tribe as there was, and he was saying in front of everybody that I, notwithstanding my marvellous knack for putting the same words in the same order that somebody else had once put them in, a waster in an old oilskin with its pockets lined with Ryvita crumbs, full of rough whisky and with breath that smelled of peanuts, was at his right hand. So we stood there, feeling satisfied and proud of the little slice of joy and excitement that we'd brought into being which, god knows, everybody needed.

I don't know how long we stood there, but it was long enough for the axe men to come back, brilliantly full of themselves with all limbs intact and a small tree, which they heaved onto the fire in one go. It crashed down through the middle, sending clouds of sparks into the air and catapulting burning sticks out into the grass around us. They were delighted and stumbled about, burning their fingers and cursing excitedly as they chucked bits back into the fire. By then quite a few people had drifted home, we were maybe like a dozen left, including the axe men who'd headed back to the edge of the trees in search of their next victim.

Pressure Drop had taken a break from his drumming to roll a spliff the size of the Olympic torch and survey what was left, and while he was lighting it somebody took what he'd been drumming on and chucked it in the fire. 'That'll be the bell for last rounds then,' he said, as it went up in flames.

Martin nodded and said, 'We're heading back to the house – you keep an eye on Adi, yeah?'

I didn't hear what Pressure Drop said back to him because inside my head I was too busy dancing around and singing, 'He said we ...'

Pressure Drop passed the spliff, saying, 'One for the road?' and Martin took a drag and we headed down the hill.

The warmth of the fire peeled away from my back. The air was cold on your face as soon as you'd gone a few steps, you could feel the dew hanging in it, getting ready to fall. We stumbled on the tussocky ground and got the giggles at smacking into each other but by the time we'd found the path he had his arm back around my shoulders and I had mine around his waist. I really needed a pee but I didn't want to move away from him. Then we started laughing about the size of Pressure Drop's party spliffs, at the idea of having to build scaffolding to hold them up so you could smoke them, and then Martin just went helpless with laughter. I couldn't get it out of him what had him doubled over like that, but finally he managed to gasp out at me that the thing Pressure Drop had said when he'd asked him to keep an eye out for Adi was, 'That boy, he could fall in a barrel of tits and he'd come up sucking his thumb.'

And that was it, broken by the image of Adi doggy-paddling in a vat of breasts I had to run for the shadows before I pissed myself. I just got my pants down in time and I was still laughing so hard while I was pissing that it came out in spurts, which made me laugh even harder, and I could see Martin holding onto his own knees and roaring with laughter on the path having seen me suddenly rush across the grass clutching my fanny. And then when I was on my way back over to him there was a crash and a leap of flames from up at the bonfire and whooping and giddy swearing – the axe ment had brought another tree. We could see their lurching silhouettes swooping round the flames as they enjoyed the carnage and a huge plume of sparks billowed up into the night. And while we both had our faces turned towards what light there was, I said, 'So are we going to do this then?'

'I don't know,' said Martin, 'Are we?'

'Yeah,' I said, 'Yeah we are.'

'Right,' and he took my hand and kissed me on the end of my nose, saying, 'That's enough for a first date.'

I was laughing again and gave him a punch in the arm with my free hand.

'Well come on then,' he added, 'Let's get home – those fish aren't going to catch themselves in the morning.'

And so on the way home, walking along holding hands like that, I guess I got scared, or maybe I was trying to protect myself, and I said something about us both being grown-ups and that there was no sense in deciding that we were married just because we'd gotten drunk around the same bonfire, and that's when it all kicked off because for Martin there absolutely was sense in that.

'Whatever you've done in the past, it's none of my business,' he said, 'but I'm not going into this lightly. I've tried, over years and years, to take care of my heart, to not wring every drop from it for the excitement of one thing after another when none of them are the real thing, to not wear it away with just fucking for fucking's sake. I've made it this far through my life without snapping so many bits off it that you wouldn't recognise its shape, and I made my peace long ago with the idea that I might never find anybody I could really, really be with. And then you show up, after the end of the world, full of silly-clever ideas, cursing in Spanish under your breath and giddy about the early morning, but if you don't want to go all the way then I'm not going anywhere at all. I know that you and Sarah have your mission, and I'll have to stay here with Julie for a while, but then I'll come and find you, not straight away, but when Julie's okay and I'm ready to sail that far, I'll come. But I need to know that if I do, you'll be waiting for me, not shacked up with some Frenchman from the mountains. This life, it's something I plan to keep on living, and I would love to live it with you, but there's far too much at stake to not do things properly. I've always known that, and maybe you still haven't realised it, even with things as they are. So if you're going into this half-heartedly, I'm not going anywhere at all.'

By this time we had reached our road, and I was drunk and too hurt at the sudden possibility of rejection to think clearly about anything he'd said, so I just said, 'Fine, well, I'll think about all that then, if I'd known we were leaving the bonfire early just to have a stupid argument I'd have stayed where I was – see you in the morning for fishing.'

He'd let go of my hand some time back to gesticulate so there was nothing to stop me stomping up the steps and into the front room alone, which is what I did. I got undressed angrily and huffed my way into bed, jealous of whatever late-night fun Pressure Drop and Adi were having and unable to get rid of the feeling of Martin's lips on the end of my nose. And the next thing I knew it was morning, and he was waking me up to go fishing.

I felt pretty groggy. I was out of practice and I'd not had many hours sleep, but I pulled myself out of bed, into clothes and to the kitchen. Martin was getting things ready, and I could see he was the worse for wear too. We didn't really speak. I pushed myself into autopilot: tea in thermos, Ryvita sandwiches in bag, legs in oilskins, out the door and mechanically down the steps I'd stomped so heavily up a few hours before. We headed to the beach. The sun was hidden behind a heavy bank of cloud along the horizon, and the glarey grey light seemed to smooth out the sea. We got the boat out on it and fed the string of bright feathers into the water, then settled down, not really speaking to each other, to wait. I was thinking to myself that strange and awkward as it was, of all the things I've had to get up too early for after too late a night, this wasn't even the strangest or the most awkward. Then Martin produced the end of the bottle we'd had at the bonfire. We put the dregs of the whisky into our tea and leaned back against the rucksack in the front of the boat, our arses down in the damp and our feet up on the bench in the middle.

As the sky slowly went from grey to blue and the mug of the thermos went from one to the other, the feeling of the night before seeped back into my body and I could feel myself going soft around him, slipping into the shape that fitted against him, pooling around his body like the water in the sandy hollows around the rocks on the beach at low tide. When we'd finished the spiked tea he said, 'So, last night you said you'd have a think about it, but I reckon you just passed out.'

'Yeah, that is what I did,' I admitted, 'but drinking is better than thinking anyway.'

'Well then, having had a drink about it, are you in?'

'Yeah, I'm in.' And that was it, and all I could feel was his beard against my neck and his cold fingers picking through the layers and slipping into the gap between my trousers and my jacket and when I managed to get my hand through his three layers of trousers his cock was so hard you could've cracked your teeth on it.

'I don't know how much of this you've done in dinghies,' he said, 'but in my experience we should head back to shore, because at best it ends with soggy clothes and inexplicable cramps and at worst with falling overboard.'

'Oh yeah – all that time you spent waiting for your Disney moment, how'd you become such an expert on the dangers of small craft?'

He just grinned at me and started the outboard while I pulled in the fishing line, a mackerel on every feather. I just left them flopping still on the hooks in the bottom of the boat around my knees while I tried to suck his cock and he tried to steer us towards the shore, and when it became apparent that the combination of oilskins, jeans, long johns, and boxers along with a cramped sitting position and a steering thing made that completely impossible he pushed my hand into my own trousers, saying, 'Trust me, there is no chance I'm not going to be hard when we reach the beach, especially if you're doing that.' And he was absolutely right. And the sex was ridiculous – not just that time, every time. Literally, every time. I've slept with more people than average, but then you'd probably be surprised how low the average is. Was. Whatever. Anyway, it's not like I've slept with with more people than I should've – though I definitely slept with some people I shouldn't have bothered sleeping with – but I've slept with plenty. Enough to know I'm not lying when I say that I never truly saw what all the exorcist-eyeballs, crucifixion-arms, banshee-howls fuss was about until him. And even though you're never going to see the entirety of the factors making reality into a head-exploding fairy tale I know it was not because we were perfect for each other, but because we made each other perfect. The whole business was unreal, seriously, it was hallucinatory, made me think my skin was covered in blue flames or that my body was suspended on points of light or filled with mercury or was the wax model for a statue when they pour the molten bronze in, melting, vaporising, disappearing and being remade as something that's shining and forever. When I take the time to remember those moments clearly enough, I feel like I will never in my life be as beautiful, as strong, as free, as true, will never be more me than I was with his cock inside me.

Maybe that me, the one I was with him, maybe that was actually the real me? Sometimes we are not best placed to judge what's real and what isn't, the things that seem real turn out to be nothing, while what seems made-up turns out to be real.

That's how it was when we heard the Beacon-like noise as we came near the *Château*. There was some of that chaotic babble at a distance, and it was unusual enough to hear the sound of a small crowd of people that it stopped us on the road. I've been part of a lot of crowds, shouted and danced and sung along with a lot of crowds, listened to a lot of crowds, felt how much they're enjoying something, how drunk or stoned or on one they are. This crowd had the bass rumble of football fans in a beer garden with the sudden chanty crescendos ending in the high-pitched, male-laughter-of-disbelief of a stag night. It sounded scary, but the fear seemed unreal because at that point it still felt silly to be scared of something like that. But the fear was real, it was the feeling silly was the made-up bit.

Also, I was uncertain of my own instincts – I think the allopregnanolone was fucking with me. I never really used hormonal contraception, but I'd heard about bad-ass wedding planners making their brides come off the pill six months before the wedding so that they knew they were really sure about the groom, and strippers who were on the pill earning less tips because they weren't acting as sexy, so it didn't seem unlikely to me that my impulses would be weirded by it. I'm pretty sure that a certain amount of the chaos and confusion in my brain now, the wild oscillations between optimism and desperation, is not just lack of sleep to the point of nausea but also a slow resettling of the whirling hormonal snow globe. In the maelstrom it sometimes feels possible that everything could be real at the same time. All possible truths are rolled out in parallel and I'm just switching between lanes as I try to keep moving forward without crashing. Anyway, the veneration of constancy as a cultural paradigm probably has more to do with Greek and Roman civilisations forming amongst trees that don't lose their leaves on the shores of a sea that doesn't even have any tides than with the actual state of the human psyche.

Put simply, my experience of first hearing the *Château* was unsettling and I didn't manage to articulate my uneasiness very well at the time. Given the outcome, I probably should have tried harder. Pressure Drop wanted to go and see on the bikes, saying we could get away quicker if we had them, and Adi agreed with him. Sarah wanted to hide the bikes and go and see on foot, saying the bikes were too much to risk losing and then Adi agreed with her too. It was like he was weighing up user failure versus method failure for escaping on bikes, and decided user failure was more likely. He was seriously struggling then because his ribs made both riding a bike and lying on a camping mattress extremely painful and the combination of constant tiredness and constant pain meant he didn't know what he wanted most of the time.

Twenty-twenty hindsight and all, but I knew we should stay away, I just didn't believe my knowing was real. I sided with Sarah, and not just that, but I insisted that we go back down the road to hide our bikes in a building rather than just putting them in the ditch. We'd passed a sort of hangar with a big gate that had been a little bit open, so we went back there.

I hadn't insisted on much up until that point in the journey. It was mostly Pressure Drop who'd do that. For example, he had very specific ideas about the names of places; he'd insisted on Fairlight, and he vetoed Hardelot and Berck as landing places, saying we were going to Fort Mahon because if ever we needed a strong arse it was when we were planning to cycle hundreds of kilometres. He believes in puns as something sacred, as if the forms of words soak through the roof of your mouth, maybe pressed by your tongue through your hard palate and rise up into your mind and lodge there. And once lodged, your thoughts have to flow around them like water around the boulders in a river, having to either wait for a flood or to slowly, slowly eat away at them if it wants to change its path. It's all part of his certainty that everything you put into your body, idea, word, food, air, whatever, becomes a part of you forever.

And he reckoned the story of your life was the same, and so we started in France at Fort Mahon because of a bad bilingual pun, half of which was in Irish, a language that he did not actually speak to any real extent, but he felt it would speed us on our way all the same. And maybe it did, maybe those years of sticking to weed in the face of heroin in Dublin's inner city really did lead him to Jah in South London, whose hand was now guiding us along the red, gold and green brick road. The thing is, when nothing makes any sense anymore and nobody really knows anything, in a way it doesn't matter why you make a decision, the important thing is to make one, to feel sure of it, and then to jump. Because you have no idea. Maybe at Hardelot somebody would have been waiting on the beach to stab us, maybe at Berck somebody would have welcomed us with open arms. We went on to Fort Mahon and had trouble enough, but actually any number of things could've gone much worse.

Who knows how many times we've saved our lives by irrational gestures? Maybe it's not even helpful to call them irrational, maybe it's like those super-experienced firefighters who have a premonition that a building is about to fall down and suddenly order everyone out on a whim seconds before it collapses. Our bodies and brains have had millions of years to practise not getting killed, maybe they're actually quite good at it.

So we took our bodies and brains back down the road to the hangar and discovered it was a recycling depot, with stacks and piles of glass and paper, which made it a great place to hide the bikes because it was a mess and because there was almost nothing anyone would ever want in there. We found a way between the bales of cardboard boxes and wheeled the bikes down into it and then Pressure Drop got us to wheel them out again and put them back in facing the other way, saying you never know whether a minute and a half will make all the difference. And I took off my goldfinger necklace and hid it by lifting off my saddle and slipping it down inside Sputnik with a knot wedged into the split in the seat tube under the quick-release to pull it back out with.

Thinking back, I do wonder what the fuck we were doing going near the *Château*. I mean, okay, Adi was hurt and not sleeping and our progress was a bit slow, but we didn't even need supplies – we had kilos of rice and lentils in the panniers, we'd picked up some tins in a couple of houses and most buildings still had a full water tank if you could get in and get to a hot tap. We didn't bother boiling it, but we used the filter straws, just in case. No, what it really was is we were thinking like before. We were thinking like people who'd got out of London, who'd travelled without incident, who'd met, just like that, possibly the only person in the south of England who had the knowledge to take us across the Channel, and the pregnant sister so that we had knowledge to trade. And then we'd crossed, and survived, and Fort Mahon had been safe enough and quiet enough and the weather had been fine enough that we'd been able to dry all the stuff that had got wet between *Seabird* and the shore. And that had only been days ago, a week at most, and since then the going had been easy: flat roads, lots of shelter, we still had food. We were thinking like we had the gods on our side.

And so, like idiots, we retraced our path, back towards the noise that all of us were scared of, though none of us had the sense to act on our dread and get back on our bikes and pedal in the opposite direction. It's only when you have to run and hide for real that you suddenly understand the point of all those games you played as a child, that the heart-thumping breathlessness of watching somebody's feet from under the bed, or the air bursting in your chest as you sprint away, make sense.

For all that we were scared – though clearly not scared enough – we were giggling like kids. Walking softly, we came round the bend in the road to see high walls, and followed the wall into the bushes to find somewhere that felt a bit hidden to scramble up and get a look over.

The *Château*, you have to hand it to Charles, was a fucking handsome spot. It had been turned into a luxury hotel at some point but it actually was an actual castle: towers, pointy turrets, skinny windows, gravel drive, becoming-informal gardens, the whole bit, complete with fucking peacocks that, as soon as we stuck our heads over the wall, saw us and raced off shrieking across the no-longer-manicured lawns, alerting every sorry fucker on the premises to our presence. Peacocks are cunts.

We dropped to the ground, Adi breathing sharply and wincing in pain, and tried to make ourselves invisible in the undergrowth. I lay there with leaves tickling me and twigs digging into me, regretting the beautiful brightness of my fluorescent trainers. Even in our hiding we were amateurish. We'd seen the knot of people over on the far side of the lawns beside the castle; we'd have had the time to scramble back to the road through the bushes, giving ourselves at least a minute's lead on them. As it was, we were right there lying in the weeds when three or four of them looked over the wall. Pressure Drop was the first on his feet, and got himself together with a speed that made it clear that in his life he'd got in shit more than most people.

He stood tall and pulled his shoulders back and got his declaiming voice on, 'Friends, we are travelling to Africa as He' – here he jabbed at the sky – 'intended. We are looking for clean water and will then continue our journey. In helping us you will be doing His' – another jab at the sky – 'will.'

And then, to me, Adi and Sarah, he broke into a thick Irish accent, not his Dublin one, and said, 'Speak English, don't whisper, but speak fast and in a weird accent, and listen to them carefully but don't let them know you understand any of the French they're speaking. Stick together and do not mention the two-wheelers, okay?'

Sarah, Adi and I nodded.

'Right – what're they on about?'

Sarah's weird accent was Birmingham, which surprised me, though I don't know what I'd been expecting. She said they thought we were mental and were trying to decide whether they should tell us to sod off or to bring us to someone called Charles. They decided to bring us to Charles. Again, at that point maybe we could've said no, I didn't think they would have beaten us up – although Pressure Drop did, on the grounds that you should never underestimate the likelihood that fuckwits will start a fight – but politeness clung to us like sleep in the morning.

We used to take the piss out of Adi for his properness but we were just as bad, me and Sarah. For all we thought we were freethinking rebels, if an angry mob said, 'This way please ladies,' we'd feel our bodies stutter in that direction in an involuntary obedience, born of years of normality, generations of relative safety and control shaping our epigenetics in a way that primed us to act like nothing could really go that badly wrong, even when something deep in our brainstem was saying that it really, absolutely, certainly, definitely could. More fool us, we followed the men in.

The *Château* was a cesspit. The time there was long, and the longer we stayed, the worse it seemed, and the more responsible we felt for trying to make some small part of it better. Sarah really believed she could do some good, in an 'even in the stoniest ground a seed can take root' sort of way. And in fairness she probably did. Pressure Drop was unconvinced from beginning to end. I was mostly just trying to avoid getting felt up. In many ways, including the only way that really counts, it was hardest on Adi.

Almost everyone was out of it a lot of the time, and nothing was ever clean or secure. A project to build an enclosure for animals would get half-begun and then abandoned just at the point where broken pallets full of rusty nails were strewn all over a section of lawn. One of the wooded areas on the far side of the grounds had been designated the dump and everything, empty bottles, animal bones, shit, torn clothes, dirty sheets, would just be thrown in there.

I'm pretty comfortable with relaxed attitudes, but they drank in the daytime and fucked in the open whenever they felt like it. I came back from pissing in the bushes at the edges of what used to be flowerbeds one time to find somebody fucking someone over the edge of an ornamental fountain, her face inches away from the thick, green water. It was tiring.

Like, I'm all for sex outside, the great outdoors is exactly that – one of the reasons why it felt so brilliantly teenage with Martin was definitely the having sex under the sky in the daytime, having my body filled up with stars and then coming back to reality looking down at him with shingle digging into my knees and my fingers soaked and sticky from my cunt, or suddenly becoming aware of the rough bark and the stubs of broken branches that were digging into my back, or his hands on my shoulders and the cold wet ground along one side of my body and the smooth pale stems of the long grasses running sideways past my eyes up towards a slowly lightening sky. Is it any wonder that it ended how it did?

For the first couple of days we kidded ourselves that we were being discreet, keeping it to the fishing trips. We certainly never got to the point of sleeping in each other's rooms. That was just because we wanted to keep it to ourselves though, let it be sparkling and new, and not let day-to-day life rub the shine off it straight away. Obviously everybody knew, but apart from grins from Pressure Drop, they were kind enough to leave us to it – no small feat on their part.

The afternoon after the Beacon Bonfire, my body still quietly vibrating like a struck bell from the fucking on the shore, we cooked and ate the mackerel that Martin and I had caught that morning and talked a bit about the bonfire and the people who'd been there. Then Pressure Drop told us all to stay out on the patio for a minute while he went into the kitchen. We could hear him rattling around in drawers and moving chairs about and then he called us in. There were two chairs, identical, beside one another and two tea towels, also identical, folded on the seats.

'Pick a chair, any chair you like, and sit down on it,' he said to Julie.

She gave him the raised eyebrow.

'Go on,' he said, 'you said last night you wanted to know if it was going to be a boy or a girl, so we'll all turn our backs and you pick a chair and sit down on it.'

So we all faced away and Julie sat down.

'Right,' said Pressure Drop, 'You can all look again. Up you get.'

Julie got up and Pressure Drop lifted the folded tea towel off the chair. Underneath it was a scissors with the blades splayed wide open.

'Girl,' he said. He lifted the other tea towel to show that on the other chair there was a little paring knife, its sharp point towards the front of the chair. 'That's for a boy,' he said.

Julie was laughing, Sarah too, 'Well that's a new one,' she said, 'and I've seen quite a few methods in my time. Who showed you that?'

'A Traveller in Walthamstow,' he said, 'He wasn't a midwife, but he'd had a fair few kids of his own to test it out on. He was a seventh son of a seventh son and if you put two fleas on a saucer he'd have bet on which would jump out first. He had second sight.'

'Did he always win then?' asked Adi.

'No, he said sometimes you had to bet even though you knew you were going to lose, otherwise it'd anger the fates.'

Sarah was laughing again, 'Well, I think we'll find out soon enough whether his method works or not, though to be honest, I've always thought a fifty-fifty chance was pretty good odds.'

A couple of days later, Julie went into labour. Sarah, though she'd always say the body can surprise you, knew it was coming, and things had changed a little in how we spent our time in the attic. I never told any of the guys what we actually did up there. I don't think Julie did either, and Sarah wasn't ever in the business of telling you something if you hadn't asked about it and she wasn't trying to teach it to you. It was our ritual, wash our hands, wash our fannies and go up there at the end of the afternoon, do the internals, do the theory, wash our hands again and come down and start preparing dinner.

But a few days before the bonfire we stopped doing the internals – which, frankly, was lucky because, from then on, I was full of spunk half the time – and instead we were doing much more breathing stuff: trying to create or relieve pressure in your abdomen by blocking or releasing your breath. And she was getting us to do a lot more feeling Julie's belly, learning how to feel where the baby was, the hard, movable lump of its head, the long smooth line of its spine, the little sticky-out bundles of its arms and legs.

It was only really then that I realised Sarah was training Julie too, like, obviously I knew already that she was training her to give birth, but she was trying to get all the basics in there so that Julie would be ready to help somebody else when the time came. She had us both doing it all, working out how close to the pelvis the baby's head was, which way it was facing. Obviously Julie was huge by then, belly like a hot-air balloon with her belly button popped inside out, and a thick line of dark hairs leading down from it.

Hairiness is one of the weirder elements of the grand new way of things. It's like a sort of constant gentle reminder that everything has changed, basically any scene you witness involving humans has more hair now. The men have beards and floppy hair, the women have hairy legs and hairy armpits and, if you happen to see one, big hairy muffs. It's only after it's all grown back and on show that you realise the crazy amount of time and energy that went into keeping it in check. Weirdly, having smooth legs is probably one of the things that I miss most about before. Stupid but true. Is that the scars of patriarchy running deep, or is it that I really did used to rip the hairs off my legs because I liked it? Will we ever know? When I was a kid, my mum used to go once a month to a woman, Ana, who was a paediatrician at the hospital, but on the side she had a secret recipe for a magical mixture that removed the moustache of any Cubana, from girls younger than me to great grandmothers, who didn't want to look like a hero of the revolution. I mean, obviously she was sometimes getting rid of more than just moustaches, but that's what you noticed on the women who walked back out her door.

Her son drew a poster for her. He was just a few years older than me; his name was Nestor and he used to draw all the time. I remember him sitting at the kitchen table with me while I waited, legs swinging, for my mother to come out of the bedroom, listening to the sometimes muffled exchanges of, '*Listo?*' '*Sí,*' and the slightly scary ripping noises. He would just draw and draw and draw: the stuff around him in the kitchen, what he could see out the window, stuff from photos in a book or magazine he'd found, anything. Anyway, the poster he drew made him locally famous because when the local *Comité de Defensa de la Revolución* got wind of it his mum got in big trouble. It said on it, '*Mezcla Mágica de Ana – Adiós Bigotes!*' and showed, as if stencilled, Che, Fidel and Martí, exactly how they looked on walls and buildings everywhere: Che with his beret, Fidel with his patrol cap and Martí with his forehead, but instead of their moustaches they just had neat red patches on their upper lips. It was a great poster, and obviously he didn't mean it badly, but wow was it taken badly.

He arrived at our door one day with a sealed envelope – his mum had written down her secret recipe and she wanted my mum to get it to her cousin in another town if things got too difficult for her – she wanted it to be useful to somebody. He brought his poster too, because he didn't know what to do with it. In the end his mum sorted things out with the CDR – on her block the CDR were almost all women and they didn't necessarily want moustaches and neither did their mothers or their daughters. At least some of them must have seen the funny side of it, and a few waxes would have been a small price to pay to continue her sideline.

When it became common knowledge that we were leaving to go and live in England, all kinds of people brought us all kinds of gifts, from the surreal – a bowler hat that had spent the best part of thirty years in a box on a shelf and which the giver was certain would be essential for my father when he reached his native land – to the hopeful – my classmates gave me an address book with all their addresses written into it – to the surprisingly practical – Ana's magical mixture. Ana's parting gift to Heike was her recipe: two cups of sugar, a quarter of a cup of lemon juice and a quarter of a cup of water, boil it till it's copper coloured. That's it. That was the secret.

My mum used that recipe to get rid of her own moustache for the rest of her life, and she kept the poster too. She brought it back to London with us and she put it in a frame, when she came across one in the right size at the charity shop, and hung it on the wall. When I was in my twenties I used to say that one day I was going to go back to Cuba and start a business making Ana's magic mixture from organic Cuban sugar and call it *'Adiós Bigotes!'* and put Nestor's drawings on the box. But it was too easy not to, I suppose.

I wonder if this summer it'll be justifiable to take two cups of sugar and a lemon and use them for something so non-essential. There's bound to be a lemon tree somewhere, but sugar ... On the one hand, there must be a lot of sugar knocking about, in houses, in supermarkets, in depots, all that. On the other, it is probably the last sugar there will be for a very, very, very long time. On the one hand, sugar is bad for you, on the other it's a great preservative. On the one hand, it is silly to use a finite if plentiful resource for something so frivolous, on the other, happiness is not frivolous and it would, however irrationally, make me feel happier and stronger and more like one of the goddesses building the new world rather than a refugee from the dregs of the old one to be doing it with smooth legs.

I don't think you can blame the patriarchy for that, I mean, you can if you want, but you have to admit that it's a complicated sort of blame. Cleopatra shaved her head and wore a wig and a fake beard. Queen Elizabeth I plucked her eyebrows off. Sarah wrote a magnifying mirror and a pair of tweezers into her essential travel kit. We all assumed they were professional tools, and they are; I myself saw her use the mirror to show Leïla the crown of her baby's head through the lozenge of her stretched vulva to encourage her that she was going to get it out through there, and the tweezers to hold the end of the thread when she stitched up the episiotomy she then had to perform when it turned out that Leïla couldn't. But they're also so she can get rid of her chin hairs.

At the *Château* – where ripping through tons of sugar to make everyone in possession of a vagina look more like a plastic model of somebody in possession of a vagina would have been highly commended – there was no way I was breaking out Ana's secret formula, and I definitely didn't want to shave my legs with the seemingly endless supply of disposable razors that Charles made sure were available, and we were there all through the summer. Even though that was only a few months back, it feels very long ago. Now, in the midst of this vortex, I need to imagine some things that connect me back to who I was before as well as forward to who I'll become. The idea of smooth legs is about the boundless possibilities of how I used to live and also – in my best, most hopeful, imagination – it's how I want to be found. I imagine myself here when the warm weather has come, stalking the lands like Françoise, in a straw hat and knickers, with Leo tied in Sarah's pagne on my back and the goldfinger necklace around my neck. And the legs on the me-that-I-hope-for are smooth and strong and tanned rather than the pale, flaky sticks that I see every now and then as they go from one pair of trousers to another in the firelight. I'm still playing me in the film of my life, and in it, warmth, bare legs and hair removal are the future as well as the past – just not the present.

Though by now there are days when you can find a sheltered corner in the sun and it's like being reborn, the great motor of all things seeping into your skin, into your bones. Jean-Luc says that the hardest stretch is from solstice to Easter. By the end of April it will be beautiful, March is easier than February was – already there are constellations of blossom bursting out on the grey bare-branched hillsides, like white milk-splats, and there have been a couple of days when I've been able to get bare chested myself without the bite of the air stopping the flow. In February you just have to take comfort in the thought that it's a short month and enjoy *Chandeleur*. Jean-Luc and Françoise decided that *Chandeleur* would happen when they had enough eggs to make pancakes for us all. There's a whole load of chickens, a whole whatever the collective noun for them is – flock, gaggle, murder, charm, all of them are wrong for chickens: with chickens it's more like a puddle. You go out with a bucket or a basin and they come racing out of the undergrowth and flood around your ankles trying to get stood on and pecking each other out of the way of whatever you're chucking at them. Jean-Luc and Françoise call them *Les Poules de la Mort* because they got them last spring when they started going around to farms and hamlets where friends of theirs had lived to try to get a sense of who or what was still alive.

I don't really know how it went with animals – I don't really know how it went with humans either for that matter – but back in Fairlight, Julie once told us what her boyfriend had said about the animals dying. He had been a park ranger out towards Beachy Head, so he saw what happened on a couple of farms as well as out in the countryside. His explanation was that the animals and birds caught it from people and then it spread among themselves, so if they were living in a house with humans or were all crammed in a shed or pen or cage or whatever they mostly all died, but wild animals, and some animals that were out in open fields, tended to live. Although some of it could've been down to starvation, what Jean-Luc and Françoise had found seemed to bear that out. They found farms where the cat had died in the house but a pair of donkeys out in the orchard had lived, or where where the hens packed in the henhouse were dead but a handful of hissing geese in the field by the river were alive.

Wherever they went, they let the animals go and they brought any live chickens back with them, in cardboard boxes strapped to the backs of their bikes, full of scritcheting claws and wobbling combs and beady eyes. They didn't even need to build a chicken coop, the *Musée* already had a bunch of big enclosures out the back for a few chickens whose job was to be an exhibit of living dinosaurs – or, that's how they'd sold it to the *Musée*. Their real job was to lay eggs for Jean-Luc and Françoise. It's less mental than it sounds. Though my idea of mental was flexible before, and these days it could probably do a one-handed cartwheel and land in the splits. Obviously that's a flexibility that doesn't extend to body hair. Yet. And it certainly didn't when it was me, Julie and Sarah in the attic – every time we got our pants down I'd have a moment of being amazed at how hairy they were, like, I'd just want to shout, 'Muff!' at the top of my voice. I've never been that hairy down there, but both Julie and Sarah had proper lapels, like, the kind that come out across your thighs in points. When we did the classes at the *Château*, nobody was like that, and by then I suppose I did find it slightly weird to see everybody so tidied up, but hey ho, the visual habits of a lifetime.

Despite her striking lapels, it was the line of hairs down Julie's belly that always struck me most, like, if you drew her naked you would have this big dark arrow of thick hair pointing downwards from her navel. Her birth went really well. Sarah says that at its most basic, a good birth is one where you get the baby out of the mother, everyone is in one piece afterwards and the mother isn't completely terrified at the thought of ever doing it again. Julie was not afraid of giving birth. She was coachable. She'd been a champion swimmer when she was young, with those big hands, long limbs and broad shoulders she shared with Martin, the coaches must've been delighted when they saw her coming. Anyway, Julie had decided that Sarah was her coach; she trusted everything Sarah said, and she believed, utterly, in her ability to physically prepare her body. And she wasn't scared of the pain – she said she'd spent enough time throwing up at the poolside to know that aching muscles were not to be afraid of. What she was scared of was the baby being outside of her, because while it was inside she felt she could protect it.

Sarah reckoned that seeing the woman with the baby at the Beacon Bonfire was what made Julie going into labour a few days later possible. She said that the morning after the bonfire, when she and Julie were in the kitchen getting breakfast, she could see that Julie's belly had changed shape, that the baby's head had dropped down into the pelvis. It's hard sometimes, what with all there is to take into account, to know what to believe. If it was back in the old days and Sarah said that, I'd probably have been looking up at what point in pregnancy the head normally engages and whether it could happen in one go and if it did could you see it, and I'd probably have found a whole load of contradictory possibilities, and in a wide field exceptional cases will occur, but the fact is, that afternoon when we went up to the attic it was clear that the baby had clunked down into place.

Sarah said that despite the mother of the baby we'd seen being tired and scared and lonely, Julie saw her baby, and the baby was okay, so this world was one in which a baby could be okay. It was Julie's body's way of expressing its confidence in her child, its confidence that Julie could bring it into the world, its confidence in her ability to make a protected place for it, and Sarah saying that was just as much part of her knowledge as knowing how to use a Pinard stethoscope. As Pressure Drop would say, who needs the truth when you have reality?

So maybe Julie's labour began when she saw the baby at the bonfire, or maybe it began a few mornings later while Martin and I were out fishing and fucking, so when we got back she had started having contractions and everyone was a little wired. Or maybe it began much later that day, because after a morning of contractions Julie ate some lunch and then lay down and slept while we rattled about the house, uneasy and unable to think about doing anything because we kept expecting it to start again. Sarah did not rattle about. She quietly got a couple of things ready and sat down and had a cup of tea while we all walked around bumping into each other, and then when we'd been doing that for about half an hour, Pressure Drop said, 'Right then, let's go and find the rock.'

So we were all, 'Rock? What rock?'

And he said that in Ireland, out in the sticks and back in the day, if a birth was difficult the men of the house went out and found the biggest rock they could lift and carried it three times round the edge of the farm, and that was supposed to help. Sarah got a good laugh out of that, and then said that, rocks aside, if Julie's body was resting itself now then it'd be a long night, and the best thing any of us could do was get some rest. She took herself upstairs to lie down and told me I should do the same. I went to bed too, but stuff kept running through my mind: how to help with the breathing, how long things should take, how the heartbeat should sound. In the end I fell asleep – even with somebody about to give birth above my head I've still got my special talents.

I woke up in the late afternoon. I could hear voices outside, some laughter, Adi getting excited about something, and footsteps upstairs. It was beginning. It was amazing watching Sarah, like, there's always a pleasure in watching somebody do something well, but there was something really special about seeing Sarah on the job. All her slightly awkward self-consciousness melted away and she became shining-eyed and strong-handed – people say 'full of herself' as an insult, but that's the best way to describe what she was – full of herself. It's mad to think she didn't even set out to become a midwife.

Sarah never told me that, I found it out from Jean-Luc at *Chandeleur*. I don't actually know what *Chandeleur* is. Pressure Drop said it's the same as St Brigid's day and *Imbolc*, but he doesn't really know what those are either, except you're meant to have a fire and make triangular crosses out of rushes. Whatever a triangular cross is. Jean-Luc said it was actually *Lupercalia* and that we should find a naked young man to slap my hand for a lucky birth – he and Pressure Drop both declined on grounds of age. Anyway, Françoise insisted it was *Chandeleur*, and that for *Chandeleur* you eat crêpes, but it's not Pancake Tuesday either.

We had arrived at Jean-Luc and Françoise's door a few weeks beforehand, hollow-eyed and stringy, winding our way down through the valley from above. Pressure Drop's weed was running low and I was mostly just trying to keep the split skin all over my hands and feet from getting infected because it would've been too fucking dumb to get basically all the way there and then die of chilblains. The rocks were insane, folded strata all around us, zigzagging and shooting off diagonally at hysterical angles. The last bit of road to the *Musée* followed a valley that became a ravine, winding its way between walls of black rock that reared over us like waves about to crash until we came out at river level and willows elbowed them out of the way. We passed a towering cliff covered in fossil ammonites the size of motorbike tyres and it felt like we'd finally lost our minds. And then we reached the gates and wound our way up the steep path through the trees, pushing our bikes past a theatrical waterfall, all fairy caverns and dripping moss, that Sarah said was petrifying, by which she meant that the water slowly but surely turned things to stone. Sarah wasn't petrified, but she was in ribbons from the stress of finally actually being fully in charge of taking us the right way now that she was on home territory and the doubt of not knowing whether she was actually taking us anywhere at all. But she was.

When we came up round the final bend Jean-Luc and Françoise were standing in their doorway and they ran out towards us, hugging Sarah around her handlebars, saying they were sure it was her when they'd seen us on the road below, but hadn't been able to believe their eyes. They helped us unhook the panniers from the bikes and ushered us in. Sarah was in floods of tears, shaking with relief. We sat down around the kitchen table and Jean-Luc poured us each a glass of water from a jug and a shot of something like brandy from a bottle he took down off the top of the dresser, glancing at my belly and at Sarah before he handed me mine, but she just waved her hand and said it was the least of our worries. There was a fire burning and a kettle on the stove. Sarah introduced us between sobs and sighs, and Françoise said, '*Bienvenue, faites comme chez vous.*' The words imbued themselves with a solemnity worthy of one of Pressure Drop's word-bombs, and my eyes welled up too as we sat and drank in silence and let it soak in.

For the first while after we arrived Jean-Luc and Françoise just fed us and tried to get us to sleep a lot. Sarah told them bit by bit about how we'd got there. There was no hurry. For so long, it had constantly felt like we were falling behind, waiting in Fairlight, time slipping away from us at the *Château*, losing days trapped by weather through the mountains. Now, suddenly, the future rolled out around us in all directions and time wasn't a worry anymore.

I shook the accumulated dust out of my rucksack and laid the bag in the bottom of a cupboard. I spent about a day and a half mending my trainers. I put the photograph of my parents and the cigar box of spores on the mantlepiece in my bedroom, thinking about inheritance and wishing I had something of Martin's to set beside them, for me, but also for Leo. I wanted the object equivalent of the birth-canal passage, something that would leave shreds of Martin all over him as he entered the world, a raiment of protection for all his days, moulding him, in both senses of the word, into who he'd become. Maybe he already had everything he'd need from Martin, but I still wished I had something – an icon or an amulet, a knife or a scarf, a ring or a tooth – to watch me from the mantlepiece as I slowly let myself settle. I washed my clothes and hung them out to dry and then folded them and arranged them in drawers and on shelves in my room, marvelling at the genius of drawers and shelves. I lay in my bed in the morning listening to the others laughing in the kitchen. I cleaned my bike and put it in a shed. I tended my chilblains until they healed. I helped a little with simple chores as Jean-Luc and Françoise's routine expanded to fit us into it.

By the time *Chandeleur* arrived, we had made ourselves at home. The pancake making was more symbolic than nutritional because there were almost no eggs – *Les Poules de la Mort*, despite our continued scraps-and-peelings support, were still deep in winter mode and no ill-defined and poorly understood calendar event was going to shake them out of it. So we had two pancakes each, as dessert at lunchtime, but to make it feel festive we lined up all the jams in the place down the centre of the table, mirabelle and quince, apricot and greengage, redcurrant and plum, glass jars glowing like jewels.

Jam is something that there must be a lot left of around the world, certainly we came across a fair amount of it on our way here. Maybe it's something that people think they like more than they actually do, because almost every kitchen you search will have two or three unfinished jars of it knocking about, leftovers of a marvellous magical process that lost much of its power due to ubiquity, like plastic, or music. As if turning last year's sunlight into dessert isn't amazing. Without bread to put it on, it's not that much fun though, even when you're completely energy depleted you can only eat about half a jar of jam straight up before you start to feel queasy, and bread is in short supply.

The crêpes were pretty exciting, we tore off shreds of pancake and loaded each one with jam, switching flavours every mouthful.

And when we'd finished, Jean-Luc said, 'So, Sarah, a poem!'
Pressure Drop and I exchanged a glance.

'What?' said Jean-Luc, 'She doesn't tell you poems?'

That's when we found out that Sarah had studied English Lit. and that she'd made her name as somebody who always had the right poem for the moment in Paris on a university trip to see the bookshop run by the woman who published *Ulysses* and the cafés where Wilde and Hemingway hung out. Surrounded by classmates who'd been across the Channel before and who were less interested than she was in gawping slack-jawed at the silhouette of the Eiffel Tower, she left them as they headed off to pick up tins of *crème de marrons* and wheels of brie at *Le Bon Marché*. She wandered instead through the Latin Quarter, soaking up grandiose facades and tiny backstreets, with French filling her ears like the sound of waves on a beach, until suddenly she realised that some of it was being aimed directly at her. An impossibly French-looking group of young people, students like her she imagined, were calling, '*Hé, l'Américaine!*' and gesturing her over to their table outside a café.

They'd ordered her a coffee by the time she'd explained she was actually from London and asked her a dozen questions in mangled English by the time the scowling waiter brought it. At that point they all jumped in to warn her not to finish it, because if they all finished their coffees the waiter would give them the boot. She looked round at them, the half-finished stone-cold coffees, the ashtray overflowing, the urgent questions still coming, about the monarchy, The Rolling Stones, the Black Panthers, the miniskirt, the unions of the steel industry, the relative merits of eyeliner versus lipstick, and she found herself laughing, because here they were at last: people who believed she had something interesting to say.

Their questions tailed off at her laughter, faces turned towards her in a ring, waiting, leaving her space and time to let the words rise up inside her and say, '"If the fool would persist in his folly he would become wise. Folly is the cloak of knavery. Shame is pride's cloak. Prisons are built with stones of law, brothels with bricks of religion. The pride of the peacock is the glory of God. The lust of the goat is the bounty of God. The wrath of the lion is the wisdom of God. The nakedness of woman is the work of God. Excess of sorrow laughs. Excess of joy weeps. The roaring of lions, the howling of wolves, the raging of the stormy sea, and the destructive sword, are portions of eternity too great for the eye of man. The fox condemns the trap, not himself. Joys impregnate. Sorrows bring forth. Let man wear the fell of the lion, woman the fleece of the sheep. The bird a nest, the spider a web, man friendship."'

At which point they all whooped and clapped and banged on the table and pulled bits of change from every available pocket and ordered a bottle of red wine and, counting heads, nine glasses, and the waiter scowled even harder at them, and they all laughed as he went off, muttering and gesticulating, to get it.

'Now you can drink the coffee,' Jean-Luc said to her, 'but we must not finish the wine.'

I wonder if they slept together that week in Paris, but then, I also wonder if she slept with her friend who had the baby. I've never found the right way to ask her about either, and she'd never in a million years volunteer something like that. Anyway, she and Jean-Luc wrote to each other, tracking each other's addresses. She settled in Streatham and, in the years while he was on his way up through the edges of the Sahara, his brief, battered notes with exotic stamps arrived at hers while a stack of letters from her to him accumulated at his parents' house in Digne.

One of the first things Jean-Luc did when he and Françoise arrived there and he found them was write to her and tell her to come and visit. Which she did, every year from then on, making the journey down through France, driving through the night, sleeping sitting up in the front seat in an *aire de repos*, with a thermos of coffee and a road atlas for company. And every time, a day or so after she arrived, after the table had been cleared and people leaned back in their chairs, their hands folded over their stomach or rolling a cigarette, she'd tell them a new poem.

And so, there among the sticky teaspoons, she began: '"So joys Ulysses at the appearing shore; and sees (and labours onward as he sees) the rising forests, and the tufted trees. And now, as near approaching as the sound of human voice the listening ear may wound, amidst the rocks he heard a hollow roar of murmuring surges breaking on the shore; nor peaceful port was there, nor winding bay, to shield the vessel from the rolling sea, but cliffs and shaggy shores, a dreadful sight! All rough with rocks, with foamy billows white."'

I couldn't listen to her without thinking of Martin out in the boat. It was all sharp rocks, monstrous waves and cliffs. I felt dizzy from the sugar and my blood was beating in my ears. I did my best to zone out. There was torn skin and unhappiness, misery and rushing currents, briny torrents and the arms of death. She paused for a moment, and it was at that point, sitting around the kitchen table with the licked plates and the jam, that I realised that, wherever Martin was, we had actually arrived. And maybe that was the beginning of my labour, though I didn't give birth until ten days later, but who really knows where the beginning of the end starts and the end of the beginning finishes.

Sarah glanced around at us, uncertain, as if checking we were all there, before carrying on: '"Now parting from the stream, Ulysses found a mossy bank with pliant rushes crown'd; The bank he pressed, and gently kissed the ground; where on the flowery herb as soft he lay, thus to his soul the sage began to say: 'What will ye next ordain, ye powers on high! And yet, ah yet, what fates are we to try?'"'

Later that afternoon, Sarah explained to me how she'd switched studies. When she got a place at university it was a big deal in her family. Her parents had their sights set on her becoming a secondary-school teacher. But then, when she was in her second year, one of the girls in her class got pregnant. This was in, like, I guess, the early seventies. The girl's parents were horrified and the guy wanted nothing to do with it – except to let his father offer her £200 if she'd turn herself in to a mother and baby home and let the Salvation Army take the child away without a trace. She lost her place at the university on grounds of immorality and was about to be kicked out of halls because of that. Sarah told her she'd be mad not to take the money, but that once she had it in her pocket she could do what she liked. The boy's family weren't really buying an adoption, just buying the right never to think about her again. She started going with her to the appointments. At the beginning she was just being a good friend, but after months of watching her friend be patronised, lied to, humiliated and, in the end, physically harmed, she was radicalised. She had a subscription to *Spare Rib*, another to *Overthrow*, she'd dropped out of her English Lit. course and moved, with her friend and the new baby, into the top-floor flat of the house she one day came to own on our old street in Streatham.

She got herself some dungarees. She wrote a letter to Nurse Fiona, one of the nurses who'd been kind during the birth, thanking her and saying that she wanted to train as a nurse and asking how. Finally, a phone call came at a moment when she was able to run down the three flights of stairs in time to grab the receiver and they arranged to meet the next day at eight in the morning when Fiona came off shift. They met at a caff in Brixton where a tiny Ugandan Indian couple wiped tables and doled out bacon sandwiches and cups of tea that they poured, already milked and sugared, from a huge and seemingly bottomless steel teapot, so large that they had a specially made slanted wooden plinth so that you didn't need to lift it, you just tilted it and the elixir of life would pour forth. Nurse Fiona, or, just Fiona when she was off duty, called the woman who ran the caff 'Mum', as did all the other regulars.

The caff opened at six in the morning so it was a hub for nurses, bus drivers, postmen and drunks. Fiona said that Mum was the local matchmaker for those who worked unsociable hours. Sarah sat down and told Fiona about what she'd seen and how she felt and that she'd dropped out of university and why she wanted to be a nurse. Fiona drank her tea and told her, firstly, she was mad to want to become a nurse, that if her A-levels were good enough she should at least aim for midwife, because then she would actually get to deliver babies, and secondly, she was going to have to lie through her teeth. If any of the matrons got wind of the fact that she'd been to university they'd say she thought she was too posh to wash and she'd be cleaning bedpans all year, and for the love of god get a nice blouse and a skirt because nobody was going to give her a place if she went in in those dungarees. What she needed to do was dress up prim and say that, for example, she'd read this awful thing in the papers about Africa and she wanted to go and help the poor women who were over there having more babies in grass huts than they knew what to do with.

'The thing is,' Fiona said, 'if you say you want to make things better here, they'll make life hell for you if they even take you on, but if you say you want to go off and help the savages they'll be all for it. You do that, and then keep your head down, your mouth shut, your nose clean and your chin up, and in time you'll be able to help.'

And so that is exactly what Sarah did, she got her place at King's and she led a double life. She'd head out to the hospital in shined shoes and a skirt, change into her uniform, be brisk and sensible, go to the midwifery classes, come home, change into her dungarees and head out to the meetings at the library. And she stuck to her Africa story, so if anybody got curious about her asking questions about knowing how to do things without asking doctors, she'd wheel it out as why she needed to know. She didn't make many friends in either camp – the students thought she was stuck-up or a nut-job missionary, or both, and the other women's libbers thought she was a spy or a coward. But by then she was used to every tribe thinking she was too much part of another to be one of them.

She made good on her Africa cover story by heading off to Senegal, encouraged by a friend of a friend of Jean-Luc's, who himself had been inspired by the then-nascent Médecins Sans Frontières and a cholera epidemic. She went to Saint Louis in the north, and became known, to her wry amusement, as '*la toubabess*'. She travelled up along the river to villages where the women sang to hippos and rode crocodiles, and she learned from *les mères des accouchées* never to move the blackened knife at the head of a baby's bed in case evil came calling. And then she came back to London and became a community midwife.

Before, it was hard for me to imagine how slow the process of finding people who thought like you was, when, for a time, all we had was systems that funnelled anyone similar together. You get more of an idea now how it must have been. Sarah joined, on the quiet, the Association of Radical Midwives and sent letters to anyone who wrote about pregnancy or childbirth in *Spare Rib*, but she was worried about being seen going to meetings with other dreadful women's libbers.

One day, tucked into her copy of *Overthrow*, there was a letter from the mailing team, saying that they'd noticed that there were two subscribers on her street — did she know that? And, in the interests of solidarity, did she want to be put in touch with them? She did want to be put in touch. She was hoping it would be another woman leading a double life, a secretary infiltrating an advertising company to sabotage its sexist ad campaigns, or a teller in a bank who was actually writing a great feminist novel. What she got, after a month of fevered imagining, was Pressure Drop. You can totally see the two of them, looking at each other across a doorstep, her having hoped for Joan Didion getting a fresh-faced Irishman with burgeoning dreads, him having hoped for Angela Davis getting the close-cropped curls and shiny shoes of a public-sector stalwart. They stayed on nodding terms, but their mutual disappointment, along with Sarah's fear of blowing her cover, stopped them from becoming friends.

They were a good match though, and despite all their obvious differences they both clearly knew a fair amount about living your life between two stools. On the rare occasions when I saw them interact with each other without them thinking anyone was watching you could see they got on and that they looked out for each other. After we left the *Château* we were all shaken, but Sarah seemed to have left her anger there, whereas Pressure Drop was angry all the time. There wasn't much to say or do about it, but you could see something in the angles of his elbows as he rode and the angles of his knees as he sat.

The first couple of nights we hadn't rested much, we hadn't wanted to go near buildings because we were too scared of meeting anybody else while we were still on their territory. We'd slept under bushes and in a dry drainage tunnel that crossed under the road and in the lee of a little kind of building in the middle of a field that Pressure Drop said was a pumphouse. Sleeping under the stars is shit. It's cold and noisy and you get soaked in dew, you have to be really exhausted to get any sleep at all and you wake feeling even more tired.

After a few nights of that we stopped feeling like we desperately had to put distance behind us. We found a haybarn piled with hay, which must've been from the year before because the fields around were full of long silvery-green grass that bobbed and bent like the surface of the sea. We made a false wall of bales that we could wheel the bikes behind and hollowed out a fort up on the top so that when we were sitting in it, we were hidden. The land all around was gently rolling. When you sat up on top of the hay bales you could see out a long way, with the edge of the galvanised roof suddenly cutting blackly across your vision like the brim of a visor. Pressure Drop was sitting looking out with his legs dangling off the edge. 'We'll stay here a while,' he said, 'we need the sleep.' Sarah nodded. I was fine with that. I thought it was them that needed the sleep but that night I went down like a brick through muddy water and in the morning it was only desperately needing a piss that dragged me back to the surface.

When I sat up, Pressure Drop and Sarah were already down below, talking about rape, as you do. Pressure Drop was in full flow: something that began with rape being about ripping somebody apart, that rolled into every child born in Ireland between the twenties and the eighties being a child of rape because they told you so little about anything that happened between your navel and your knees that how could anybody fucking consent to fucking anything if they had no idea what the fuck was happening to them. Sarah was just listening to him.

'It's to tear something, to tell somebody they're just a hole in something, it's always fucking violence: banging, nailing, shagging just means shredding something, like fucking tobacco. And those fuckers back there, there'll be more and more children, and they're going to finish by raping the children. Because it happens every fucking time: David fucking Koresh, Warren fucking Jeffs, the whole fucking Catholic fucking Church, every time some fucking fucker thinks they're the only one with a direct line they end up raping fucking children.' He was up and pacing, his arms shooting out in loose-jointed anger that made him look like a puppet.

Sarah was sitting on a bale looking at her hands, running her thumbs over the cycling callouses that were forming at the base of each finger.

'He's not there yet anyway,' she said, 'it's not like we were armed to the teeth, and we got away, didn't we? You did a great job of putting the evil eye on him – did you go to church when you were a child?'

'Not church, "Mass", with Nanna, my mother's mother, and not just when I was a kid either! No questions asked – she did the whole bit, scapulars in every colour, collations on a Friday, annual retreats at Lough Derg, and when I was a teenager it didn't matter where I was on Saturday night, on Sunday I had to be at hers, on time and compos mentis enough to go to Mass, no breakfast beforehand, hold it together until it was finished and then she'd make a fry-up when we got home. If I looked a mess she gave me such stick. That's what kept me off the hard stuff – I knew if I got into it then sooner or later I'd end up missing Mass, and if that happened I'd never hear the end of it from Nanna. There was a lot of heroin knocking around Dublin then, you'd see a whole herd of junkies coming through, looking for somebody who was dealing that day, but I stuck to the weed because Nanna's piss-taking meant I had to go to Mass. That's not where I got the incantation though, that's powerful stuff that is, I got that mitching school to avoid the Jesuits and sitting for hours in the waiting room of Connolly station while it rained. The incantation was the Irish translation of the list of station rules.' He broke into the huge voice he'd used, incomprehensible words rumbling out of him, and then their translation, 'Do not litter! Do not allow dogs to foul the platform!'

Sarah started to laugh, Pressure Drop too, spluttering on through it, 'Do not spit.' The pair of them cracking up, Pressure Drop taking huge gulps of breath between shouts of laughter, 'Do not beg.' It got the better of him and he gave up, just laughed and laughed. Then, wiping his eyes, he said, 'What about you though? I mean, reciting those rules is mad enough I'll grant you, but where the fuck did you get the idea to show them your parts?'

Sarah, who was wiping away tears of laughter at his performance, had to take a few deep breaths before being able to tell him, 'I saw it done once, in a village upriver in the north of Senegal. One of the men had done something, I can't remember what it was, maybe I never knew, but whatever it was, all the women knew he'd done it and he was denying it. So the older women got up before dawn and stood in a circle around his hut and started chanting, and when he woke up he came to the door all puffed up with anger and was about to start shouting at them when they all lifted up their skirts. You could see all the fight go out of him. He froze, and then he tried to run, but every time he tried to get between them they moved towards each other and he'd recoil back. Eventually he broke through and ran. He never came back to the village as long as I was there. The women said it was the most powerful gris-gris there was – that if it gives life it can take it away.'

'Fuck's sake – an old grey minge and some rules for civilised behaviour in a railway station and that's all she wrote. Fucking great.' He sat down on a bale and flopped backwards onto it, letting out a huge sigh. I remembered that I needed to piss. As I climbed down he gave me a wave, and Sarah nodded to me. I grinned at them, but their laughter had been between them, there wasn't a part of it for me.

Anyway, over forty years or so Sarah delivered – though that makes it sound like she was putting them through letter-boxes, she'd say birthed – thousands of babies. And you could absolutely see that when she was at Julie's side. At anyone's side I suppose.

At the *Château* her classes were obviously the best bits. In fact, they were the only bits really that were at all bearable. They were at eleven in the morning because by then pretty much everyone had got up and pretty much no one was drunk yet. The classes were the deal for Sarah. I guess given the setting it was always going to be the case that somebody was pregnant, and when Sarah saw that somebody was she felt she had to stay. I think in a way the place bothered her least because she was doing what she'd been doing her whole working life: trying to keep the pube-shaving, the extra stitch for the husband and the distaste for breastfeeding at bay for long enough to get a baby out and onto the tit.

She could just shift her mind back a decade or five and then get her impenetrable wall of purpose up around her and nothing could get through. Also, you can't deny that being, as far as the henchmen were all concerned, old, and that made her life easier.

Pressure Drop couldn't take it there at all. There were so many people he expected better of. He just hated the fact that all that limitless freedom could result in something so dickishly constrained, that of all the possible worlds that could've been created they had decided on that one. There were about fifteen women and four men, plus a few other men who'd visit regularly, and Charles, who was the boss. The idea of leaving was a complicated one. Technically, none of the women were prisoners there. Technically, neither were we, and we had a mission and a means of transport with ready supplies stashed just up the road, but we ended up stuck there too.

At first I couldn't understand why Charles was the boss, or why everyone thought he was such a ladykiller. I'm sure a lot of it got lost in translation, but I began to get a bead on it as time went on. I didn't get to know anyone well – I didn't speak any French when we arrived, but everyone there was really ordinary, like, men and women that you just would not have noticed if you'd stood behind them in the supermarket queue. Charles and the henchmen offered food, shelter, protection and, as they saw it, good times, in return, essentially, for sex and for being made to feel that their provision of food, shelter, protection, good times and sex was the best food, shelter, protection, good times and sex that had ever been had.

Before we'd arrived, sure, our progress had stuttered. Adi's injuries meant that we had no sense of how far we were really capable of going, or how long it would normally take to make or break camp. Later, it was easy to feel like we'd been wasting time, but in fact, if we'd continued at that pace, we'd have been absolutely fine. There was a lot of daylight and we covered thirty, maybe forty kilometres a day: keeping away from houses, skirting towns, camping in the corners of fields, searching for clean water, lowering our standards for what we considered clean water to be. The countryside was like the south of England: green and gentle and without great excitement except for the hedgerows, which were wild. It felt like they were trying to seal the roads back up, everywhere there was grass and weeds bubbling over onto the edges of the tarmac like the froth of waves running up a beach, and branches and brambles still bendy with the sap of that year's growth reaching from one side towards the other, ready to whip your legs and snag your arms as you rode by.

Then, when we were trapped, it was only the creep of the vegetation that let us know time was passing during the long summer months: the weeds rose, the green of the trees darkened and that of the grasses lightened. We seemed caught in loops, going nowhere, rolling from day to night, from teaching to forgetting, from chaotic party to ineffectual clean-up. Nothing went forwards, just round and round. Even Leïla's belly didn't seem to get any bigger – though she was a funny podgy shape, so it was hard to tell. We knew it was getting near the birth because Sarah told us to keep our rucksacks half-packed or be ready to lose what wasn't in them. After the hassle we'd had getting them there was no way we were letting them go at that point.

When we'd first showed up Charles twigged immediately that we hadn't just been walking down the road with our hands in our pockets so he, ever the gracious host, offered to send somebody to pick up our bags for us. Obviously that wasn't going to happen because we didn't want them knowing about the bikes, so we said we'd hidden them in some bushes and it would be difficult to explain where exactly. So then Charles offered to send somebody with us, for protection and to help carry stuff back. And that's the kind of place you start to see it – it was all about control. He wanted to know everything possible about what resources we had. Maybe he didn't believe our Africa story, whatever, he was just fishing for leverage. But polite. Because he'd realised that's what works best on normal people – you act polite. You run them down a bit, but you act polite, you make it clear that you're in charge, but you act polite, you accidentally touch their leg when you're sitting beside them, but you act polite, and that way it's harder for everybody to put their finger on what's going wrong.

Like with his barbecues. One of the men had a gun – not a little tuck-it-in-the-back-of-your-waistband gun, a big long one, the sort you put up against your shoulder to aim, a rifle or a shotgun. And so, every week or so, Charles would give this guy a handful of cartridges from one of the locked cupboards and the guy would head off into the fields around the *Château* and shoot a cow or a sheep or something. And then he'd come back, on foot, and he and Charles would take the quad bike and head out to where he'd shot it and come back with the animal, or at least huge recognisable chunks of it, strapped to the back of the quad bike. And they'd always ride up the driveway revving the motor and scaring the shit out of the peacocks with Charles sitting at the back, on top of the carcass and holding the gun. Even though it was never him that did the killing, it was always him that brought home the bacon. And he and the guy would drag it off the quad bike and over to where the barbecue was, and butcher it as a great spectacle of how grand their largesse was, of how plentifully they were feeding all of us but also as a great spectacle of how well they knew how to use a big knife to cut a body into little bits.

It annoyed the hell out of him that Pressure Drop wouldn't eat any of the meat, but he made sure that was hard to see – just like Pressure Drop made it hard to see how hungry he was most of the time. Sarah was worried for him, she even said to him at one point, 'You know, they don't hunt on a Sunday.' But Pressure Drop said that your physical state bearing witness to oppression was as important as your mind doing it. He really, really hated it there.

I ate the meat, cooked to the point of it being cremated. Sarah encouraged it, despite the uncertainties about how safe it was. By then it had crept up on me.

I've since seen Pressure Drop eat meat. The first time was when we were coming through the first set of mountains. One day we came over a high pass and everything opened up out in front of us. We could see a wide valley in the far distance, a river in the hollow of it, fields stretching out either side. I thought that was it, that we were going to arrive, but Sarah said no, we had to cross that valley and carry on into the mountains on the other side of it, which seemed to go on forever towards sharp snowcapped peaks in the distance. And so, with that discouraging thought lodged in my guts, later that day we found ourselves once again trying to make it to shelter in pissing rain driven at us by the wind, except that time the rain turned to whirling snow. It was magical in a terrifying sort of way. Everything started to disappear around us. First the mountaintops smudged away into the clouds, then the land around us dissolved into blankness, then the road we were following became just a flatter bit of featurelessness.

The bike tyres crunched into the surface, but at any speed beyond walking they skidded all over the road, so we were soon pushing them through the erased landscape back towards where we'd seen a house. We got inside and then we were once again trying to find enough fuel to warm a room and dry our wet clothes and shoes, once again going through shelves and cupboards searching for food. We only had a couple of cups of rice and lentils left, so if we could find anything else to eat, we ate it. Often any carbs had already been destroyed by mice, plastic packets nibbled to confetti and the remains scattered with shit pellets, but we took whatever was still edible. The real prize was tins, which we emptied into the pan and ate heated as quickly as possible in whatever combination they came in. Tinned tomatoes with tinned potatoes. Tinned sardines with tinned beetroot. Tinned sweetcorn with tinned beans. Tinned chickpeas with tinned chickpeas.

Nothing ever felt like enough calories. Even when I was just beginning a meal I would know that at the end of it I would still feel hungry. It was impossible to tell if I was losing weight because I was, confusingly, getting bigger all the time. Pressure Drop didn't really have anything to lose, and had maybe for years been getting most of his nutrition somehow from smoke, but there was less and less of Sarah, her face just hollowing out beneath the skin.

So while I got wood in from another blessed woodpile and Pressure Drop lit the fire, Sarah searched the kitchen. She came back in with her eyes gleaming, although her face was anxious. She was carrying a stack of three huge tins. 'Pressure Drop,' she said, 'you're not going to like this, but I really think it's what you have to do.' The tins were *confit de canard* – duck in duck fat. I was busy trying to sort out our sleeping stuff before it was too dark to see so I didn't catch Pressure Drop's immediate reaction, and then I went outside with basins and saucepans from the kitchen to collect a load of snow in the hope that it would be warm enough indoors for it to melt overnight.

The sun had gone down behind the mountains we'd already crossed but it was not yet night. The moon had come up over the mountains we had ahead of us, the ones that were now hidden behind the mountains we were in. It had stopped snowing and the sky had gone from total cloud all around your head to big wads of it scooting across the sky, their edges glowing with the last rays of the sun or the first rays of the moon. It was as if the real world had been reprinted in white and blue and indigo, and the snow sparkled like glitter when you turned your head.

I began filling the basins with a ladle as quickly as I could – not just because this was well after we'd first heard wolves, but also because the cold was impressive. It wasn't the cold that comes at you on the wind like the blades of a knife, or the cold that trickles into you from a grey sky, this cold was monumental. Solid. Just existing in it was doing battle with it – for the living heat of your body to be present you had to constantly smash the cold out of the way, every little metabolic action in your cells working away like microscopic pneumatic drills, chipping a little warm hole the shape of you out of the huge cold mass.

It was probably only a few degrees warmer than zero indoors, because the mounds of snow I brought in defrosted so slowly that they were not fully melted by the next morning, but the relative difference was so noticeable that you could feel all your face muscles relax a little when you came into it.

My stomach muscles probably did the same because Leo took advantage and tumble-turned inside me.

Pressure Drop was sitting near the fire. He'd taken his shoes off and his huge, long feet were stretched so close to the flames that it looked like they were about to burn. I came and sat beside him and did the same. Taking your shoes off is a tough one, because although the fire heats the bits of your feet that are facing towards it much more effectively, the other side – and there is always another side where the heat of a fire is concerned – gets cold much quicker. It's the only way though. Pressure Drop is a fan of the leave-your-socks-on-and-dry-them-on-your-feet technique, but he's clearly so wrong: taking off damp socks and putting on dry ones is a sacrament, especially when in between the two pairs you can stretch your feet towards a fire and let even the crevices between your toes dry, pulling them away to put the dry socks on only when the warmth actually becomes painful to your soles.

I found my dry socks by the light of the candles Pressure Drop had set up. Sarah was surrounded by bits and pieces from the kitchen, pouring flour from a glass jar – take that, mice! – into a big bowl. She opened the tins of *confit de canard*. The fat inside them was hard and yellowy-grey. It looked like glue. With a spoon she scraped as much of it as she could out of the tins, excavating around the pieces of duck that were in there so that they looked vaguely archaeological, and she put the fat and a few handfuls of snow in with the flour and mixed it all together into a dough that she could knead. The fat that had been left in the tins had been melted by the fire by then, and she tipped the duck legs and all the liquid fat, now golden in the firelight, into a deep frying pan and put it over the fire. It immediately started sizzling, and the thick, greasy smell made my head spin. I looked over at Pressure Drop, and I could see that whatever the moral and theological fight that had been playing out in his mind was, the winner had been decided.

Sarah put a small frying pan at the other side of the fire. She made little balls of dough, stretched and flattened them between her hands, patted them in flour and flapped them onto the pan where they puffed up in bubbles. She flipped them, showing the blackened blisters on their undersides, and when they were speckled all over she slid them into a clean, folded tea-towel. I actually dribbled into the fire with hunger when she asked me to turn the meat in the pan, my spit sizzling on the embers like sap does when you put green branches in the flames.

We stuffed ourselves, burning our fingers on the meat, cramming the flatbread in our mouths, licking the plates. When we'd finished Sarah drained the last of the melted duck fat from the tins into the pan, set it back on the fire and threw in a few handfuls of sugar. It crackled and smoked, and when it darkened to bronze she poured it onto one of the heaps of snow I'd brought in, where it trickled and set like lava running down the sides of a volcano. We picked it off and crunched it to shards while we built the fire back up.

The whole meal was mesmerising, I'd never seen her do something like that before, never seen her put special care into anything except her work. I'm certain she was doing it for Pressure Drop, to honour his internal struggle. It was her way of making the food be more than just food, more than just him putting another creature into himself. Making it instead be hope and love and future.

Pressure Drop's certainty that we become everything we have ever put into ourselves makes more sense now, in that I tell myself that I have, in some tiny way, become Martin. I put him inside me, and we put Leo inside me, and now forever more I will carry fragments of Martin floating within me, as if I'm a lump of amber. While Leo was in my belly, his cells with their little packages of DNA, mine and Martin's all tangled up inside them, will have crossed the placenta into my blood. They'll have lodged in my heart and my brain and my bones, and they will stay there, maybe forever. It comforts me to imagine that whatever the future holds, somewhere in the shallow eddies of my bloodstream, there, like quietly multiplying piles of river-smoothed stones, are cells that are ready to list the dark hair, the broad knuckles, the easy smile, the thrown-back head, the nose, the swinging stride of someone that I once put inside me. Even if one hopeless day I forget what he looked like, those cells will gently roll through me, pebbles in a stream, rattling off what they still remember. And somehow I will hear them, even if I don't understand what they're saying anymore – when we're given signs and wonders, hearing and understanding are not necessarily bedfellows.

Like with pregnancy. For me, you can divide the very early signs of pregnancy into daytime signs and night-time signs, but the thing about both sets of signs, if you notice them at all, is that they feel pretty much like other stuff. The daytime signs felt like I was just about to get my period – slightly less flat-chested, not wanting to spring out of bed in the mornings and a weird kind of heaviness around the inside of my sacrum, as if the earth's magnetic field was suddenly exercising a stronger pull on that part of my body than any other, drawing the iron molecules in all the blood that was starting to collect in that spot towards it. The night-time signs of early pregnancy felt like I was just on the edge of coming up on pills – when I lay down I could feel the palms of my hands glowing as if I could've shot laser beams out of them and there was a strange business in my body, not tense, just busy, a kind of excitement at a cellular level, all the little fibres of my being whispering to each other that something was waiting in the wings and sending quiet cascades of signals through me, flipping switches so that circuits of fairy lights were all connected up and ready to come on. But there was no great soaring epiphany-like explosion of light, no sudden rush that throws your head back and pulls your chest open, no tooth-clenching wide-eyed grin, just the constant flow of it, energy reorganising itself to stream through a system down new pathways.

There's movement, and there's stuckness. Once, after my parents died – years before the world went the way of all things, back when both your parents dying relatively suddenly and in quick succession was unusual – I went to a hypnotherapist because a friend said it might help to connect some of the dots that'd been blown apart. I didn't actually think it would do anything, but that is some properly weird shit – your toes tapping out Morse code for your unconscious while you're stuck immobile in an armchair slurring like a drunk. Anyway, one of the things my unconscious said while I was under was that I had to be more like a river, all flowing in one direction, instead of being like the sea, waves pulling in and out but not going anywhere. I don't know about that, always preferred the sea to rivers and I'll not be held responsible for the New Age shit my unconscious spouts, but one of the many, many things that made being at the *Château* so unbearable was that we were completely stuck when my body was putting everything in place to push ahead.

Sarah says women are locked to the future, that just the existence of periods and the fact of being able to count in time and know that in a certain number of days you'll bleed makes you project into it, and that pregnancy is like that to the power of pregnancy. All you can do is push on. At the *Château* it felt like I was the Trojan Horse for a juggernaut that was being built inside me and would, when it was ready, crash out and drag us all onwards behind it. But there we were, jammed, blocked tight in a place where it felt like the only thing that flowed freely was the constant stream of lies and innuendo from Charles.

My French wasn't good enough at the beginning to know exactly what Charles was saying about me to his henchmen, but the humour was broad enough that I could get the gist. The thing Charles had, his big old ace in the hole, was that he was an amateur radio enthusiast. Obviously in the world of before this was surely something that made him almost unfuckable but now it was glamorous and powerful – all it takes is a total disruption of our way of life and everyone starts thinking a little differently, right?

In the tower that he'd taken as his quarters, one of the rooms was set up as his radio listening post and once he knew I spoke English, German and Spanish I ended up spending a lot of time there. Any free time I had I was supposed to sit in the office and listen with him, or sometimes I'd be sent for because something would come through in one of those languages while I was working with Sarah in the mornings or sleeping at night and I had to rush to his side to simultaneously translate and then respond if he wanted a message sent back. Though more usually I had to rush to his side to be told I hadn't been quick enough and then sit there making call-outs in the hope that whoever it had been would respond.

And then when we walked out of his office there'd be some of the henchmen hanging around and he'd pretend to do up his flies and pat me on the shoulder and say, in simple

English that they could all understand, something like, 'You go and clean yourself up, yes? Don't forget to brush your teeth!' or, 'Very satisfactory, thank you.' And they'd all laugh, and I would say nothing.

Anyway, radio is a weird thing. When you're used to stuff being on a screen and it feeling small and far away, radio feels really close and life-size. Adi had a wind-up radio that he'd got on one of our supply trips before we left the Arches, back when we were filling up our wish lists with amulets. In Fairlight he'd sometimes take it out and tune in to the BBC Emergency Broadcast Service, where a cleaning lady and a really young sound technician were the only people left in the building and they'd just sit and talk to each other about what the weather was like or what they were going to eat next or where they wished they were in a way that felt like they'd entirely forgotten that anyone might be listening. But then, once in a while, one of them would break the sonic fourth wall. If it was the cleaner, she might break off when he was annoying her and she'd speak to everyone, to 'All you listening', she would tell us not to worry, that it was all part of the Lord's plan and that if we'd let Jesus into our hearts we'd be at His side, and soon.

If it was the sound technician, he did more of a show: he'd tap out a jingle on the desk or do the pips coming up to the hour and then say, 'This is the BBC Emergency Broadcast Service and you are not alone.' And then he'd talk directly to people, like, 'Okay, this is for Natasha in Bristol – anyone know a Natasha in Bristol, pass this message on,' and then he'd tell stories about everything, like, really everything, that he and Natasha or whoever had seen or done together and when he ran out of stories they'd go back to bickering about Hula Hoop flavours and whose turn it was to make the tea.

Adi said once he'd turned it on really late at night and he could hear her snoring. They must've had an emergency generator for their building because you could hear that they had an electric kettle. The sound of it was intensely nostalgic.

The guys – because they were always guys – that I heard on Charles's set were completely different. For a start, you have to be a particular sort of person to own both a radio transmitter and an emergency means of creating electricity to run it. It's also different because it's call and response. People say something and they're waiting for a reply. But it was like pulling teeth. Everyone was so fucking cagey. They all, Charles included, seemed convinced that they had their hands on a wealth of vital information and that sharing any of it would result in their downfall, but they were all trying to get information out of whoever they were talking to. Even when it was a call sign that Charles knew and he'd decided he liked the guy, they'd both be super wary that other people would be listening in. The number of times he went on at me about not giving anything away. But he wanted me to reply, and I'd have absolutely nothing to say to them. If I replied with questions – which was what Charles always told me to do, with an intensity that made it seem like he'd been to some kind of pickup-artist training where they'd told him it was the key to all communication – they wouldn't tell me anything anyway. It was all so childish. Even if I'd wanted to pass on information, there fucking wasn't any. I had none. They had none. Nobody knew fuck all about what was happening any farther away than their fingertips apart from the weather. It was like trying to play tennis without any balls. Which obviously meant that Charles could make stuff up, and as my French got better, I realised that's what was happening. Basically he was giving everyone the impression that through fragments of information cunningly gleaned from the air he had a clearer, broader picture than anybody else of what was going on. The reality was that he didn't know jack, but he'd planted armed militia and random violence in the minds of everyone in the *Château*. I was perfect for him because not only could he claim to have learned things in languages that nobody else spoke, but my French was too hopeless to put anyone straight.

At night, when the ionosphere collapsed, things came through in all sorts of languages, sometimes languages I recognised but couldn't speak, like Dutch, Italian, or Portuguese, sometimes mad-sounding shit that could've been Vietnamese or Arabic or Turkish or Finnish. Charles knew the call signs for different countries, and when people's call signs were from far away he was less twitchy about what I was saying, and when we were in the maritime band he cared least of all.

It was clearly different at sea. When a sailor came through, they told you almost immediately who they were, what their boat was, where they were and where they were going, as well as how many people were on board and what the weather was like, and in detail too. It must've been training. Listening to them give their name, position and direction I'd keep my eyes fixed on the notepad in front of me, if I closed them, even to blink, I'd be out there drifting in the emptiness, the floor pitching under my feet.

It scared the shit out of me if I thought about how far Martin would have to sail, a tiny speck on the blue-black. Whenever I could, wherever they were, I'd try to get word to him; 'I am Audaz, this is a message for Martin, captain of *Seabird*, location unknown: I am alive, I will meet you where we planned.'

I'd ask whoever we'd intercepted to pass it on, to tell anyone they spoke to, repeating it in whatever languages I could, the intensity of wanting the message to reach Martin making me feel like I was transmitting it myself, physically bursting it out across the airwaves. And then they'd be gone. It was pretty horrible doing it in front of Charles, worse after what happened with the antibiotics. We both knew that my desire made me vulnerable, and that it was only a matter of time before he would find a way to exploit that vulnerability. But until something bounced back, he had no hold there. That's real radio, messages in bottles, names written in the sand, your voice going out into the nowhere with no idea if it'll find the ear it's destined for.

Getting the boat from Fairlight to Fort Mahon had been bad enough. It took much longer than any of us expected, we were unlucky with winds and tides and, apart from Martin obviously, we were totally incompetent. Too many times we felt it all go wrong, the little sounds of the boat and the water become uneven and staccato, and its movement fall out of rhythm. Adi would rush to the side to hurl and no one except Martin would have the slightest idea what to do about it, so he'd be snapping at us to grab this or shift that and we wouldn't know what this or that he was talking about, and the boat would flop about like a fish on the hook. Once it happened when he'd gone to lie down for a couple of hours because he'd been up all the short night at the wheel. When he came up on deck to see Adi boking while the sail flapped uncontrollably and the rest of us uselessly picked up and dropped various rope-ends, he was so close to rage that he couldn't look at us. And that's before even getting into when we actually reached Fort Mahon and needed to make it to land.

At Fort Mahon, after I'd managed to get the dinghy from the shore to the boat I had to just sit and shake for a while.

Sarah wrapped a blanket around me and helped me to put on all the clothes I had in my bag then wrapped a blanket around me over them. She bandaged my hands with some clean cloth and gave me a cup of hot water and sugar to drink, then had to take it off me, tip half of it out and re-bandage my hands before giving it back to me because my shaking had spilled it all over me.

Meanwhile Pressure Drop, Adi and Martin began loading the dinghy – bikes and boats, never not a rubbish combo. The dinghy butted against the hull of our boat like a calf looking for the teat and we had to keep buoys in place to stop them damaging each other. The drop to lower things down into it was probably a couple of metres. Pressure Drop was in the dinghy trying to settle things into it with the weight evenly distributed, and Martin and Adi were passing stuff down to him.

Martin kept saying, 'One for the boat! One for the boat!' meaning that whatever they were doing Adi should keep hold of the boat with one hand and move stuff with the other. It seemed to be impossible for them to get enough free hands close enough to each other without their bodies getting in the way. Time was short, the tide was coming in and every minute the sea covered more of the beach and our landing place got a few metres farther away.

Obviously they were having a total nightmare of it, snagging ropes and hands and pedals and cursing in unison, but I was suddenly full of goodwill and energy and wanted to help. I was good for nothing – they'd ask me to pass something to them and I'd just not see it, even if I was actually holding it. But despite my hopelessness, or maybe partly because of it, a cloud of euphoria billowed up inside me, blowing the last of the tinnitus out through the top of my head and making everything I was watching a hilarious slapstick performance. Which is part of why I was so unprepared for what happened to be so serious.

Adi lunged for something with both hands at the moment an odd wave hit us, and he slipped and lost his footing as the boats swung apart. The buoys wedged between them fell out of place, Adi fell overboard, and the boats swung back again, slamming together around his chest in a swift, effortless movement. I think it's impossible, but I'm sure I heard the crunch.

I couldn't see his face, but I could see Pressure Drop's. The boats moved apart again, and Pressure Drop reached out and grabbed the shoulder of Adi's jacket before he slipped underwater. Martin was yelling at me to get the buoys back in place, but he was drowned out by the sound of Adi howling in pain as Pressure Drop tried to pull him into the dinghy. It took forever to get him in. The whole time he was moaning and flailing, unable to bring any strength into any bit of himself for leverage or lift. Finally Pressure Drop got him half in and he managed to pull his legs up and push on the side of the boat with his feet to roll crumpled into the dinghy on top of the bags, whimpering. He inched his way towards the front of the boat and got himself into a sitting position. There was no blood. Sarah called down to ask Adi whether he felt like he could breathe, and he nodded feebly and said he thought so. Pressure Drop moved closer to him, rocking the boat as he did so there was more howling from Adi, but after listening for a bit Pressure Drop agreed that Adi was breathing pretty normally. With a great grin of relief Sarah said, 'I think it's probably just ribs then, just broken ribs.'

Pressure Drop whooped and Martin, who'd been looking seasick himself, gave a huge sigh of relief. They finished loading, and the poor little dinghy was sitting so low that it was impossible to get aboard without water slopping in over whichever edge tilted downwards. Whatever spilled in immediately soaked into the rucksacks piled in the bottom so was impossible to bail.

Sarah and I climbed in. We distributed our weight as best we could. Pressure Drop and I were sitting either side, one oar each with the wheels of the bikes layered horizontally over us, locking our legs in place. Sarah was at the back, Adi, hunched over and dripping, was at the front. Everything that wasn't our cramped legs was bags. I finally understood a little better why Julie had been so up in arms about the deal with Martin to take us across.

Back in Fairlight, as the time got closer, she'd been dead against it; she couldn't see why he had to take us, couldn't see why we had to go at all. In a way she was right, things were good in Fairlight, but Sarah and Pressure Drop had their missions, Adi was quartermaster-in-chief, and I still thought I was invincible. I had no fucking clue. Still, I understand better now the kind of rivalry there was between us, because obviously Martin wasn't the father of her baby but he was the head of the household. She must've put a fair amount of energy into fighting down the feeling that I was just some brazen hussy out to steal her safety. But Sarah had cut the deal, and the deal, I discovered later, involved Martin taking us across and then going back to take care of Julie.

I only found out the details when Sarah made it clear to me that she thought I was pregnant. It was when we were leaving Fort Mahon that she brought it up. We spent a few days there, camped in a hollow in the dunes where soft, short grass was studded with golden flowers with silver leaves. Our kit was sodden when we got ashore and it was too heavy and Adi too hopeless to get farther. It was soothing, listening to the sea and the rattling of the scratchy marram grass on the dunes that surrounded us. It was relatively easy there to make soft-ish places where Adi could half-sit half-lie, which was literally all he was capable of doing without help, so it wasn't a bad place to nurse him and wait for my hands to heal enough that I could grip my handlebars. At night, salty driftwood filled the firebox stove with blue and green flames and we spent the days stretching our belongings in the sun and wind, making sure everything that had got soaked on the way over was dried to a crisp and had the salt crystals shaken out of it before we set off. One afternoon, Sarah and I were spreading sleeping bags on the grass, trying to get them to stay, stilt-propped on its strong bendy stalks so that the air would suck every last scrap of moisture out of them, and I was complaining about not sleeping, feeling too hot, fizzed up.

Not sleeping was a new one on me. Though when I consider things now, to think I called that not sleeping? Wow, fuck me. It would not even scratch the surface of the tear-jerking face-punching exhaustion of the early weeks with Leo. The first few days I was so confused by the exhaustion that even daylight seemed like a kind of aggression: the half-light of the fireplace and the doorway of the room, a few slivers of sharp pale light between the slats of the shutters and the soft-blue blob of the face of the Casio on my wrist were all I could handle. I was in the depths, whacked out of my head on nitrogen narcosis and scared I'd blow myself apart with the bends if I came up too quickly. The setting on my watch had been changed to twelve hour and it didn't even matter – night feeds and day feeds bled into each other; both would just loom out of nowhere in the darkness, Leo wailing and a thousand microscopic needles jangling in my nipples.

The others floated in and out of the room now and then, down into my abyss, eyes wide as goggles as they adjusted. They brought their own air supplies – the edges of their clothes smelled bright with the outdoors clinging to them like a halo. Sarah would press my belly and poke my fanny and check that Leo was glugging back mugfuls of me and reassure me that everything was fine. Françoise brought baby food, but for me: soup, condensed-milk porridge and a sort of sweet grainy paste she called *tamina*.

From time to time one of them would take Leo away and change him and I'd feel intensely relieved and miserably lonely at the same time. I just wanted to stay down there in the dark with my undersea monsters, floating between the three simple points of pain: my stinging nipples, my slowly contracting womb and the siren of Leo's crying. As long as I was under there, nothing was real. I knew that if I came back up to the surface that I'd have to reconcile the contradiction: you spend your life being told that impossible things don't happen, but the truth is that all the things that really matter are made entirely out of impossibility.

Slowly though, I was hand-signalled back up towards the surface. Sarah came in at some point, a few days after the birth, and I was sitting up with suddenly enormous milky tits up around my neck like a floatation device. They were drum-tight; when I weighed them in my hands they felt like small melons. She said it was time for a wash. She and Françoise set pans and kettles boiling and gently bullied me out of bed. They poured shining water into the bath in the bathroom – a room I had never even seen used. In the winter air the steam filled the space like whipped cream and slid out through the crack of the open window in dollops. I left Leo with them and got into the water.

My body was like a totally new landscape to me. My tits bobbed out of the water, taut and bulging, the skin pale and shiny as if the milk beneath the surface was glowing through. Past them I could see my belly, fat and floppy, wrinkled like a deflated balloon, deep creases forming and disappearing as I breathed. When touched, it moved in a weird way, the skin slid around on top of me as if the surface wasn't really attached to the flesh underneath it anymore. It gave way in the middle; the skin was loosely draped across a vertical rift in my stomach muscles. They had split apart underneath the skin, as if I'd been unzipped there to get the baby out. It didn't really feel like me, more like something I'd been left inside to take care of.

When I sat up to wash my hair, my tits, confused by the transition from warm water to cold air, started to weep, pearls gathering at the tips of my nipples and plunging into the bathwater where they disappeared. It was pretty weird, like being a leaking tap or something, but it seemed like a waste. I kept washing my hair one-handed with my left hand, but I rinsed the suds off my right hand and carefully slid each drop of milk from nipple to fingertip before it could fall and licked them off as they ran down towards my palm. They tasted of nothing really, just a little sugary. My sugar though.

By the time I was clean, the air had completely cleared and the now-cool water was misty and opaque, thick with the sloughed-off remnants of me: blood and milk, sick and skin, sweat and piss. I pulled the plug, throwing the baby-maker out with the bathwater, wrapped myself in a towel and opened the door a crack. Following Sarah's instructions I'd left my birth-encrusted clothes in a pile outside the door. They were gone, replaced by a new bundle, folded neatly on my slippers.

I could hear the rattle of housework, Sarah and Françoise were talking to each other in busy voices and Jean-Luc and Pressure Drop were in the kitchen chopping and chatting. It was the beginning of the afternoon. All the shutters were open and the low winter sun threw lines of light and shadow across the floor. It all looked very hard and shiny. I slid the bundle of clothes towards me through the door with my foot. I didn't want to make their clean, bright world murky with my edgeless presence. Pulling on the pair of period pants that were on top of the pile, I remembered Sarah taking dozens of pairs from a Primark somewhere like Haywards Heath and my moronic astonishment that she knew such a thing was available there. My trusted old pinstripe trousers from the glory hole were there, clean, as well as a cotton nursing bra, a vest, a flannel shirt, a thick, soft cardigan, a knitted headband and some warm socks. I got dressed, put my slippers on, gave my hair one last rub with the towel and pulled the headband on. I picked my goldfinger necklace up from the edge of the sink where I'd left it, slipped it, heavy and cold, over my head, and tucked it in under my clothes.

I opened the door again. It sounded like everyone was in the kitchen. I was suddenly pulled under by a wave of panic that Leo was cold or hungry or alone and ran, quietly, down the hall to my room. It was empty, hollowed out with light. The shutters were wide open and the freshly mopped floor gleamed. Seeing my shadowy reflection in it I suddenly remembered that at some point in the deep-sea darkness I'd got out of bed for something and what felt like litres of blood had just fallen out of me, splashing onto the floor. Someone had soaked up the worst of it with a towel soon after, but since then everyone must've been stepping over or around or through a huge patch of dried blood every time they came into the room.

The bedsheets had also been changed. The room smelled of woodsmoke and lavender and vinegar. I was turning to leave, the wave of Leo-panic building again, when Françoise walked in.

'Ah, good!' she said, 'Okay, take off the jumper and the shirt and arms up.'

I did what she said, and she took a long, thin roll of fabric from the pocket of her apron. She wound it round my hips and gave me the end to hold under my chin and then she looped and twisted, looped and twisted around and back and around and back all the way up my body to my underneath my tits, hugging it tight around my pelvis and my belly and my ribs.

She patted my shoulders, happy with her work. 'It's not closing the bones, but it'll do. So, now you should eat a proper meal, no?'

I was looking at myself in the mirror, managing to just see past the hollows under my eyes and the crazy inflated tits, the fabric hugging me into something like the shape I used to be. I put the shirt and the cardigan back on, feeling the binding like armour underneath. It made me want to pull the necklace out from under my clothes and have it shining as a celebration that maybe I was still in there after all.

Then Leo started crying in the kitchen and straight away I felt both my tits well up at the thought of him, and milk soaked through my top.

'Come on,' said Françoise, 'I think everybody is hungry.'

And she was right, and Leo has stayed that way, and so I get drunk. Not that way, as in he drinks me. It is like having a pet vampire sucking the life out of you all night.

The whole idea of succubi is pretty unfair – like, who fucking invented these magical women who go around secretly sucking the life out of people in the night when as a general rule, throughout human and in fact mammal history, it's been females having the life sucked out of them in the night? And it happens again and again and again. And just when you think you've found some kind of pattern or rhythm and are able to imagine that the night, though shattered, will at least be shattered in such and such a way, that this shattering can be planned for, *vlam*, the vampire turns into a bat or a puff of smoke or whatever and you're screwed all over again. It seems that looking after a baby is fine as long as you do not try to do anything else, like pee, or eat something while it's still hot, or sleep, at the same time.

Anyway, what I called not sleeping the way I experienced it at Fort Mahon, when the signs were trying to make themselves understood, I put down to getting used to nature being noisy, the constant babble of wind and waves and birds and insects and grass all constantly shuffling and huddling around.

'Maybe you're due your period?' Sarah said.

I said yeah, I was, had been for a while but that didn't normally stop me sleeping.

Sarah nodded, and then, when she could see I wasn't going any closer in my head, stood up straight and stopped trying to straighten the sleeping bag so it would stay on the smooth, wobbly grass hummock and picked it up instead. She shook it, flicking sand in my face, then, while I was blinking, gently floated it up over the hummock, where it landed and stayed, rustling wildly as it settled into place.

'In fact,' she said, very precisely, 'how long exactly have you been waiting for your period?'

It's not that I believe that everything is predestined, I just don't see what difference it makes if it is or not. Sarah's question was like zooming out, falling upwards away from the

Earth, seeing the sperm meet the egg, his cock push inside me, us meeting Martin on the road in the mist, the route of the bikes from London to Fairlight, Pressure Drop's stubbornness, Sarah's dream, Adi's bike skills, Julie's hope, their father's love of the sea, my mother's skill with the single-celled, my grandfather working at the dairy and making the payments on a house in Streatham, and onwards and onwards forever, like falling upwards away from the surface of the Earth with the sense that it would go on and on, becoming more and more intricate and more and more tiny, and maybe if you got high enough you could see everything turning on its axis and rolling round to meet you. Obviously Pressure Drop would say that if you got high enough of course you could see everything. But you'd have to get really fucking high.

We'd talked about having children, me and Martin, but not really talked, joked maybe, or not quite joking but storytelling, when we were looking for his boat. He'd sailed all kinds, delivering them across the Mediterranean and around the UK and he knew what kind he wanted. I had no idea they even made boats out of steel, I mean, ferries, yeah, but I never imagined a sailboat could be made out of something so un-floaty. Anyway, that's what he wanted, so after Julie's baby was born, we went on an expedition, me and Martin, down the coast. I never got beyond calling Julie's baby 'the baby', although Julie named her Detta straight away. Sarah was the one coaching Julie through the early days, but we all shifted our behaviour to make space for Detta one way or another, being quiet when she was sleeping and trying to keep the doors closed to keep the place warmer.

So Martin and I abandoned the new household with its new centre and headed off on the bikes. Like a sort of secret honeymoon, but better because of having a plan: find and steal the perfect sailboat. In Pevensey Bay we'd climbed up and around the spikes of the barriers, almost falling sideways into the sea from getting caught in a fit of laughter when the back of my jacket snagged on one of the spikes and I hung for a moment, cartoonishly, before a perfect sound-effect ripping noise sent me thudding onto the concrete.

We were going up and down the jetties with Martin trying to get me to understand what to look for – I didn't even fully understand the names of the bits of boats he was on about, let alone know how to pick out the distinguishing features he was on about – when I saw a movement out of the corner of my eye, a curtain twitch or something. I grabbed Martin's hand and dragged him down crouching. Encountering strangers was complicated, my expectations were half we-come-in-peace sci-fi and half Hollywood gunfight.

Obviously there were neither aliens nor cowboys, instead a scratchy little voice came creaking across the water to us, 'What exactly are you two up to then?'

An old lady was living on one of the boats, on her boat, her and her husband's, but he had died. She reckoned it was safer and it was more set-up for getting on with things. There was fuel, food and water supplies, a little cooker, all that stuff. She wanted a chat. Oh my god, but she wanted a chat. She wanted to tell us all about all the places she and her husband had ever sailed to which was, like, everywhere in the world. At another time that would have been a really interesting chat to have, but I was too excited by the idea of being off on an adventure with Martin to want to share his attention with anybody else. He wanted to listen though, asked questions even, and because I was jealous of him listening to her, when she asked again what we were up to I butted in and said that we were looking for a boat to sail to Santiago de Cuba, but that it'd have to be big enough because we were planning on having half a dozen babies on the way. Martin looked at me like I was a total idiot, but he looked at me and that was all I cared about.

Although I really wish he was here with me, I'm also relieved he's not. I am a fucking wreck. Before I even got around to trying to deal with Leo, the mountains utterly did for me. We were in such a bad state when we arrived, gaunt and strained, our lips chapped and our eyes sunken. Sarah's joints clicked so much that she sounded like a bag of clothes pegs, and Pressure Drop had a cough that shook his whole body when he lay down at night. We would've made poor eating.

After we'd come through the fruitful lands, and before the wolf-school, at one point we came through a small village. Pressure Drop had just got a puncture and we walked in towards the main square to have somewhere sunny and comfortable to mend it. We'd pretty much decided the place was completely empty, and Sarah and I went off to see if there was any food worth scavenging in the houses around the square. We didn't find much, but we didn't have much time, because when we came out of one we saw that Pressure Drop was talking (I say talking, it was mostly gesticulating) with a man and a woman by the bikes. We went over and Sarah took up the communication. Even after the *Château* my French was still not great, and their accent seemed pretty full-on. They were a funny-looking pair, him all sinewy and tortoise-necked and her pink-faced with a sweaty sheen. The man swallowed like a lizard and the woman rubbed her pudgy fingers against her thumbs as he spoke. It seemed they were inviting us to stay, but whatever she was getting from them, Sarah was uncertain. Pressure Drop got the puncture fixed, packed the kit away, and a minute or two later

Sarah shook her head and thanked them and said we would carry on.

They stood in the square and watched us go. Something was off. Sarah said she couldn't put her finger on what she didn't like, but she didn't like it. Weirdos are weirdos – we were ready to leave it at that. On the way out of the village we passed a small graveyard. It was full of skeletons. That was not unusual, we'd seen a few places where it was clear that, for want of a better alternative, bodies had simply been laid out in lines somewhere, and in the time that had passed they'd become skeletons. The one good thing about the months at the *Château* was that while we were stuck there we'd missed travelling through the goriest, most maggot-ridden stink of the summer months. But the remains in this cemetery were not all laid-out skeletons with their now-oversized clothes flapping around them, there was also a heap of bones in one corner, disjointed and partly discoloured. We did not stop, but I felt sure that had we examined them we'd have found what I think archaeologists would have called butchering marks.

We didn't talk about it then, we rode. Who knows, maybe they were animal bones, or maybe they were human bones collected from the village and brought to rest on sacred ground, or some other anodyne explanation, but none of us wanted to try to give it to each other. That night we camped without a fire and shared the couple of tins of peeled tomatoes we'd found.

At one point I said, 'That graveyard...'

Sarah shook her head and said, 'The rising tide of consciousness does not lift all boats, but it does expose those who don't float as wrecks, and they end up lost in the deep.' We didn't talk about it again until we were telling Jean-Luc and Françoise about our journey.

If only we'd had some wariness when we arrived at the *Château*. When we were brought to meet Charles he was clearly a weirdo too, with his shaved head that no more hid his early onset male pattern baldness than his t-shirt did his discreet paunch. At the beginning he agreed that we could have a room together. This was, he made clear, a special favour he was doing for us because normally the women slept in rooms along the 'ladies corridor' — because it was easier to protect them like that. Obviously. But with the twenty-five or so people that we were, there still were whole floors of rooms that hadn't yet been touched. The doors all had those electronic keycards so they had to be smashed open. This led to the advantage, for Charles, that they could never be properly closed again, never mind locked.

Charles and one of the bigger henchmen, sledgehammer and wedge in hand, led us up the main staircase and smashed a door in, giving us two interconnected rooms, one with a double and the other with two singles. Charles made grinning comments about who was going to sleep where and tried to work out if there was some sexual relationship between any of the four of us, finishing with a laugh and a 'but that is not my business, eh?' — which obviously meant that he would absolutely make it his business to find out — while the henchman stood there, fidgeting with his potential weapon of lethal force and looking from Charles to us like a dog watching his owner at the fridge. Even so, it was really hard not to just jump up and down on the beds and throw the way-too-numerous pillows around the room.

The hotel had been all tricked out in muted satin, classy grey and navy blue, big heavy curtains and discreet luggage racks. The way it was all so neat and perfect made it feel like everything would work, like you could walk into the gleaming bathroom and turn a tap on and warm water would pour out of the over-large shower head, like you could lift the remote up off the fingerprint-less table and flick through the channels, like you could piss in the toilet. Seeing something that threw your mind back so immediately to how things were before gave me some idea what it was like to be Adi – I think everything was like that for him.

Pressure Drop went and had a look out the window.

'Third floor,' said Charles, 'Safe. Nobody can get up.'

Meaning, obviously, nobody can get down. We glanced at each other and nodded to Charles, like as if, yes, nice room, we'll take it. Everyone carefully preserving the illusion that we had any kind of choice in the matter.

At that point we were still thinking that we would leave in the early morning, so we followed Hammer and Charles back along the corridor and down the main staircase. The thick carpet felt weirdly spongy underfoot and it was just bizarre how much 'indoors' there was. When we reached the lobby Pressure Drop broke out the weed, partly because smoking his way out of a problem was clearly a favourite tactic of his, but also as a distraction. He played up his crazy Rasta act to the point that one of the henchmen pulled enough English together to ask him whether it was his father or mother who was black.

Pressure Drop in no way looks black. He looks very much like what he is – a lanky Irishman with dreads. In reply he launched into an oration about Rastafarianism, Saint Patrick being a slave, Bob Marley being Irish, the brotherhood of the oppressed and about people being transported from Ireland to the Caribbean.

'All those poor fuckers, dragged from their homeland, stripped of their faith, orphaned by the loss of their mother tongue. Cromwell sent thousands to the Caribbean, and when they started dying of heatstroke, their cheap pale skin blistered like fucking pork crackling under a sun it was never designed to withstand, he sent children, thinking they'd just get used to it. Took them from the streets, from workhouses, threw them onto boats and shipped them halfway across the world to a land of tropical plenty, full of fruit they didn't know they could eat and insects they didn't know could kill them. Imagine being twelve and being taken from some fucking barren fucking hillside in Connacht where your family has been scraping out a living since the dawn of fucking agriculture, turning the grey stones out of the soil under a grey sky with the grey sea shifting in the distance, and they take you from there, on the coffin ships, to a land of translucent lagoons and coral sands where you can walk barefoot with warm dry feet for maybe the first time in your fucking life, surrounded by palm trees and hibiscus flowers and hummingbirds. And yet this paradise has been rotted through its core by Babylon's never-ending hunger for the toil of human flesh ...'

And while he was doing his thing, he was building one of his scaffolding-requiring joints. Charles and the guys were watching, maybe understanding some but more sucked in by the general tone than anything else, and you could almost see Charles trying to do the calculations; if Pressure Drop put that much weed into one joint, and he had that much in his pocket, how big a bag of weed did he have in the rucksack that we had supposedly hidden in the bushes somewhere down the road?

Pressure Drop, switching back to his thick farmer's accent, said to me, 'Fucking go and find the best fucking way out of here while I have them occupied.'

Some of the women had wandered into the lobby and I could see Sarah looking them over while I asked Charles where they used as a toilet. He said anywhere outdoors. So Adi settled himself beside Pressure Drop, the joint got lit and passed and Sarah and I walked away from the speechifying and I never found out who the Irishmen in the Rastafari hall of fame were.

We looked around the outside of the *Château*. Because you've seen films where people are able to do stuff like climb down drainpipes and shit like that you imagine you'd be capable of those things, but when you look at the actual physical world with the eyes of the actual physical person who'd be actually physically climbing down the drainpipe you realise that's bollocks – what you're actually physically looking for is a fire escape. There was one. And when we found it, that's when Sarah said we couldn't leave because one of the women was pregnant.

And so that night, after an evening of negotiating between ourselves under our breath while pretending that we were being hosted rather than just getting stuck, we went back up to our room, taking a detour on the way to wedge open the door to the fire-escape stairs. We agreed we'd stay for a bit, a couple of weeks, time for Sarah to teach some basics and Adi to sleep in a bed while his ribs recovered. I would go and get a small rucksack each from where the bikes were and then hide them in some bushes on the road near the *Château* – then we could let Charles and the henchmen escort us out to find them, and no further questions would be asked. We spent an hour or so waiting and quietly listing what we thought I should bring or leave, and then, when it all seemed mostly quiet, I headed out.

Walking without making a sound is much harder when everything is silent around you, even on thick carpet. Concrete stairs are surprisingly resonant in the empty night, and gravel is a total fucking nightmare. There was half a moon in behind clouds, and by its light I followed the ruts left by the wheels of the quad bikes across the drive and headed onto the lawn. The moon came out from behind a cloud when I was standing in the middle of it and I was so scared of being seen that I froze and actually felt my bladder clench in a way that nearly made me piss myself.

And yet, what the fuck was I so scared of? Like, they had a couple of guns but I am pretty sure that they would have been really unlikely to shoot me. So basically I was scared of rupturing the surface of social pretence, of arseholes thinking I was rude, which, seriously, who gives a fuck? I made my legs work again despite the moonlight, and got to the edge of the shrubbery. I couldn't really go into the shrubbery because there were too many twigs to snap and snag on, so I just pulled my hood up and sort of hunched to the height of the bushes. When I came round to the front of the *Château* I could see the little dancing orange glow of the burning tip of the guard's cigarette, hovering as he drew in on it and then twirling around his head and hands. I thought maybe its light would make it harder for him to see me and kept moving.

There were trees behind me by then and I straightened up, moving in little bursts, a few steps at a time. Whenever I saw the moon edging out from behind a cloud I'd hunch down or tuck in near the trunk of a tree and try to breathe quietly until another cloud moved in. The guard finished his cigarette, which meant there was no longer any way of knowing where he was, and I discovered that the last stretch to cover was bare gravel at the base of the high blank wall beside the gateway. I started crawling, and when the moon came out I flattened myself on my belly, imagining myself as a shadow or a puddle.

I didn't dare look around. When we played *las escondidas* when I was a kid, we were all convinced that your eyes had a supernatural power to draw another person's eyes to you. When you were the seeker and you spotted somebody you shouted their name followed by, '*El blanco te traiciona!*' meaning the whites of their eyes had given them away; their gaze had drawn yours to them. I was too scared to even look up to try to see when the next cloud was coming, but finally it did. I skittered round the gatepost on my hands and knees, scrunching in the gravel but fast enough that by the time the guard had got his torch on and swung it to where I'd been there was nothing there and he could tell himself that it had just been an animal.

I crouched on the other side of the wall, too scared to shift my weight to stand in case it made a sound, and tried to steady my breathing, and then as soon as the guard switched his torch off I was padding down the road as quickly as I could go without making any noise. I was so whoopingly excited to have got out and so full of adrenaline that I don't remember much else about getting to the bikes except a blur of moonlight and hedgerows, or really anything about trying to sort a certain amount of stuff into rucksacks either.

I cannot emphasise enough the extent to which I was totally shitting myself the entire time. Telling it like this makes it sound like I somewhat knew what I was doing, which I did not. Me even existing to tell this story might make it seem like I'm somebody hyper-competent and exceptional, or that this was my destiny or something. People always talk about history being written by the victors, but actually who gives a fuck who's writing the past, it's the future that's written by the victors. And victorious right now boils down to one simple thing: being alive. And I am still alive, so right now the future belongs to me. But the fact that I'm alive is just a heady blend of chance and design, and nobody will ever know how much of each there was in the mix, or even really whether there is any difference between the two. Design is born of consciousness and consciousness is just down to chance – just another weird quirk of the evolutionary process, like toxic spit or iridescent tail feathers or the ability to metabolise the outpourings of deep-sea hydrothermal vents. The fact that human consciousness turned out to be one of the most destructive forces on the planet is just chance too. And so is what or who gets destroyed by it.

I'm pretty sure the henchmen spiked his beer the night Adi got destroyed – like, just with alcohol, he wasn't used enough to drinking to have noticed, it wouldn't have taken anything more. Sarah and I thought he was out with Pressure Drop who was smoking on the front steps, and Pressure Drop thought he was with us up in the room. We never found out what they were 'just playing' with him – Adi couldn't remember and they wouldn't tell us – but Pressure Drop caught them on their way back in. Two of them had his arms around their shoulders, but there was no pretence that he was walking between them. Pressure Drop shamed them into bringing him up to our rooms. The tips of his trainers dragging behind him left a trail in the thick carpet of the corridor. His head was slumped forwards and there was vomit all down his front. They made out like he just couldn't hold his drink and went off laughing and shoulder-barging each other.

We gave him some water. He threw it straight back up. Luckily we managed to aim him at the bathroom, and water vomit is one of the less gross to clean up. I wiped most of it into a corner while he lay on the floor dry heaving. We decided not to put him in a bed and poked a couple of bath mats in underneath him so he wouldn't be lying on bare tiles. We got him to drink a few last sips of water and then left him in the recovery position with the door open so that we could keep an ear out for moaning and retching.

It wasn't until the next morning when he woke up whimpering about the pain that we discovered the state of his foot. Basically, something jagged and dirty had ripped through the side of his trainer and stabbed him at an angle up through the arch. Sarah was devastated that none of us had noticed the night before – it had bled quite a lot in the night, but the blood had mostly just seeped into his sock and filled up his shoe.

Sarah sent me and Pressure Drop off to get a pan of hot water and some salt and a couple of clean pillowcases. By the time we'd negotiated those items she'd got Adi cleaned up a bit and he was sitting on the lid of the toilet with his injured foot propped up on the edge of the bath, looking so sorry for himself, poor fucker, and either swearing off alcohol or apologising for the state he was in every thirty seconds. The wound in his foot oozed and the skin all around it was red and puffy. Sarah had him soak it in salty water as hot as he could bear, and when he took it out it looked a bit better, but maybe it's just that the heat made the rest of his foot puffy and red too so there was less difference. She bandaged him up while we tried to get out of him what had actually happened the night before, but he had no real idea.

Pressure Drop stayed with him while I went with Sarah to give her class and when we got back she opened up the bandage for another look. The wound had gone back to being just as puffy and oozy as before, and a red line had started snaking away from it, to his ankle, up the inside of his leg and towards the crook of his knee, as if something was burrowing slowly into his body.

Sarah said, 'I'll go and get the hot water this time,' and she and Pressure Drop went off, leaving me with Adi. He was still feeling dreadful, mentally as much as physically. He felt awful about the fact that his ribs were part of what had led us to stay and now his foot was going to keep us there even longer. I tried to get him to see that Sarah would have wanted to stay anyway, Leïla being pregnant and all, and that whatever had happened the night before wasn't his fault, that it wasn't because he'd been drunk but because arseholes had acted like arseholes, but I had limited success.

When the others came back we soaked his foot again, and then he fell asleep. He slept fitfully and whenever he woke he didn't seem fully awake. He was confused about where he was and got mixed up between his ribs and his foot being hurt. His forehead got warmer, his breathing got shallow and he started to have bouts of shivering. While he was asleep, Sarah told me that he needed antibiotics, and we needed help to find some, because we had no real idea where we were.

She left us with a damp cloth to hold on his forehead and went back down to speak to Charles again. By the time she got back, the red line had reached his groin and the skin of his leg was mottled, like when you hold a hot water bottle too close for too long. Sarah said that Charles had made a big deal about how hard it was to find antibiotics these days, that it was a highly difficult and dangerous mission – 'You will need to thank me in advance for this,' he'd said. Sarah explained that Pressure Drop had already offered to plant some weed in the grounds of the *Château*, but Charles wanted something more immediate, more obvious, and, much more importantly, he wanted everyone to know that he'd got what he wanted. Pressure Drop wouldn't look at me, but Sarah did. I agreed – what else was I going to do?

Sarah and I went together to talk to Charles. Medicalising it and getting her to do the bargaining in French made it a bit more transactional, which felt easier. She made it official that in my condition sex was out of the question, because of the risk of birth defects from STIs, and that you could still catch syphilis or gonorrhoea from a blowie, so that was off the menu too, but that I would jerk him off if they'd then go and find some antibiotics. Sarah stood outside the door to wait for me.

I went into it feeling ready, I'd been through it in my head and rationalised it: up-down hand movements equals Adi's foot gets better. I guess the contract should've been more detailed, because what I wasn't ready for was all the stuff that went along with the up-down hand movements. As soon as he got me in the door I was backed up against the wall and he was all over me, breathing on me, slobbering on my neck, his hands up my t-shirt trying to get it off, grabbing at my crotch through my pants, and talking all the while, telling me that he knew it was what I wanted, and that I should let myself enjoy it. What got me through it was that by chance – or by unconscious anticipation? – I had my tightest sports bra on and it was like armour, there was no way for him to get into it without serious help on my part, or a scissors.

I tried to un-feel him as much as possible and thought of milking the cows at the farm on the way to Fairlight. At the end he pulled me towards him in a way that left me with spunk all down my front and then sent me back out into the hallway with a wad of tissue paper to clean myself up in full view of the sniggering henchmen, waving his hand to indicate his mess and saying, 'Sorry about this, next time we will do it in the mouth, it will be cleaner, okay?'

Sarah looked from the sniggering henchmen to Charles, and asked when they were leaving, and he shrugged, saying it was late and would soon be dark and that they'd go in the morning. They all nodded in the most dismissive way possible, as if she had a bee in her bonnet about something trivial, and then it wasn't until the next afternoon that a couple of them headed off half-heartedly to ostensibly search for medicines.

By then Adi's whole body was covered in ragged bruises like dark clouds. No amount of soaking his foot in hot water had prevented the wound from becoming claggy and foul-smelling and it was surrounded by little pus-filled blisters. Sometimes he seemed to wake, but when he had his eyes open he wasn't really there. He was confused about what kind of reality he was in. At least some of the time he thought he had got shot in a computer game that had become real, and a good part of the rest he was worrying about letting his mum know that he was going to be from uni.

When it was me, I just went along with it and tried to reassure him on those terms – that I'd called his mum, that the gunshot wound wasn't serious, that the paramedics were coming, whatever. By the end of the day his whole leg was dark purple and massively swollen and the toenails were black. His babbling had stopped, given over to shuddering, shallow breathing and little childlike noises of pain.

We took turns in the night, overlapping, stints of a couple of hours, two sitting with him while one rested. He was mostly asleep or unconscious. You could smell the seepage from the wound even with it bandaged. Sarah was kept awake by her quiet furiousness, barely managing to keep her rage from propelling her into pacing the room. Pressure Drop came in to relieve me, settling himself down, humming and singing to himself, low under his breath. I stumbled to my bed and was asleep in seconds.

Sarah came and woke me sometime before dawn, her eyes red and runny.

We sat around his body together until the sun came up, until life stirred down below, not talking really, except that at one point Sarah said, 'How Adi died, that's how women die when whoever is delivering their baby hasn't washed their hands properly.'

I nodded, absorbing it, a bit taken aback that she wanted to use Adi's death as a teachable moment. Pressure Drop realised that wasn't what she was doing though. He buried his face in his hands and let out a long sigh.

Sarah looked at him, his long fingers with their knobbly knuckles completely hiding his expression, and then back to me.

'That's what could happen to Leïla,' she said.

I nodded again.

Pressure Drop let out a long, low groan. 'So,' he said, 'We're here for the duration, that's what you're saying.'

'If you'll both agree to it,' she said.

Pressure Drop slid his fingers up between his dreads.

'How long?' he asked.

'Late September,' she said, 'or early October.'

Finally understanding I said, 'Right up to the birth?'

Sarah nodded and said again, 'If you both agree.'

It felt like she was trying to give us a choice where there really wasn't one.

We dug the grave on a hill in a field beside the *Château*. It took us fucking forever and it wasn't even that deep. They never show how long it takes to dig one in films. Charles and the henchmen kept trying to get involved – they just liked the idea of the challenge of making a big hole, wanted to go off to a nearby farm and come back with a mini digger or something. We wouldn't let them help. We carried Adi there on the top of a folding table, still wrapped in the sheet, our arms and backs aching from the digging, and half-lifted half-slid him in, clumsily trying to manoeuvre his body in a way that felt solemn.

Sarah asked Pressure Drop if he would say something, saying that she couldn't, and so, lifting his eyes to the heavens while Sarah bowed her head, he began: 'Why is it the wicked live, become old, are mighty in power? Their seed is established in their sight, and their offspring before their eyes. Their houses are safe from fear, His rod never punishes them. Their bull breeds, their cow calves, they send forth their little ones like a flock and their children dance. They take tambourines and harps and flutes and celebrate. They are rich until the day they go to the grave. But I say, let the candle of the wicked be put out. Let their destruction come. Let them be as stubble in the wind, as chaff that the storm carries away. He stores up iniquity for them – they will get their just rewards and they will know it. Their eyes will see destruction and they will drink the wrath of the Almighty when their number is up. Some die in full strength, at peace with everything, their pails full of milk and their bones full of marrow. Some die in the bitterness of the soul, having known nothing but pain. They all lie down alike in the dust, and a blanket of worms will cover them.'

When he'd finished, Pressure Drop stepped back and Sarah put Adi's mobile, with all the photos that he'd taken so carefully to show how hard he'd tried to make it work in it, on his chest. I put his rucksack at his feet, and we started to bury him. As the soil covered the last patches of its brightly coloured canvas,

I started sobbing that he'd never loop his arms into its straps again. All the efforts he'd made to pack everything we'd need for the journey, from the hours I'd spent as his runner-slash-minder prowling the boxes of the glory hole, to Decathlon, to Watches of Switzerland, to going overboard and smashing up his ribs at Fort Mahon so as not to lose a thing, to the night we arrived at the *Château* when he'd revised and re-revised and re-re-revised his list of essentials before I went and fetched the rucksacks from the bikes, all that had brought him no farther than a fucking shallow grave.

The night when we'd arrived at the *Château*, when I was carrying his rucksack along with all the rest of ours, I remember how the tiredness suddenly came down on me. The bags felt heavier and heavier. We'd agreed that I'd bring the rucksacks off up the road past the *Château* in the opposite direction to the hangar before I hid them, and when I'd finally passed the gates and hidden them in the gateway of a field, I could just feel the energy draining out of me, head down to feet. I had to really force myself to keep going back towards the *Château*. Which I think was my body manifesting its disbelief and disappointment that I was making all these efforts not so that we could leave but so that we could stay. I got back in the same way I'd got out, crawling, crouching, edging, creeping, and then back to the room. The other three hadn't really slept while I'd been gone, and while they were glad I was back safe, you could also see that Pressure Drop was gutted that it was all settled and that we'd definitely be there for the foreseeable.

So when it came to the moment, months later, when we were finally actually leaving, and the henchmen were all riled up that we were taking the contents of my belly with us, I mean, obviously we were scared and we were angry, and we were sad, but what really propelled us through the moment was that it felt inevitable, we just knew we had to leave.

It was half pantomime, half prison-break. We came storming down the stairs, everyone shouting at everyone but none of the henchmen quite ready to escalate it into actually manhandling us. When we got out the front door Pressure Drop started declaiming, his arms spread wide and the incomprehensible words full of guttural phonemes rolling out of his mouth like boulders crunching down a scree-covered hillside. The henchmen weren't sure whether they were supposed to knock him out, fall under his spell or shrug their shoulders and make a small farting noise with their lips.

They came at us, but got sucked in, and when he finished hexing them with the rules for how to behave at a Dublin railway station, Sarah lifted up her skirt and went, as Pressure Drop put it, the full Sheela-na-gig on them. They stopped dead for long enough for Pressure Drop to throw the still-lit butt of his joint into the dried-out oily weeds that filled the flowerbed where the quad bikes and jerrycans of petrol were. We ran, leaving them stamping and cursing as the little flames spilt like water across the ground.

We couldn't run as far as where the bikes were hidden – it was a fifteen-minute walk so that would've been beyond us at the best of times, and the months at the *Château* had left us soft. We did what Sarah called a 'scout's walk', running for a hundred steps then walking for fifty, glancing over our shoulders for either a column of smoke or a quad bike. Neither appeared. By the time we got to the hangar I probably wouldn't have been able to hear the quad bikes arriving over my hard breathing and the pounding of blood in my ears.

The hangar was still there, and the bikes were still there, but they weren't ready to roll. The tyres had deflated, the panniers were a mess after my scramble to pack rucksacks the last time I'd been there, and mice had rampaged through everything. They had completely destroyed the kilos of rice, oats and lentils that had been in plastic packets, they'd burrowed into the sleeping bags and they'd finely shredded our road atlas, using the strips to build a delicate, spherical nest. It was like a message to us about the futility of thinking we had some kind of control or understanding of the journey we were on. We breathlessly repacked the panniers, throwing handfuls of mouse-shit mixed with food onto the floor.

A few months later, in the mountains, we carefully sifted through similarly destroyed packets of pasta, tipping droppings out of individual penne and putting our faith in the boiling water they'd be cooked in to disinfect them.

The houses in the mountains may have been empty, cold and mouse-ravaged, but they were kind. They had walls stacked with firewood and the larders of people who drove hours to get to the nearest supermarket and had no intention of doing it every week. And, more often than not, the doors were unlocked – really, it was like somebody had broadcast a message that was only audible above a certain altitude telling people to leave them that way. It was so fucking humane, it made me want to cry.

Breaking and entering always seemed wasteful, even if it was sometimes exciting. I don't count shops, I think technically that would be looting anyway. Getting into the boat with Martin was the first real breaking and entering I did. My stunt of saying to the old woman that we were going to sail to Cuba was not entirely successful because, while Martin did look at me, he was soon looking at her again. She went down into the cabin of the boat and came back with, I kid you not, a tray holding a bottle of sherry, three small crystal glasses and a tin of fruitcake.

'Come aboard, a plan like that needs celebrating,' she said, pulling a folding chair open for herself.

So we stepped onto the deck and leaned against the cabin and, sipping sherry and nibbling fruitcake, Martin explained to her what he wanted. She clearly approved. They had a detailed conversation about lengths of boats and sizes of waves that I quickly lost track of, but the old lady had all the kind of knowledge that Martin wanted, and she seemed to think she knew every boat worth knowing about on that bit of coast; 'We don't know the racers or the Sunday sailors much, but the tourers, we know them, and that's what you're after.' She talked about herself in the first person plural, linguistically unable to process the fact that her husband wasn't with her anymore – she'd even seem to look for his agreement on things, finishing her sentences with an almost imperceptible pause, a beat in which she was maybe silently providing his affirmations to herself.

She said there was nothing there for us – mostly all plastic with a few, like hers, in wood. She tried to push Martin towards wood, saying that you could always fix wood with wood, but when she saw he wasn't moving she said she reckoned he'd find what he was looking for in Brighton Marina.

She described the exact boat, *Seabird*, even knew the guy who owned it – not well, but well enough to say, 'If he's not living on that boat right now, well then he's not going to need it where he's gone.'

She reckoned it was late to be heading for the marina – best to set off in the morning.

'Besides,' she said, 'this is the best hotel you'll find anywhere on the south coast – all these boats, they've got beds, water, most of them have a cooker and dinner and breakfast tucked away too. And the receptionist likes you. Come on, I'll show you to our best room.'

She leaned behind the door leading down into her boat and dragged out a crowbar, then we stepped back out onto the jetty with her and followed her lead.

'We never liked the fellow who had this boat, nor the boat, did we, but as a room for the night it's probably as good as it gets.'

As we made our way along the jetty, I could see that Martin was not impressed with the boat. It was a motor yacht for a start, and even I could see it was ugly.

'A right Sunday sailor, not even in fact, more of a Saturday-night sailor if you see what I mean, and not always with his missis either!' She handed the crowbar to Martin. 'Go on then – he's not going to be back.'

I kept looking around as he did it, worried that somebody would appear and start shouting at us, but of course nobody did. It was incredibly loud, the crack of the plastic, the screech of metal twisting against metal. I've since discovered that in this world there is almost never anybody watching, and if there is, they, like spiders, are probably more scared of you than you are of them, but I hadn't discovered it then, so I was all eyes and on edge by the time Martin managed to force the lock.

When the door finally sprang open I could see exactly what being a Saturday-night sailor was all about. There was a little kitchen with a very well-stocked bar on the right and a banquette along the left, padded in red vinyl. Through a door into the front bit I could see a big bed with satiny sheets in the same colour red, and an implausibly large and weirdly wide and flat chandelier hung from the ceiling.

Martin burst out laughing and the old lady was delighted at his amusement.

'Well we'll leave you to it then,' she said, 'I'm sure you can figure it out.' And she was off to make her tea.

So we went in there, giddy with adrenaline and I was totally hyped with the idea that we were going to spend the whole night together, and not even in a ditch or a bus shelter or something but in an actual bed underneath a massive, weird, ugly chandelier. I wanted to get naked and fuck straight away but Martin insisted we go and borrow the keys to the gate off the old lady and bring the bikes onto the jetty for the night, so I slightly sulkily went along with that, inching away when he started to get into another long conversation with her, this time about navigation, imperceptibly shuffling my feet towards our boat willing the invisible cord between us to twang him after me, which it eventually did.

I managed to infect him with some of my giddiness while we went through the cupboards to find dinner. Better than dinner, we found board games and crisps. Packets and packets of crisps, all kinds of flavours: sweet chilli, Skips, salt and vinegar, Worcester sauce, pickled onion Monster Munch and more. So instead of starting to cook anything, I went through the games while Martin set himself up at the bar with a tea towel, a bottle of tequila, another of tonic, and a couple of solid little glasses, and then we ate crisps and drank tequila slammers and played strip Connect Four.

By the time the sun was going down – it was near the end of May and the evenings were long – I was completely hammered. Having got Martin down to his t-shirt and jeans relatively effectively I was on a losing streak and only had my pants and socks left. I was full of booze and bubbles, talking trash about how I was going to make a big comeback, but pacing myself has never particularly been a talent of mine, and so when Martin went out to piss off the side of the boat I passed out. So that was our great night of Saturday-night-sailing together.

I woke up the next morning, alone in the bed and lying in a position that made it look like I'd fallen from a great height. It was daylight, but only just – fishing hour. I was woozy and dry-throated, but mostly the tequila had paint-stripped all the serotonin off my synapses. I was dying with hungover embarrassment that I'd pissed what I was – correctly – certain would be our only night together up against the walls of a sleazy cabin.

It smelled of food, baked beans, and something frying. Martin was in the kitchen making breakfast. I was going to have to go in there, and I knew he was going to laugh at me and I was pretty scared I was either going to dissolve in tears or explode in anger if he did.

The thing is, I actually used to really love the feeling of a truly terrible hangover, the kind of hangover where you crawl out of bed at about four in the afternoon, slightly hysterically amused by your own incompetence as a human being, and in order to carry out the most basic steps of moving forwards into the day you need to do a sort of running commentary in your head, like you've become your own private sports commentator: 'Ah yes, I can see she has managed to put her other foot in the other leg of her trousers, well I must say this is truly extraordinary work here.'

My internal sports commentator always leaned a bit towards the camp crickety end of things, a regression to voices

I absorbed intermittently at odd hours of the day on my dad's long-wave radio when I was still little, but maybe also because they always seemed to commentate on nothing much actually happening.

'Well, this is really quite remarkable, I do believe she is going to attempt to pull them up – but will she lie back on the bed to do it and lift her arse in the air? Or will she, no, wait, this is incredible, she's going to stand up! This is it, fully vertical! Amazing, we haven't seen anything like this since three or four weekends ago!' And so on.

The best time for this sort of hangover is November, because by the time you make it out of the house it is already getting dark again, and there's comfort in the darkness, because the darkness of the night before was kind to you, picked you up, twirled you round, showed you lights and laughter. It is the morning that hurts. And so you manage to get dressed and leave the house with, clamped firmly between the teeth of your mind, a linked series of small achievable task such as: 'Buy eggs. Buy bread. Come home. Make fried-egg sandwich. Eat fried-egg sandwich.' And once you're out in this new beginning of a new darkness, your flayed nerve endings are all quivering and the world feels raw and new and hilarious and strange and beautiful. Sometimes I loved hangovers even more than I loved getting wasted.

But not that morning. Not when there had been something at stake, something that had been missed, dropped, lost, probably forever. I shifted quietly across the bed to see if I could see where my clothes were, thinking if I could get them on first then at least I'd feel like I had some kind of protection against the vision of my own idiocy, but he saw or heard me and called out, 'Alright sleeping beauty?'

I just groaned in reply, making out I felt worse physically than I really did. The business of being physically mobile was going pretty well. I was on my way to dressed, I still had my socks on from the night before so that was an easy win, all fairly smooth really.

'It's all-day-breakfast from a tin and fried tinned potatoes. And there's tea, but no milk.' He leaned back from the cooker to look through the doorway, 'How's the head?'

'Still attached to my body apparently, but trying to sever all diplomatic ties with my stomach. What happened?' I knew exactly what had happened, it was just part of the 'poor me' act. I finished pulling my jumper on and came and sat down on the banquette, sliding along in behind the table he'd folded down in front of it.

'Well, I think what happened was you tried to fake your own death to avoid losing at strip Connect Four after bragging that you'd never lost at strip anything in your whole life. I came back from having a piss and you were keeled over.'

He put a plate of mostly beans and potatoes and a mug of black tea in front of me, grinning, and continued, 'So I put you in the recovery position and went and got off with the old lady. She was a bit dry and wrinkly but what's a fellow supposed to do, eh?'

I knew he was joking, but I was so fragile that I must've looked devastated by the idea of it, so he didn't push the humour, just got his plate and slid in beside me, patting my leg and saying, 'Eat up, yeah? You'll feel better for it.'

It was a weird feeling, the hungover breakfast was such a thing of before. I'll probably never even eat baked beans again; we didn't encounter a single tin on our journey, it's like they don't even exist in France, and I think the emotional weight of a hangover would probably crush me to death these days. The breakfast and the warmth of Martin's thigh and shoulder against mine did their work though, and little by little I felt more human.

He must've sensed it because he then said, 'I actually did go and see the old lady last night.'

'What?!'

'No, idiot, I went to talk about the journey. I told her the truth, where I'm actually going to be sailing. It's much more dangerous you know, to sail down around Europe and into the Med than sailing across the Atlantic. Crossing the ocean is easy, you just set your sails, read a book for six weeks and hope you don't arrive in a hurricane. Anyway, she gave me a present. She said it's for us both.'

He turned and lifted something out from the shelf behind our backs. It was like a cross between a large leather camera case and an old jewellery box.

I immediately thought of being on the doorstep with the woman whose name I never knew, giving me her gold. She had been half-hiding behind her front door, which itself was half-hiding behind her hedge, and the way she motioned me over. Quick little gestures and brightly coloured fabrics made her look like a tiny hopping bird. At that time everybody was wary of everybody else, all the talk was still of germs and fear and hoarding. God there used to be a lot of fucking talk. I do not miss that.

I had been on my way home from the allotment. Despite my incompetence and, let's be honest, lack of interest, it was still producing – nothing like it did under my mum's care but producing all the same, and my expectations of it were so much lower anyway. The summer bounty was past, but I had a rucksack of greens, kale, leeks and chard sticking out of the top of it and some gone-to-seed parsley in the side pockets. I was grateful for the veg because it was harder and harder to get any in the shops, and at that point the allotment had yet to be raided.

I thought she was going to ask for some of it, so my expectations of getting ready to give something away made me confused and slow to realise that she actually wanted to give something to me.

'You're Heike's girl, yes? She was always nice with me, always.'

Here, then, was another woman that my mother had decided not to make friends with for one reason or another. She pulled me into her hallway.

'You take this.' She pushed a lumpen plastic bag into my hands, grabbing her hands around mine so that I couldn't let go of it to look inside it.

'My daughters are gone now. Their daughters too. My sons are men, they don't need this. One of them will come for me soon. You take this. You will need it. Your mother, she was always, always nice with me.' The weight and feel of the bag still made no sense. 'You take it.'

She waited for me to nod acceptance of the gift before taking her hands off mine. I loosened my grip on the bag to look inside. It was so much gold that it didn't look real, and it being shoved in a plastic carrier bag didn't help its case. I thanked her, asking again and again if she was sure and, surreally, offering her some greens in return.

'No, silly, my son will come soon to take me with him, take it, go, thank your mother for it.'

'My mother, Heike, my parents, you know, my parents are dead.'

'Yes, of course I know, but that doesn't mean you don't talk anymore though.' She pushed me back out the door and shooed me down the path away from her house.

I went home and took a bottle of rum and the bag of gold up to my bedroom and put everything on, piling chains one on top of another and linking earrings on necklaces when I ran out of piercings, wondering if her son really was coming for her, thinking about women all over the world since who knows when who'd slipped metal of last resort around their necks and wrists, through the lobes of their ears, hanging it onto their body, because you never know. I drank a rum to Heike in the mirror and said thank you.

And Pressure Drop made the gold into something I could carry with me, because you never know. Obviously it's not good for anything now, you can't eat it, but gold's not fear for the future anymore, it's hope. And it's beautiful, and beauty is a happiness in itself. I loved wearing it from the moment I first put it on. Apart from slipping it down Sputnik's seat tube before the *Château* I only took it off twice on the way.

The first time, we were not much more than a week, maybe two weeks, away from the *Château*. Our first days on the road were just scrambled progress and crooked sleeping positions, but after we'd rested up a bit in that hay barn we did better. We started to feel that they probably weren't coming after us or, if they were, they weren't coming the way we were going. But then we arrived at a river. A proper, big river, broad and dark and muscular, sinewy at the soft sandy edges of its islets, humping itself easily over the irregularities of its bed, and so smooth in the middle that nobody would have imagined trying to ford it. We followed the path we were on, between the farmland and the riverbank where trees and bushes had been left to explode, noticing each time a little track veered off it towards the water's edge and imagining anglers with all their khaki paraphernalia, and slowly realising that when we found a crossing point it was likely to be patrolled.

Summer had ended and the leaves were falling: oak and alder, hawthorn and birch, bright against the blank soil of the path like plant-book autumn. After we moved to London, we still spoke Spanish when we were together at home and all the best English my mum ever learned was the names of plants. After fifteen years in London she was still living everything in the present simple and saying she was going to make things instead of do them, but plant books were her dictionaries and she'd have known whether the dried-up umbellifers that stretched their skeletal fingers towards us were once hogweed or cow parsley.

It felt like the path, well-worn as it was, was not going to be there for many more seasons. The day had been dark and cloudy, and it was getting near evening, that moment when you think the sky is getting brighter but in fact it's just that it looks more luminous in comparison because there's less light to fall on anything else. The round yellow leaves glowed on the darkening earth like scattered coins. Then suddenly Pressure Drop stopped us dead, saying he could smell smoke on the breeze.

We moved a little bit away from the path and sat down on a fallen tree.

'We do it differently this time,' Pressure Drop said, 'We trade what we have to for a quick, safe passage. We don't have time to do anything else – no matter what. Are we agreed?' He looked hard at Sarah.

She nodded.

'Okay, get yourselves organised then.'

He pulled his pillow out of the top of his rucksack and decanted a significant amount of weed from it into his pouch and I scrabbled through my layers and unknotted the goldfinger necklace from around my waist. Of all the things I've ever dry-swallowed in my life, those beads were definitely the worst. Not so much the size, the end of my middle finger isn't that much bigger than a large paracetamol, but that said, anything you have to swallow seems much bigger in your mouth than it does in your hand. It was more doing it again and again, twenty-four times. There's only so much saliva a body can produce, and then they'd twist and go down sideways and I could really feel the edges of the flat end scraping down the inside of my throat. It made my eyes stream – which seemed even more unfair because if my body could've produced that liquid in my mouth it would've been much more useful. It took me significantly longer than I expected and it burned raw down behind my sternum afterwards.

'Fair play,' said Pressure Drop, standing up when I was done. 'Shall we then?'

By then it was too dark to cycle safely so we wheeled the bikes along the path. The sky had gone from grey to dark blue and we soon knew there was light somewhere up ahead. It wasn't that we could see it flickering through the trees, more like a sixth sense that the darkness was less dense in that direction. We couldn't tell what sort of light it was. We worked our way towards it, stumbling on the odd tree root and complaining quietly about how much noise my fancy freewheel made. The sound of the river was constant, rushing and rustling along beside us.

Soon, the trees ended and across the scrubby ground, we could see the fire. It was a bonfire on a roundabout and the roundabout was at the beginning of a suspension bridge that stretched from the flickering light across to the true dark on the other side of the river. We could see that there were several people sitting around the fire, not doing anything in particular. We looked at each other and kept moving towards them.

When we got within what we thought was the limit of the light Sarah called out; '*Bonsoir messieurs, nous sommes trois voyageurs dont une vieille dame, un pèlerin et une femme enceinte. Nous sommes de passage.*'

The men were up instantly.

Sarah continued to explain that we wanted to camp by their fire that night and cross the bridge in the morning, but they weren't interested, they were running at us waving sticks and shouting at us not to move. We didn't. They surrounded us. They took our bikes out of our hands, twisted our arms behind our backs and pushed us towards the fire.

As we came fully into the light Sarah muttered, 'Stick your belly out,' at me in that Birmingham accent she'd used back when we arrived at the *Château*. The men got us to sit down on the ground facing the fire and one of them stood over us with a big stick while they went through our bags. Sarah tried to speak to them but they told her to shut up, that if they wanted to hear from her they'd ask.

They were really thorough with the search, completely emptying the panniers, shaking out sleeping bags, unrolling tents, running their fingers through the rice and lentils and peanuts in the Tupperware boxes, getting me to build and dismantle the firebox stove to prove that all the pieces were part of it. And then they searched us, or, they searched Pressure Drop, right down to his holey flapping boxers, and they told us we could either let them search our clothes or we could wait until a woman arrived in the morning but if we chose to wait they'd have to tie us up overnight. We let them search us.

After all the bullshit of the *Château* it was a relief to see it, to have the violence and the danger out in the open. I got down to bra and pants and Sarah had no bra so they let her keep her t-shirt on but got her to stretch its fabric against her body so they could see there was nothing but her hidden under it. It was easy to see that my belly had a significant effect and I pushed it out as far as it would go. I was past halfway then and the bump was in its photogenic phase – better defined than the thickness around the middle of the early months and not yet the waddle-inducing blimp nose cone of the later months.

Sarah says that people unconsciously know that a pregnant woman is neither a danger nor an opportunity to anyone except herself and her child, and given the smallest chance they will act on that knowledge.

She was certain from the beginning that my pregnancy was a 'good thing'. I spent most of the day after she pushed me into an awareness of it staring at the sea, distractedly turning our spread-out tents in the sun every now and then. The sand dunes were calm but noisy with the wind and sea and they were full of insect life, flamboyant stuff. Butterflies came by to investigate the Day-Glo bits of my trainers. Most commonly they were red and iridescent black with spots, like what you might imagine a ladybird would turn into if it were a caterpillar, but the actual caterpillars you saw were stripy black and yellow ones – straggly looking plants with raggedy leaves and moth-eaten, yellow flowers, were often dripping with those caterpillars, like branches filled with fruit.

When evening arrived, Sarah sat down beside me while Pressure Drop was lighting the fire and said, 'There's no going back, you know.'

'I know,' I said, slightly snappily. I didn't need reminding. I'd watched from the dunes, aching and nursing my raw, seeping hands while *Seabird* sailed away.

'He's not going to come back either,' she added, 'the deal is Martin will stay with Julie for at least a year.'

'A year!' He hadn't told me that it would be that long. He'd dropped hints. Or, maybe if I think what he'd actually said, he definitely said that he wouldn't be competent enough with the boat to leave that summer and that he wouldn't do the journey in winter. So, actually, I suppose he had told me, I'd just not heard it. Or not that starkly and definitely.

'It's the most dangerous part of a human's life, the first year,' said Sarah, 'Julie and the baby need all the support they can get.'

'A year though – that means I'll be alone.'

Sarah looked at me, 'Alone like Julie was?' she asked.

'No, I know, I didn't mean that.'

'I know what you meant, I'm just pointing out that it's nonsense.'

In the evening, the bug life of the dunes changed, almost everything would go off to bed, but these massive shiny dark-backed flying beetles with big antennae would come out as the sun started getting low. They always seemed too heavy and ungainly to perform whatever aeronautical manoeuvre they were attempting. They'd come zooming towards you like a noisy black shuttlecock, carried forward by their own thrumming momentum, detect the obstacle far too late, attempt to bank and turn, fail, and smack into your shoulder or the side of your head with considerable force for an insect, then they'd bounce off and try to right themselves while they zoomed off in another perilously obstacle-ridden direction. They really freaked Pressure Drop out, I think he thought they'd get stuck in his hair. That's why he alway took charge of lighting the fire there, he thought they didn't like the smoke. As far as I could tell they weren't capable of avoiding things they didn't like, but it meant he took care of the fire so hey ho. He called them cockchafers, though I was never sure if that was an insult or what he thought they were really called. So he was busy with the fire and Adi was busy trying, in micro-movements, to find a position in which his ribs weren't constantly screaming at him, while Sarah was talking to me.

'This is a good thing you know,' she said, 'you just have to look at it clearly. It is a good thing for so many parts of the future. It is a good thing because it will protect us on our journey, because a pregnant belly is the oldest talisman there is. It's a good thing because it propels us; it catapults you forwards, into where you're headed, and at the same time ties you back into your past. It's a good thing because if you're going to be a midwife everybody is going to ask you if you've given birth, and if you haven't they'll find it harder to trust you. It's silly really, nobody thinks a fireman can't be a good fireman if his house hasn't almost burned down but with midwives that's just how it is.'

Pressure Drop, who was listening as he fed bigger and bigger bits of driftwood, smooth as bones, into the firebox, snorted and said, 'That's only because people are fucking morons. Of course having your house almost burn down makes you a better fireman. That's the difference between memorising something and learning it.'

'They're pretty much the same thing really,' Adi said.

'No,' said Pressure Drop, 'learning it doesn't just mean being able to list the points of something, learning something means it becoming a part of you, so that your muscles, your nerves and your unconscious mind all work away underneath your brain to make the right thing happen. It's like an upside-down swan.'

'An upside-down swan?'

'Swans are actually bastards, but that's not the point. People always say, oh swans, they look all graceful gliding down the river but they have these stupid flappy little legs paddling wildly and pushing them along below the waterline. If you've really learned something, all people might see is the stupid flappy little legs but there's actually an immense weight of graceful understanding giving them reason and sense. If all you've done is memorised something, then it's all just legs.'

Adi, though there was no real point because it was clear Pressure Drop was getting on a roll, said that you could remember something and that information would be useful to you in dealing with the real world.

Pressure Drop just shrugged. 'You can say that,' he said, 'but even in real life people usually manage not to learn anything from the things that happen to them. Like, you haven't a hope of becoming a better fireman from your house almost burning down if nobody's told you it should make you a better fireman. And anyway, just because you understand how something happened it doesn't mean you understand what has happened.'

'But,' said Adi, 'isn't knowing how something happened more important?'

Pressure Drop looked at me, nodded at my belly, and said, 'Audaz, you understand how it happened don't you.'

Adi looked mortified at being witness to such a question.

'Well, yeah,' I said, 'obviously.'

'Right, birds, bees, storks, cabbages, the whole fucking rigmarole, fine. But do you understand what has happened?' And that was Pressure Drop doing 'understand'.

It felt like the sand was slipping away from under me when he set the 'understand' word-bomb off, as latency made a bargain with crystal clarity. He'd got Sarah too, I could see by the way her shoulders dropped and the muscles in her face relaxed.

He went on. '"Understand" is a terrible word, "understand" makes you feel that you're beneath something, that you are below it, as you would be the heavens, looking up and trying to grasp something greater than yourself, and that is not just not what the word means, it's not even where the word came from. In Old English, "under" meant to be in the presence of something, to be in the middle of it while at the same time it's in the middle of you. It's all around you and running through you and those two things are the same thing. The reason a belly full of new life is a sacred thing is because it is the physical embodiment of the true meaning of understanding.'

He was drawing breath for the next round, but instead he flinched to backhand away one of the giant beetles while I took a moment to settle into the feeling of being just a skin between the world and itself.

Regaining his balance and then checking the bug had fucked off threw him off his flow, so after he was sure it wasn't coming back in for another round, he finished with, 'Just to be completely clear though, I don't want to know anything about how it works – that's your business, you two,' gesturing towards me and Sarah, 'All the squishy stuff, that's the curse of Eve and I don't even want to think about it.'

Sarah was probably right about the belly being a talisman. Though it did the opposite of help us at the *Château*, but that's because I didn't have it when we arrived, because its appearance got woven into a story of there when it actually had nothing to do with there, so there was confusion about its contents.

But once it was in place it conferred its protection, and standing in my underwear by the fire on the roundabout while our belongings were searched, I imagined I could feel the gold I'd swallowed a few minutes before magnifying my belly's potency from within, sending out its aura to shield Sarah and Pressure Drop too. I watched the men around us and tried to see myself in their eyes as they squeezed the clothes I'd handed to them, wondering whether I looked like the past or the future, like hope or like despair.

They handed our clothes back to us and offered us chairs from a huge pile of those fold-up camping chairs that have a cup-holder in the armrest. Decathlon again. If any of their chief executives are still alive, I bet they're wishing they'd run ad campaigns about their products surviving the end of the world. Pressure Drop sprawled into one, his own angles echoing its angles so that his shadow looked like an enormous spider, and tucked his pouch into the cup-holder.

They asked us questions. Sarah's French was better than any of their English, so she did the talking. She told them mostly the truth, fudging dates, leaving out the births and glossing over the horribleness of the time at the *Château*. She said she had been a nurse, as agreed, and that we'd stayed while she taught everyone some basic first aid, and that we were going to Digne-les-Bains to start a nursing school. They seemed mostly satisfied with our answers, even grudgingly impressed that we planned to cycle the whole way down France. She only faltered once. I hadn't understood the question, I wasn't even really trying to decipher any of the language, just feeling the tone and the rhythm of their voices, watching their gestures. She went suddenly shaky and breathless, couldn't answer. He'd asked her how she knew her friends in Digne-les-Bains were still alive.

They decided we were not a threat, and it seemed that our arrival was sufficiently anomalous that the odds of there being another event that night were vanishingly small. They said we could sleep near the fire. We set up our tents and re-packed our bags. They let us cook our rice and lentils on their fire. Pressure Drop skinned up and most of them happily accepted a smoke. While I was cooking and he was smoking, Sarah was, I thought, negotiating the toll for crossing the bridge, but it turned out there wasn't one. They weren't there to collect, they were there because there was a nuclear power plant a few kilometres away on the other side of the river.

It was fucking insane to me that you would build a nuclear power plant on this beautiful tree-lined river, but Sarah didn't seem at all surprised. I suppose everywhere is lovely until you ruin it really. One of the guys used to work as security at the plant, which explained the thoroughness of everything that followed our initial capture, and he was the one who told Sarah about the lights going out internationally. She explained it while we ate.

Apparently when people started dying, like, really a lot of people dying, the scientists running the power plants realised they couldn't do it – a couple of people in their team would die and they'd realise that nobody knew how to do some super-complicated thing that stopped the whole plant going Chernobyl. So they started getting in touch with other plants, first in their own countries and then all over the world. Then when people didn't stop dying they realised they'd have to shut everything down, so they agreed a date and began the process, without saying anything to governments or anything because they didn't want to be told not to. They created and printed off massive instruction manuals telling whoever was left in the place what they should be doing because it seems it takes years, decades maybe, to properly shut one down. They knew that once they'd got past a certain point they probably wouldn't be able to communicate anymore because knocking out the power would, in most places, set off a chain of events that would shut down everything else too, and then the lights would go out all over.

So when they weren't keeping an eye on the bridge, the guys at the roundabout bonfire, as well as most of the other adults in the area, took turns trying to follow the steps they'd been given to decommission and enclose, and they didn't want anybody interfering with their work. A fair few of them believed that the whole outbreak had been initiated by Artificial Intelligence – one of them said: 'Well, if you were of greater intelligence than humans, wouldn't you look at the world and think that humans was the problem?' which I couldn't really disagree with – so they'd cut every dead electricity cable that linked the plant to the rest of the world in case they became conduits for some kind of machine-infection. They were organised – they had systems, rules, protocols, rotas. Although they had no communication with them, and didn't even know where they were, the ex-security guy said to Sarah that he felt connected to the other groups of people all over France, Europe, the world, who were doing the same thing, he felt them by his side, all of them, instruction by instruction, bucket of water by bucket of water, bag of cement by bag of cement, slowly, quietly, carefully, saving the world.

He was listening to Sarah tell us what he'd said, and he came in, in broken English, to say that their village up the hill from the roundabout had grown since the deaths stopped, because when waifs and strays did pass through, they often decided to stay. And although they were running out of most kinds of food stocks in the surrounding area, they had managed to plant some fields of root vegetables and cabbages that they thought would get them through the winter, and there were fish in the river. The younger people looked after the fields and the fishing instead of working at the power plant – because of the babies, he said, nodding at my belly. I had a moment of freak-out, thinking that there was some hidden cohort of women and babies being looked after in the village and that Sarah would insist on us staying, but he meant because of the eggs, the sperm and the radioactivity. 'No good saving the world if there is nobody alive to live in it,' he said, and I suddenly had a sense of all the nested apocalypses, a matryoshka of disaster reaching all the way inside me, fractal cataclysms exploding inwards and outwards, stacked mushroom clouds like turtles all the way down.

We slept in the glow of the fire. It was strange to be woken every now and then by its flickering or their voices. Since the *Château* we'd already got used to being alone in the dark nights. In the morning we were packing up when the change of shift arrived, this time a mix of men and women. They had a thermos jug of coffee with them and it smelled amazing, thick and rich, like a smell that you could chew. They got the story of who we were from the night shift and from Sarah and then offered us some coffee. I should not have said yes but I did, and before I had even finished strapping my rucksack on top of my panniers I needed to shit. I was too preoccupied with that to really notice that Sarah was anxious about something.

I grabbed the soap, my mug and some clean pants from my bag and told Pressure Drop what I was doing, warning him that I'd be a while. I don't think at that point he remembered about the beads though. I went off along the path we'd arrived on, into the trees and along the riverbank, looking for a spot where

I'd be able to get down to the water. Riverbanks are motherfuckers, the water is so close but it's often impossible to get to it, there'll be a treacherous grassy overhang that your foot pushes through when you put your weight on it, or else mud that means you can't get any closer without getting soaked and filthy or the bit of water you can reach will be shallow and stagnant and not water that is useful for anything except getting in your way. I was getting more and more desperate, the caffeine grinding my unaccustomed guts and sending everything south. I found somewhere. Less than ideal, but then what would the ideal place to pick gold out of your shit with a twig be?

It looked a bit like when you see fox droppings and they're full of iridescent beetle shells. It was quite gross getting them out but not so gross it made me gag or anything. By then I was more used to being on intimate terms with my own shit than I ever thought I'd be and at least I didn't have worms. I did the best I could, rinsing them and using stems of long grass to clean out the holes in the middle. The first ones I got were still warm to the touch but everything was soon stone cold. It took fucking ages, and the whole time I was sweating that somebody was going to notice how long I'd been gone and come looking and there would be no fucking way of explaining what the hell I was doing except the truth, and even the truth was not really explicable.

I got twenty-three of them – the smallest one was gone. It had been the last one we poured and there wasn't enough gold left to fill it up to the top. I had a flash of certainty that the baby had swallowed it inside me, impossible though I knew that was. I looked for as long as I dared then decided that it must still be somewhere in my guts. I wrapped the twenty-three I had up in some leaves and zipped them into my jacket pocket – I wasn't going to put them back on the string until I knew they were really clean – and went back to the others.

When I got there Pressure Drop was sprawled back in one of the camp chairs with his head in the kind of impossibly uncomfortable-looking position that you'd normally only expect from a sleeping toddler on a long bus journey. I had a horrible split second where I thought he'd been shot but then I saw smoke rising from his far hand. As I walked towards him he shifted only his eyeballs in my direction, so that his eyes were almost all white, just a smudge of blackish-blue in the corner of them nearest to me.

Then when I got in front of him he was staring down the middle distance. Sarah was a little way away, in deep discussion with the whole group.

'What's she talking to them about?' I asked.

'She told them the truth,' he said, taking a long toke on his spliff and letting his hand drop down to his side again.

'What the fuck?'

'I know, I know.' He looked at me properly, 'I know,' he said again, 'She couldn't take it, when the women arrived she cracked, she wanted to warn them about the *Château* and check there was nobody who needed her help.'

I went and got another camp chair and dragged it over to sit beside him. I took up pretty much the same position, though my head-loll was unimpressive in comparison. 'What the fuck am I supposed to do with the beads?'

'The beads?'

'The beads, they're in my pocket, I washed them in the river but I can't swallow them again unless they're properly clean.'

Pressure Drop exhaled. I swear he could've been the pillar of a synchronised swimming team, his dreads waving like tentacles under the water and a silvery bubble of smoke in each nostril.

'Try not to think about them,' he said, 'If you think about them other people will know about them.'

I lifted my head back up to look at him. 'Because you think they're mind-readers?'

'No, eejit, because I think they're humans. If you think about the beads you'll want to check on them, you'll put your hand in your pocket, you'll fiddle with them, you'll look shifty about it any time somebody looks towards you and, sooner or later, somebody will notice and they'll come and ask you what you've got in your pocket. And then they'll know. So do not think about them. And try not to be too hard on Sarah, she's spent nearly her whole life being useful one way or another, it's the hardest addiction to kick. If she doesn't offer them help, then she doesn't know what she's for.' So Pressure Drop smoked and I tried not to think about my pocketful of gold and we waited.

In the end there were no pregnant women in the village. Sarah came back over to us and we set off. The relief gave us giddy wings and we sped through the countryside that day. Pressure Drop sang and hummed a sort of Burning Spear medley as we rolled through picturesque villages and around hills topped with pale châteaux, the dark roofs of their towers arrowing up towards the busy sky. The land was full of bounty, unpicked fruit weighing everything down and we stopped a few times to stuff our panniers with under-ripe apples and our mouths with over-ripe grapes. When we walked into the fields of vines, clouds of starlings exploded up around us, whirling and resettling out of reach to continue gorging themselves.

You could smell the fermentation, the grapes turning to wine right there inside their skins, and it made me wonder if the starlings were drunk. Were their joyous, shrieky chattering and their unpredictable jerky wheeling the products of pissed-up ecstasy? The way they'd all suddenly fold their wings and drop from the sky like a hail of soft stones seemed more and more like they were practising how to deal with passing out mid-flight. It made me laugh enough that I wondered if maybe I wasn't just full of swift-acting sugars but also a bit drunk on the grapes.

In any case, when evening arrived we were in great spirits. We stopped by a copse and as we unpacked the panniers and made camp in a clearing in the middle of the stand of scrubby trees, Pressure Drop was talking about the fruitfulness of the land, long arms shooting about in enthusiasm and tent poles waving for emphasis while he declaimed, '"There will be peace for the seed: the vine will yield its fruit, the land will yield its produce and the heavens will give their dew; and I will cause the remnant of this people to inherit all these things."'

As we threaded the poles into the flysheets, he told us that contrary to what we thought – though I had never actually thought about it – it was neither the agricultural revolution in Mesopotamia nor the invention of writing in Sumer that forced inequality on humans. After we'd eaten rice and apples he gave me a handful of little iridescent starling feathers. He settled himself by the fire, making his body look like a game of pick-up sticks, limbs in a sort of entropic equilibrium, skinned up, and continued the long conversation he'd started with himself, saying that the subjugation of beasts of burden may have fooled humans into thinking they had the right to own more than they could carry themselves, but it wasn't agriculture that reduced people to slaves to Mammon, but the idea that somebody could own the land.

I used the starling feathers to clean the beads one last time before boiling them while Sarah sat throwing little handfuls of dry twigs onto the fire so that the skinny tree trunks around us would flare into existence and then fall back into the shadows when the quick flames died down.

We were happy. Happy because my belly had worked its magic at the bridge, happy because the land was bounteous, because the weather was fine, because the hills were not steep. We were happy because we'd crossed the river, because we'd put it and the people at the bridge between us and the *Château*, so we couldn't feel Charles and the henchmen in the backs of our necks or between our shoulder blades anymore, and because the excision where Adi used to be was not quite so raw and bloody. But I think mostly we were happy because somebody else had a mission, and that made ours seem less crazy.

I rethreaded the beads when the water cooled enough to get at them. Putting them back onto the shoelace while they were still warm was like doing it the first time when they'd just come out of their moulds, but by now my skin had rubbed them golden. I tied them back around my waist, or, more accurately, I tied them above my bump because by then I didn't have a waist anymore.

I never found the littlest one. I looked for it the next morning, and many other mornings after that. Crazy though I knew it was, I even looked for it in Leo's first nappies. Maybe it is still inside me. Maybe it was left on the riverbank. Maybe it was washed into the river and swallowed by a fish that was caught on a hook and gutted by a fisherman who found the gold bead and gave it to his wife, and she wears it now. Maybe it is sitting undisturbed underneath a rock or a sod of earth somewhere between that riverbank and here. Maybe, although it's not possible, maybe it is inside Leo, lodged at the base of his spine or somewhere in his skull, lurking in his cheekbone like the adult teeth of toddlers, waiting to descend. Maybe some day, in ten years' time, it will once again emerge warm from within, poking through his gums after one of his milk teeth drops out.

Wherever it is, the moment it surfaces again to human eyes it will be instantly snatched up. We are so primed to it, that solid spark of light that burns underground and underwater, constant and unwavering. We love it, it speaks to the part of us that insists on carrying on, that longs for sunlight in the winter, water in the desert, fire in the night, to the part of us that draws us inexorably onwards, that believes that one day we will move beyond scrabbled swaps of disposable lighters and dried beans and something that flickers and flashes will once again have all its meanings.

And that was the same flickering flash that I saw in the shadow of the half-opened box that Martin held in his hands on the Saturday-night-sailor's boat that morning while I waited for the tinned breakfast to take effect on my hangover. As he opened it, I could see the shining metal, but what he lifted out was not jewellery. It looked like somebody had very expertly deconstructed a pair of brass binoculars and then given the parts to somebody equally expert but who'd never seen binoculars to rebuild.

'Sextant,' he said.

Hearing him talk about it, it was like he was describing something that was mystically alive to the forces of nature around us, so much so that at first I thought he was just inventing stuff. When I realised he was actually trying to tell me how it functioned, I entirely misunderstood how the thing worked and thought it was a machine for showing how time spins backwards and forwards or some kind of super-sensitive detector of gravitational pull.

Anyway, the way he explained it was that you made the sun set at noon, and then when it touched the horizon you spun the stars you couldn't see around your head like you were throwing on a scarf, and then you located the Three Centres, and when you knew the position of the Three Centres, suspended as they were in time and space, then you would know where on the curved, sliding blue of the ocean's surface you were. The Three Centres were the centre of the sun, the centre of the earth and the centre of you.

'And that,' he said triumphantly, 'is why you're right – we should sail to Santiago de Cuba and have half a dozen babies on the way – because you can't discover anything from two points in a line, especially when you're one of them, you need a third point to know how far away or close you are and where you're headed. Life is movement, and trigonometry is the basis of all understanding of movement.'

He handed me the sextant. It was surprisingly light and, because I didn't know how to hold it, seemed strangely imbalanced in the hand for something that was supposed to be all about stabilising the whirling orbits of the universe and locking them to one another in a geometric form. It was warm from him holding it.

'Come on,' he said, taking it back off me, 'get your shit together, we've got a boat to find.'

And he was right about the third point being how two points know the distance between them. At the moment, Leo's centre is so close to mine that the distance between us is hard to measure in anything other than the breadth of hairs or the thin film of milk and sweat that forms between his cheek and my tit.

His land-grab closeness makes the distance that has now opened up between me and Martin gape like interplanetary space, like geological time, moment after moment slipping away between us, seconds tipping over the point of a watch hand and tumbling from the future into the past like the microscopic skeletons of plankton, falling to the bottom of the ocean and accreting over the course of forevers too long for us to understand until some slow violence rips the layers upwards through the living soil, pulls them towards the sky to become the peaks of mountains, monuments to a rolling roar that this is how far things have come, this is how far away things now are.

Before there was me and Martin, and Leo was just some point of possibility, spinning out there in the quantum realm and now there's me and Leo, and Martin is out there, flickering between being alive and dead, casting out through the sea or the sky or the earth, looking for my body to bounce an echo back, throw a pale shadow on the screen, draw the needle to north. The other night I dreamed Martin in bed with me, dreamed his hands on my tits, dreamed his breath in my ear, dreamed him inside me, and in the dream that wrapped around the outside of that dream I knew it was a sign that he was alive and asleep and dreaming me at that exact moment. The knowing of it woke me, and I discovered that in fact I'd fallen asleep lying beside Leo while I was feeding him and he'd woken up some time later and latched on again in the dark. I still don't know if that counts as child abuse or infidelity but I was sobbing for a long time afterwards.

So the trigonometry has been done and that's how far away Martin is, so far away that his body is a memory being sucked out of mine by another body, like an oyster from its shell. Martin and I only got that close in secret. He never shared my bed, he never put his mouth on my skin in sight of anybody else, he never cried out for me where somebody could hear. Which is why, that morning on the Saturday-night sailboat, I was so ruined by having passed out on our only chance. But at the time, he didn't seem to hate me for it, he just showed me the sextant and said we had a boat to find.

And so we got up and out and onto the bikes and set off. Having cycled through such a lot of nowhere by now, having come through France, it strikes me that the south-east of England is so full of people it's ridiculous. There must have been people all around us that whole ride from the house in Fairlight to Brighton Marina. We were never out of sight of a house, possibly never out of screaming distance of another human. But in my head we were invisible and invincible, the king and queen of Fairlight on a mission.

I had enough sixth sense going on to be glad we'd set off early though. Also, as I discovered later, Martin had a massive knife with him. We rode towards Brighton above the cliffs but turned off early, down towards the fuzzy forest of white masts. There were loads of seagulls going mental, swooping and squawking. Martin said there must've been fish, seagulls only get that excited about food. When we arrived at the marina the first stretch was all fishing boats and while most hadn't been touched for some time, Martin reckoned one of them had just come back in, and that's why the seagulls were still going batshit. The idea that there was almost certainly somebody watching us as we climbed up and over the metal barriers, hung by our fingers and dropped down onto the access to the jetties made us try to act like we really knew what we were doing.

I still had my long hair then, they were all horrified in the *Château* when I got rid of it. It wasn't like I just decided to cut it off for no reason, it was the nits. Everybody got nits and nobody would deal with them properly. Like, it was blindingly obvious to me that you had to choose a day, treat everybody, and that's it, but nobody wanted to do that. Sarah was okay, because I forensically combed her every two days, but her eyes just weren't up to doing the same thing for me. In the end I had no idea if I was scratching because of the nits or because of the idea of nits or because of attacking my scalp so much to try to get rid of them.

Pressure Drop soaked his hair in oil and kept his head wrapped in a pillowcase that he doused in whatever strong alcohol he could find each morning. I was terrified he was going to set himself alight.

The *Château* was full of parasites of one kind or another, Sarah lived in fear that we'd all catch scabies — the fact that I didn't really know what scabies were was the only thing that kept me from living in fear too — and as well as the nits I had thrush, so my vagina burned like unholy fire, and we constantly caught worms too. Same story. Nobody wanted to sort them out systematically so you'd just be woken up every ten days or so by the skin-crawling wriggle of creatures in your arsehole and then, on Sarah's advice, have to spend days oiling your anus, scrubbing your nails and trying to sterilise your knickers in the sunlight. And you couldn't even talk about that, any conversation that went anywhere near something that partly happened in your pants would be immediately derailed. At least the nits you could discuss, but Charles wet-shaved his head so he wasn't interested in enforcing anything, and nobody wanted to be told what to do by anybody else, so it was never-ending. After a few weeks I was just fucking sick of them so I took the scissors of my Swiss army knife out and chopped my hair off in ragged lumps.

Anyway, back then I still had it long, long enough to be swishy even, so I tucked it inside my hood and told Martin not to help me with any of the climbing despite my shortness because I thought that way, from a distance, we'd look more like we were behaving like two blokes and not a couple. Not that I was really able to think of us as a couple, but you know what I mean. Apart from the maybe-there fisherman there must've been people in boats watching us go by, breath held, fingers clenched around the handles of knives and hammers and screwdrivers, waiting to see which way we'd go, but nobody made themselves known to us. Maybe they were scared, maybe they just decided we were none of their business. One way or another there was no little old lady with a need for a chat and an excuse for a glass of sherry to call out to us as we went looking for the boat she'd said would be there.

I didn't really remember – or mostly understand – what she'd said about the boat we were looking out for except that it was red, so that's all I focused on. The seagulls calmed down bit by bit – every time we noticed them a few had disappeared and they'd got a bit less shouty. We prowled, walking softly along jetties and across the decks of boats when we had to, up and over or around whatever barriers we encountered, until Martin grabbed my arm; 'Audaz, that's it!'

We'd just come onto a new jetty and there was a flash of red at the far end of it. We ran-walked to it as lightly as we could. There was no sign of life aboard.

It's always odd when you see somebody go weak at the knees over something that basically leaves you cold, and Martin was completely in love with that boat. As soon as we'd stepped on deck it had got him in a Class A way, he was touching everything, tugging at ropes, stroking bits of railing. I just stood there. He took the crowbar out of his rucksack but I could see that he really, really didn't want to have to break the door. I suppose this boat looked a lot more solid than the last boat, and a sailboat with a broken door is not so good at keeping the waves out, but also he just didn't want to hurt it. He started tapping all around the door, feeling everywhere, wedging his fingertips into every little crevice, standing back, looking, starting again somewhere else.

The seagulls were all gone by then. It was a beautiful morning; the sun was already high even though it was still early and you could feel some warmth in it despite the breeze. Having seen Martin's initial ship-struck caressing, I only realised he was actually looking for a key when he found one. He stood out from behind the mast, dangling a shiny brass key from a little blue float, smiling at the perfectness of his life. Then he was all busy, down into the boat, checking things, back up and untying and tying, clipping and screwing, hoisting and lowering, and then he looked at me and said, 'Okay, I think you should go and get the bikes.'

Bikes and boats do not mix. Everything about how they are made and used conspires to make one damage the other – or both of them damage you – if you try to combine them in any way. Compared to arriving at Fort Mahon, getting the bikes from Brighton to Fairlight was easy, but it didn't feel that way. When I was getting them, Martin edged the boat along, pulling and pushing against other boats until he got into a position where he could jump onto the jetty with a rope and pull it towards a spot where the bikes could be lowered over the edge to it. It was slow and I kept expecting him to fall in. Lowering the bikes down to the boat was horrible. A bike, when it's set on its wheels on the ground, is a lovely, solid, fluid machine, but as soon as it's dangling out over a railing, twisting your stretched arms with its surprising weight, it becomes a contraption for snagging ropes, skinning knuckles and snapping fingers. Anyway, despite the tide having dropped considerably by then, we managed it with only minor injuries.

We were so busy trying to avoid damage that we didn't notice that we had an audience, it was only once we had the bikes on deck and had sucked and shaken our pinched fingers that we saw that there were people, fishermen most likely, on the sea wall watching us. In their matching outfits, skinny legs poking out of bulky jackets, zips open and their hands in the pockets of their trousers so that the points of their elbows pushed out like chunky wings, they looked like large birds. They didn't say anything, but while we were bringing the bikes down into the cabin – another utter pain-in-the-arse of a job – they came down off the sea wall.

I was fighting with handlebars below when I heard Martin say, 'Alright, lads?'

I came out and they were standing at the railing just above where we were. They looked both less and more scary up close. They were more dissimilar, more of a mix of ages, shapes and sizes than I'd imagined, and they weren't really dressed the same, just similarly, but up close they looked more desperate than I'd thought: grimmer, jaws more clenched, eyes narrower.

One of them said to Martin, 'That your boat then?'

'I was given it.'

'Oh yeah, who by?'

'Margaret at Sovereign Harbour. Arthur asked her husband Eddy to keep an eye on it, and now Eddy's gone and Margaret asked me to come and get it.'

Martin was standing just like them, his hands in his pockets and his elbows out. He'd taken his jacket off when we were getting the bikes down but it was only then that I noticed the massive knife. It wasn't the knife we usually brought fishing, that was a sharp stubby thing in a black sheath, this one was a bare-bladed machete. He had the handle wedged through one of his belt loops, the way you would with a stick if you were pretending it was a sword and you were six. I didn't know if he was bluffing with the names, apart from Eddy obviously, and I didn't want to know, but the combination of them and the machete seemed to be keeping the bird-men on the land side of the railings.

Martin started to pull up the little front sail.

'You know how to handle her do you?'

'More or less,' said Martin, then turned and said to me quietly, 'You'd better learn fast Audaz, it's going to take the two of us to get out of the harbour.'

The little sail at the front was pulling the nose of the boat to point it out into the water.

'Where you headed then?' asked the guy, as Martin flipped the rope off the metal thing it'd been wound around on the jetty, gave the jetty a push with his foot and we were out of jumping distance in seconds.

'Cuba,' he said, looking up at the guy. 'Not right away, but we're headed for Cuba.' He grinned at me, which made me think that the difficult bit was over, and told me to get the mainsail up.

The difficult bit was not over. The bird-men walked out along the sea wall to watch us and they looked even more like cormorants out there, still with their hands in their pockets, watching. Everything on the boat happened either too quick or too slow and I was unable to judge the amount of force involved in anything. We'd be barely moving and then suddenly the harbour wall would loom out of nowhere, or the bottom of the big sail would come swinging across and nearly take my head off.

The bird-men didn't take their eyes off us. It was clearly part of the fronting up that we had to sail out of the harbour with a certain amount of competence and dignity and between jibs, booms, jibes, luffs, abouts and tos, it didn't seem to be happening. I started to get anxious. I realised that if they were fishermen, and they were almost certainly fishermen, they must have fuel for their boat and so they could just come after us if they decided they wanted to. The fear made me clumsy and stupid. I forgot the words I'd learned and misheard and misunderstood instructions even when Martin managed to give them in language I could understand.

Just as we came around the end of the sea wall the wind caught us and pushed us sideways at it. The bird-men had come right to the edge and were looking straight down onto us. Martin was shouting at me to get a buoy over the edge to cushion us but for fuck's sake keep my fingers out of the way, and although I managed to just in time the imagined screech of metal on concrete was ringing in my ears. We bounced off, and when we came out of the harbour the sea rolled at us with far more strength than I'd been expecting and I thought I was going to crown our performance by being thrown over the edge of the boat, but I wasn't. Martin did some kind of hocus-pocus with the ropes and the sails swung once more and then the boat kicked and we darted forwards over the waves.

Once we were properly moving it was amazing. You wouldn't have said really that it was a windy day, but it felt like we were fast. The water rushed along the sides of us and when Martin adjusted things and steered you could feel the whole boat twanging, like it wasn't a solid metal piece at all, but actually a hammock of guitar-strings or a bow and arrow, constantly gathering force to shoot itself forwards. The sky was blue and off to our left the white cliffs towered up with the green hills behind them like something from a patriotic hymn book.

Martin was at the wheel, grinning like an idiot. He wanted me to come and try steering. I was a bit wary after the hassle we'd had getting out of the harbour, but he pushed for it.

'Come on, what are you scared of crashing into out here?'

I stood between him and the wheel. He got me to set my legs apart a little, to feel the deck as the base of the triangle of me. The boat pushed and pulled but sometimes I would find an equilibrium where we could glide.

Martin took his hands off the wheel, saying, 'Try to feel the boat as the point of contact between the wind and the water, between the sea and the sky, if you find the right point of contact then everything will be beautiful.' He put his arms around me. 'You have to feel for it,' he said, 'close your eyes.'

'What! You're mental.'

He was laughing, 'Go on, close your eyes, it's safe. I promise, if a whale comes up from the deeps and you're about to crash into it I'll take the wheel, okay?'

At first I just felt totally destabilised, on the edge of dizzy with the movement, but then sometimes there would be moments of a sudden kind of harmony, like the lightness in your body when you take off a heavy rucksack or a thick scissors blade slicing through slippery fabric. I was concentrating hard and if Martin's fingers hadn't been so fucking freezing I might not have noticed them picking their way through the layers of clothes around my waist and in against my skin.

'Keep your eyes closed,' he said, 'pay attention. Find the point of contact.'

His fingers were so cold they left tracers on my skin, I could feel where they'd been as well as where they were as he slid them up towards my tits. The flash of cleverness I felt when I remembered that I'd been too hungover to scramble into my sports bra that morning made me know that I could talk without breaking the moment and I said, smiling in my own darkness, 'So, is this a standard method for teaching somebody to sail then?'

'No,' he said, 'This is an advanced method. A special method. Keep your eyes closed, keep your hands on the wheel, and concentrate. Feel everything.'

One of his hands, fingers still icy, was sliding back down my belly. By the time he'd got my trousers open I was soaking.

'This,' he said as he slid his fingers into my cunt, 'is the Audaz method, the all-in method.' His fingers slid back out and found their point of contact. 'This method should only be used if you and the person being taught to sail plan to have half a dozen babies together on the way to Santiago de Cuba, and it requires you to keep your hands on the wheel, keep your eyes closed, and spread your legs a little wider.'

I could feel every bit of me he'd touched glowing, his fingers, warmer now but still colder than my skin, were all over my cunt and my tits and I was so wet I could hear it.

'Feel everything,' he said, 'feel the sea holding you up, the sky pushing you down, the sun on your face, lick your lips and taste the salt on them.'

I could feel myself starting to shake inside, the movement of the boat mixing with it, and he said, 'Audaz, I am so fucking hard and I really want to feel you come on my cock, but you need to tell me when you're close because I think I'm going to come as soon as I'm inside you.'

And that was it, I was right on the edge in a darkness full of movement and I wanted him in there with me.

'Now,' I said, 'Fucking now.'

His hands disappeared from my tits and my cunt but it was already building in waves inside me. I heard zips and fabric and he pulled my trousers down and lifted my hips up and there was the sudden cold of the air on my cunt and the sudden warmth of his cock inside me and it snapped my eyes wide open and everything was blue and white and full of sunlight and sounded like seagulls.

And so that's the place I found myself back in when, about nine months later – I'm not saying that I've got anything exact on anything, but neither has anybody else so I might as well believe what I like – it was time for Leo to come out, and he and I were both having none of it. It would be fair to say that my preparation for the event was less methodical that Julie's, or even Leïla's, what with much of it taking place while we were trying not to die of exhaustion, exposure and malnutrition in the mountains. We worked through a pretty solid crammer course once we reached Digne, but a couple of weeks of eating, sleeping and breath-work weren't enough to put me in top form. I was scared that I was too weak and tired to go the distance. Sarah said she's seen women in far worse shape give birth: addicts, alcoholics, anorexics, but knowing that didn't really help. My body took a couple of dry runs at it, taking me through a few rounds of early morning contractions and then letting them peter out. I was unconvinced and I was lonely. Obviously I wanted Martin, but also I wanted my parents.

All the dreams I'd had about them the whole way down through France were no substitute. Dreams are much more vivid and feel much more important now. While we were travelling, there was something in the way sleep was always shaken up by various kinds of fear or discomfort that made things come unstuck inside me. At night, the solid blue ice of my unconscious started to break up, chunks separating and floating around on their own, isolated slabs of memory flipping and sloshing through slivers of dream fragmented by the hardness of the ground, the early light of dawn, the flapping of flysheet in the wind or other less explicable noises. Whole sections of my childhood and my teenage years broke free, the shape of them visible for the first time in decades. Often, as the pedals turned later in the day, I'd find myself turning them over in my mind, searching for some special meaning. No revelation came, but I dreamed a lot about my parents. Like, really a lot. I thought I'd worked through a certain amount since they died, but it turns out not so much after all. In fairness, the lying about it probably slowed me down quite a bit. Basically, my mum died of cancer – although really she died of a combination of not wanting to make a fuss and believing absolutely in the NHS despite all signs that it had been beaten to its knees. Before my dad and I had even fully finished the paperwork, let alone got used to her not being there, he went and had a heart attack. And so there I was, mid-twenties, lonely and broke and lord of the kingdom of house, garden and allotment that they'd left me.

Ever since we'd left Cuba there had been a trickle of people needing to come and stay – friends of cousins of colleagues and the like – which meant the house was well set up for lodgers, and it was way too big for one person, so after I'd made it through the new round of paperwork I advertised for housemates. I was embarrassed to own a house because it made me The Man, so when people moved in, I told them that my parents had gone back to Cuba when they retired.

I mean, obviously I had friends who knew the truth, but in my day-to-day home life I stuck to the line. Which made things easier because when the washing machine broke or the shower curtain needed replacing, I could make out like it wasn't really my responsibility — though I would, in my own sweet time, sort it out — but harder because the lying meant I never really processed the fact that they were dead until about ninety per cent of the people in the world were dead and I was about to have a child myself. At which point the glacier started calving and I was flooded with dreams from which I'd wake bereft, with just kaleidoscopic flashes of sensory memory glinting in the dark and a gaping desire to hold and be held by my mother and father.

I don't imagine that, had they been with me, they'd have been some kind of chicken-soup-breathing, brow-smoothing, hug-dispensing, wisdom-saturated, two-headed platonic parent-beast, I'm well aware it would have been an utter nightmare to have them along for the ride, and looking at it rationally having Sarah is basically hitting the jackpot. But, with a kind of raging sadness that rises out of tiredness and crashes unrelentingly like waves onto cliffs, I wish they were here. Even if they would've had no idea what to say when, on the third day in a row I got up with fading contractions in the still-dark early morning. Whereas when I went in to Sarah, she did.

She said that I had to bring Martin with me to the birth. She must have felt me looking at her blankly in the dark, because she rustled herself up to sitting and said, with great sensible authority, 'Go back to bed, Audaz, and stimulate your nipples, see if that gets us anywhere.' So I did, and with spit and polish what we'd set in motion together all those months ago gathered momentum and rocked its way towards its now-inevitable end. Or, as it should more accurately be known, its beginning.

Even though I'm well out the other side of it now, I still wish Martin had been there for the birth. He'd have remembered it. When you're going through it, it feels like it would be utterly impossible to ever forget what's happening to you, but by a few days later I was left with just scraps: the contractions rolling through me like the weight of water holding you up and down as you're swept through river rapids; the sudden distracting surprise of vomiting at the pain; feeling the umbilical cord lying warm, wet and heavy on my belly and snaking from there back up inside me, and how thick and rope-like and resistant to scissors it was when the time came to cut it; the weird gush of the first milk, uncomfortable but satisfying, like bursting a spot. I've already completely forgotten what the real pain felt like. I have not forgotten that it was there, but I can't remember it.

So because Martin wasn't there I don't really know what giving birth was like, not how it felt on the inside, or for the people around me. And obviously Sarah remembers, but for her it's just one of many, and they're all different. Like, coming up to Leïla's birth was completely different to the feel of things coming up to Julie's birth. Julie's was very much a family affair but at the *Château* it was chaotic but institutional, like waiting for the date of a brutal restructuring in a failing business. There was a clear pecking order among the women. It was pretty horrible to see. I was apart from all that because I had a different status as Sarah's assistant, and also because I didn't speak French so it was impossible for me to be drawn into their power struggles. It wasn't exactly based around attractiveness, although that was a factor, it was more to do with how much effort you looked like you were making. Like, what were you prepared to sacrifice of your time, your needs, your desires, yourself, in order to be the kind of person Charles and the henchmen wanted you to be. And that became part of the measure among the women – whoever slid back on their grooming regime or wasn't arsed to be personable lost currency with everybody.

Anyway, it was clear that the pecking order was going to be kicked completely out of whack by the birth because currently Leïla, as the other women saw it, got away with murder. She didn't have to help out with annoying housework, she didn't have to have sex if she didn't feel like it, she didn't even have to look particularly attractive. All she did was lie around getting a tan on the inside of her belly button. And she didn't have to pay in any way for her privileges. Yet. Some of the women there had had children, so they must have known that, once the baby was born, Leïla would pay through the nose. I think in some ways Sarah was more worried about them than about Leïla, about what it would be like for them after the baby was born, how it would feel being around somebody's child when theirs were gone. As the days rolled by, all the women got twitchier and twitchier about the impending reckoning. So while Julie's birth had been all about the physical, Leïla's became all about the psychological. Until it was all very physical all over again.

I wasn't there to see it unfolding, so I can't know what I would've done. Things just spiralled there, fuelled by alcohol and boredom and insecurity and a clawing at some kind of rank. Charles and the henchmen always made it as hard as possible not to get sucked in. That night became a party dresses night. The party dresses were a *Château* custom; at a certain point in certain piss-ups they'd be invoked as a way to create an atmosphere and the women would all head up to their rooms and get changed and come back showing more skin and less emotion. If I hadn't left by that point I always left then. So that night all we heard from our room was the usual buzz of bad music on tinny phone speakers, the usual crescendos of shouting and squeaking, the usual punctuations of small crashes and smashes. And then it got quiet enough that you could fall asleep.

We were bolted awake by sweeping torches and hesitant female voices in the still-dark small hours. Sarah was sitting up in bed snapping instructions at the owners of the voices before I finished rubbing my eyes, and was putting her shoes on by the time I was sitting up. Her torch scraped round the walls of the room as she collected her things, her voice tight and seemingly disconnected from where the torch was.

'Pack everything,' she said, 'and keep the bags with you. Get dressed, when you have everything ready come down to her room. Pressure Drop, do not let Audaz out of your sight. Not for any reason. Alright?'

The torch swung at us, blinding us one after the other, we squinted, nodding behind upthrown arms. I opened my mouth to ask her something, but her voice came from nowhere and stopped me before I could begin, 'Don't ask me about it,' she said, 'I don't know and I don't want to talk about it. Pack. Dress. Come. We'll talk down there.' The torchlight threw itself into the corridor and she was gone.

I thought she was just being abrupt and urgent because she thought it was all going to happen suddenly, and that we should be ready to get out of there quickly, so I was scrabbling around for another torch, grabbing clothes and trying to roll up my sleeping bag all at the same time when Pressure Drop said, 'She never said hurry you know.'

'But she was in a hurry,' I said.

'She's not in a hurry,' he said, 'she's fucking livid.'

'What about?'

'I don't know. She'll tell us. Or not. But there's no hurry.'

When Pressure Drop and I got down to the women's corridor our torches showed body-con, lace and bare legs splashed across it. We picked our way over the murmuring, smoking women as we made our way to Leïla's room. Sarah was with her. All we got was hushed instructions. 'We'll have to move her.'

Leïla looked deflated, despite her enormous belly, and her eyes were wide without looking at anything.

'Keep the bags, we're going back to our room.'

We got her standing and walked her towards the door, her arms round our shoulders and Pressure Drop carrying the rucksacks. When we came into the corridor the women pulled their legs away from Sarah's torchlight and tucked them underneath themselves. They melted back into the shadows behind us as we took Leïla down the corridor and up the stairs. Halfway up she started moaning and sobbing but Sarah kept her moving. We got to our corridor.

'Take the armchair and set yourself up in the corridor. And don't let anybody in.'

Pressure Drop dragged the chair out through the doorway of our room, then ducked back in for some cushions. Sarah settled Leïla on what had been our bed, fussing with her gently. It was all so different to how it'd been with Julie; Julie's labour was like running bobsled races, slow lead-ins with not much commentary and then a sudden scramble to jump into position around her to follow her through the contraction, and then calm again. She actually found the contractions funny, not during them obviously, but after them she'd be there still searching for breath but laughing at how the pain could just disappear, it seemed ridiculous to her that something could hurt so much and then suddenly not hurt at all, like a sort of pain rollercoaster where the little train ticks along up the track, nothing to see here, higher and higher, and then suddenly you come up over the lip and you can see you're about to plunge vertically down into a full loop-the-loop yelling your head off. But with Leïla there was none of that headlong rush, everything was blocked and stuck, and in one of the long pauses during which it seemed that nothing much was happening, Sarah told us why.

At some point in the previous evening, a decision had been taken that it was time to '*mettre la machine en marche*' and so, because it is a common certainty that fucking is how you get babies out as well as how you get them in, everybody and nobody decided that all the men would have sex with Leïla one after the other. Sarah, for my benefit, was at pains to point out that the cervical sweep as well as oxytocin, whether it's from a syringe or an orgasm, have their place in inducing labour, but that the manner in which a procedure in administered has more effect on its outcome than we'd like to imagine.

The women who were prepared to talk to us about it said that Leïla had agreed to the idea, that she'd been up for it, but it was hard to believe that wasn't just their way of absolving themselves from whatever part they'd played. Everyone seemed to have had a hand in it. Leïla said they'd egged her on, laughing at the idea, joking about what position she'd have to be in, and then when it became clear that she didn't actually have a choice they'd told her, tight-jawed, to make the best of it, not to put up a fight, just get it over with. Then they'd helped hold her in place so that, with all the hammering purpose of people convinced that their nether regions have magical powers, Charles and the henchmen could take turns to go at it. And they had succeeded in setting something in motion, but it was not at all clear what.

Groups just go one way or another it seems. Personality. Geography. Necessity. After we got stuck in the snow in the first mountains, where Pressure Drop ate the duck, the snow turned to rain in the morning and the following day we were able to ride on towards the wide valley we'd glimpsed before the weather had closed in. Although it was a huge fucking relief not to be straining uphill all the time, when the valley came back in view it was slightly discouraging to see the wall of dark rock in the distance on its far side and know that we were going to have to go up and over it.

As we lost altitude the air seemed warmer and the trees got taller and more luxuriant, solid trunks, heavy branches and the open ground between them beginning to be carpeted in a thick layer of leaves, and then coming round a bend to a clearing we heard voices, laughter. There were wheelbarrows parked along the side of the road, enough tents for it to look like another ad for Decathlon, and in among the trees we could see flashes of colour, raincoats and welly boots moving rhythmically. The wheelbarrows were heaped full of chestnuts, so shiny and rich that they looked like glowing embers. An old boy in, genuinely, braces and a beret, came out from between the trees towards us, straightening up and rubbing his back, and he and Sarah talked. I could understand a certain amount by then, so I knew he thought we were mad, but he liked us all the same. He called the rest of them down to meet us.

They were a mixed bunch, maybe a dozen of them, they were from all over that area, but they now lived in one village when they weren't camping out to collect chestnuts, and what was really brilliant was that apart from the old boy, none of them knew how to do anything and they found that completely hilarious. Like, they had some snares for catching rabbits and every evening they would try to work out what kind of spot to look for to set them up in and then in the morning if there were no rabbits everyone would absolutely rip the piss out of whoever had set the snares, but thanking them at the same time because when there were rabbits, or sometimes a squirrel, in the evening they'd have to be skinned and gutted. And nobody knew how to do it, not even the old boy – he looked the part but he had only ever seen his mother or a neighbour, a hunter, skin rabbits. So they all took turns.

We stayed with them for more than a week, probably not quite two, going from one chestnut orchard to another, or whatever you'd call where you collect chestnuts, it's just like being in a tidy wood really, anyway, in that whole time nobody skinned a rabbit without going into a monologue that went something like the French equivalent of, 'Aagh, this is disgusting, I am a fucking white-goods delivery man for fuck's sake, aagh, fuck, there's blood all over my trousers, oh my god this is so fucking gross.'

And everyone who didn't have a knife in their hand would watch and fall about laughing. If you were far in the trees and you didn't know that food was in the offing, the hysteria was a good dinner bell. It got even better when the old boy said that now that we'd got the hang of getting the skin off in one bit, really we should be keeping the skins and tanning them. To do that you have to scrape all the last shreds of meat off the skin, tack it to a tree to dry out a bit and then rub the animal's brains all over it. I could just about handle gutting and skinning a rabbit by the time we left them, but cracking the little red-raw half-flayed skulls with their goggling eyeballs and stupid teeth still in them and then mushing brains mixed with skull fragments all over the skin with bits of it getting under your nails and up your sleeves and everything, well, that gave them some good monologues from me too.

Every now and then we'd shift camp, with much of the same hilarity at their own incompetence as they tried to wrestle pop-up tents back into their bags. Some would bring the wheelbarrows of chestnuts back to the village and come back later or the next day with them empty. Next year they hoped to have a horse. In fact, they said, they already had a horse but, cracking up laughing again, next year they hoped to know how to use a horse. Collecting chestnuts is back-breaking work, stomping to crush open the furry cases on the ground, then you have to bend or squat to pick the nuts up. All day long.

But then in the evening we'd make a huge fire. There was so much fallen wood that we made much bigger fires than we needed, just for the luxury of it. Also, the fires kept the wild boars away – they were pretty present, but you heard them more than you saw them, scruffling and squealing and crunching through discarded rabbit bones in the night. We had to guard the wheelbarrows full of chestnuts though. The one time I saw one clearly it came barrelling out of the undergrowth and went sprinting down the hill. It looked nothing like some fat curvy pig, it was solid and athletic, a dark trapezoid of pure muscle from its lifted snout to its outstretched hind trotters, sailing through the air between hummocks of uneven ground as it jinked between the trees and hurtled out of sight.

I shouted some kind of incoherent warning, more just a yell of surprise really, to the rest of the gang. Downhill there was a crash and screaming. The boar wasn't interested in us, but it had slammed into and overturned a wheelbarrow of chestnuts and bitten the leg of a woman who'd been standing nearby after its collision. It hadn't really gone after her, just nipped her to get her the hell out of its way, but just that had left her with a huge, heavily bleeding gouge in her calf. So when night fell we'd build up the fire to keep them away. When it died down we'd lift a piece of galvanised sheeting onto the embers. That moment, when it was suddenly much darker, made everyone quiet for an instant, and always made me think quite hard about how powerful something would have to be to make a wild boar flee for its life. Then we'd fill the runnels of the galvanised sheeting with chestnuts and laugh at somebody struggling to skin a rabbit while the smell of chestnuts roasting filled the air. Almost the best thing is that when they're roasted they're too hot to peel immediately, so you wrap them in a spare jumper and sit on them until they cool down enough to touch. You can even lie down on the leaf litter with them wedged, warm and rustling, in the spot in the small of your back where it aches.

Olives are easier on the back. A week or so after we'd left the chestnutters, we came down into the valley to a long, long bridge over the river in a town where everyone who was left had gone to live in a fourteenth-century castle that had been half blown-up during the Second World War. I know because I read the tourist-information panel while they went through our panniers. I hadn't had the time or the energy to swallow the goldfinger necklace, I just shoved it down into my bra when we arrived at the village, and luckily they weren't searching for anything that couldn't be eaten. We didn't have much to interest them in that department. They levied a bag of chestnuts and a couple of lighters and let us carry on over the bridge. They didn't care where we were going, they just didn't want us sticking around looking to be fed.

We crossed the flattened floodplains, all the while eyeing the mountains ahead, managing to salvage several boxes of cracked wheat, a random selection of tins and a highly prized tube of harissa from a couple of isolated houses we passed and came upon the tail end of the olive harvest. The olive gatherers didn't like us much, or they were wary anyway. They were going our way, working their way from one grove to the next. They tolerated that we worked with them for a while, combing the leaves of the silvery-green trees with little plastic rakes that looked and felt like beach toys – it reminded me of combing Sarah for nits at the *Château* – then hauling supermarket bags of fat olives towards a small trailer. Some of them clearly knew how to do the work, and there was a definite hierarchy between those with a practised gesture for flicking open the net underneath the trees and those who spilled olives onto the ground while they tried to tip them from the net into a shopping bag. The work was much easier than chestnuts, but they were a lot less fun. They laughed less. The chestnutters had given us a snare, and we got some grudging respect for catching the odd rabbit, but skinning them, the fleas and the smell especially, was much less bearable when it wasn't a gross-out comedy spectator sport. There was the same jumble of two-minute tents at the edge of the field, but no big fires, too much dry grass around, and there was no immediate food to cook together – olives off the tree are disgusting, one of those things that really make you wonder how people realised they were edible when they taste so awful. Maybe before plants got so domesticated everything tasted awful. At the end of the day, everyone huddled into small groups around little cooking fires and ate what they had.

  The ground around the tall, dead weeds was covered with little white snail shells and in the mornings the sun stencilled the shadows in frost and lit the far mountains in Day-Glo peach and salmon. It was a real effort to drag yourself out of the sleeping bag; the air was so cold that taking your arms out from inside it felt like dipping them into cold water, but by afternoon we were sometimes in t-shirts. And then, no matter the field, at the end of each day the sun would begin to set perfectly in line with the rows of olive trees. Their shadows would fall one onto the next like dominos so that the field alternated between alleys of bright-gold light and bands of blue-grey shadow in a way that made it look as if the ground was heaped and hollowed into banks and ditches. Walking across the illusion, with my brain telling me that a mound was rising to meet my foot when in fact the ground was completely flat, gave me lurching sea legs. As soon as the sun got low like that the cold would come at you fast and start settling into your bones.

Over several days we worked our way through a few fields with them, and then when the trailer was full we rolled it with them about ten kilometres to the oil mill, where an ancient rusted olive press had been relieved of its decorative duties, taken down off its little concrete pedestal beside the gates, and brought back into service. It was nothing like the same shape, but all the same it reminded me of *guarapera* presses at the roadside in Cuba when cane was being harvested, a queue of men, machetes hanging loosely from belts and hands, waiting for their turn with a cup. We all hung around, taking turns to twist the handle and watching the oil seep through and dribble out over the lip, spirit-level bubbles slowly rising up to the surface as it ran down into the waiting bidons. Liquid calories. They gave us a meanly small bottle of it to take with us when we carried on. We drank it, thick and peppery, a sip a day, until the bottle was no longer cloudily golden, just glass.

I was pretty big by then, like, seven months or so, more maybe – despite the five-year diary and the expedition watch that Sarah had got Adi to get for her before we left the Arches, if you don't know where you're counting from, no amount of accuracy is going to help. In spite of, in fact, because of, my size, Sarah was happy that I was working, moving. She'd worried about that at the *Château* in the long months of immobility, for me but especially for Leïla. And immobility turned out, for Leïla, to be the biggest danger of all.

Leïla got well and truly stuck. Her cervix wouldn't open. Sarah said that because other people had forced Leïla to open, her body was now keeping everything as tightly closed as possible. While Sarah was angry about what had been done to Leïla she was absolutely furious that it meant less would be learned; she had been holding on to the idea that all the other women would help with the birth and learn from it but after what had happened she felt that if she let anyone who'd had any part in it — which was everyone — near Leïla, whatever tiny progress had been made would clam shut again. She didn't even want the sound of their voices to reach Leïla's ears — she banned everybody from as much as coming along the corridor towards the door of our room, and everyone knew she was so angry that they didn't dare argue about it.

It took days for Sarah to get Leïla lined up inside for what was going to have to happen. Days with the curtains drawn in the daytime and a candle burning at night, coaching her through contractions that could go nowhere because she was pulled tight closed like the mouth of a drawstring bag, coaxing Leïla into letting herself be touched. Most of the time I couldn't do much. I stood in while Sarah catnapped, holding Leïla's hand and trying to reassure and comfort her in broken French, or sometimes even watching both of them sleep.

Pressure Drop kept sentinel outside the door, singing gently, speechifying quietly to himself, smoking. Months before, when I'd gone to get the rucksacks from the bikes, he'd told me how much weed I should take from his pillowcase; he measured the air with two hands, as if showing how much spaghetti you'd need for thirty people and solemnly intoned, '"All flesh is grass."' He'd eked himself out over a few joints a day since then, but knowing that the time was nigh, he wasn't rationing himself anymore and the smell of fresh smoke constantly filled the corridor like incense.

It felt like it would never end. If the waiting beforehand had been bad, the waiting during was fucking excruciating. We, more than anybody else, were dying for Leïla to give birth so that we could fucking leave. Now and then somebody would appear at the top of the stairs with some food or water, basically looking to exchange it for information. Sarah had told us not to tell them anything at all, not to tell them what was happening, whether it was going well or badly, not to tell them whether or not the baby had been born, not to tell them even whether Leïla was dead or alive. One time it was Charles, which was unusual because normally he'd have sent somebody else to gather information. He waited at the top of the stairs for me to come over to him. It wasn't an urgent translation need, he said he needed to warn us that there might be difficulties if we tried to leave. The 'if' and the 'tried' I hated. There was going to be no iffing and no trying. We were leaving, just as soon as Leïla's cervix got on board with her womb. I asked what kind of difficulties he was expecting and he said that the henchmen might try to stop us. More specifically, they might try to stop me.

Basically, Charles had told all the other men, or let them believe, it makes no difference, that I was pregnant with his baby. And when he told me he'd done that, he expected me to thank him for doing it, because he said he had done it to protect me because it stopped the other men bothering me.

Probably he expected me to finally suck him off for what an amazing favour he'd done me. I was so disgusted by the thought of him infesting me, as if it hadn't been bad enough spending months being crawled over by parasites, having them clambering through my hair and wriggling out through my rectum, multiplying in my vagina and hatching their next generations in whatever bit of my body suited them. But alongside that feeling of being overrun, there was the feeling of being inhabited. There was the something else growing inside me, stealing my breath and growing fat on my blood, but something I wanted to thrive. I felt certain that the bigger the baby got, the more surely it would draw Martin towards me, like a planet creating its own gravity. That Charles had dared to incite the henchmen to believe that the baby could have been his made me feel like I'd been invaded by all of them, as if they all had their hands up me clawing at my innards.

Clearly all that was made worse by the fact that at some point Charles had gotten to lord it over us. If he'd stuck to his side of the bargain about the antibiotics and they'd worked, I'm pretty certain I'd have been able to laugh about it afterwards. Even beforehand I got some good bleak amusement out of imagining how appalled Adi would be when he got well enough for me to tell him what I'd done for him – but that never happened. The henchmen had come back a couple of days later. There's no way of knowing if they actually looked for antibiotics at all, let alone how hard they looked, or whether if I'd agreed to actually fuck Charles would they have looked quicker and harder. They were empty-handed and it was too late anyway, so I'll never get to gross Adi out with an imitation of heavy breathing and a description of how one side of Charles's upper lip curled up towards his nose as he came.

I mean, even without that bubbling under, obviously it was a charged situation: Leïla was in the middle of a horribly long labour, Sarah was keeping a tight lid on herself in front of Leïla but she was right on the point of boiling over, Pressure Drop had stopped even trying to hide the utter contempt in which he held the whole situation and now I was spitting venom. Maybe Charles was actually scared of what might happen when we started walking out the door, but I felt like he was trying to turn my unborn baby into a changeling child of rape and then rob me of it.

I stormed down the corridor towards our room, spun, stormed back, hissed at him that he'd fucking better put them fucking straight because we were fucking leaving. He shrugged, said, 'You know, they will believe what they believe,' and turned to walk down the stairs. At that moment it was like some part of me stepped out of my own body – I could see it, another me, transparent, like the shadow of a stained-glass window thrown on the air in front of me – and my imagination shoved him hard in the back.

I turned on my heel and stormed back along the corridor to Pressure Drop, who was nodding slowly. 'You want to watch what that part of you does,' he said.

'What part?'

'The part that pushed him down the stairs.'

I was so angry I couldn't even talk to him about the fact that he could see my, what, my thoughts? My astral projection? My body of light? It didn't come up again until weeks, maybe by then months later, after we'd left the olive harvest behind us and headed up into the mountains. We were feeling like we could handle it, even though at the very first crossroads we started seeing signposts for a place called Die.

Pressure Drop really wasn't keen on that. He tried to talk himself out of his apprehensions, saying that there was a place called Kill outside Dublin and that they should be twin towns, but it definitely spooked him. We were only just keeping our ends together on whatever we could scavenge from abandoned larders and the slightly rancid walnuts that we sometimes stopped to pick up under trees by the side of the road. Sarah had a way of opening them, apparently unthinkingly, with the point of a knife – it was knacky enough that it made you think that whatever came out of the shell wasn't going to be gross, but it generally was.

We were settling in somewhere for the night, Sarah searching the cupboards, and I'd gone upstairs to look for any extra covers we could pile on top of our sleeping bags. I was on my way down with a first armful and Pressure Drop was on his way up to get the rest, and as he stopped to let me pass he said, 'No pushing now, eh?' I didn't really know how to ask him, like, how do you admit that you believe not just that you saw a visual manifestation of your own violent thought but that another person saw it too?

Later, after we'd eaten whatever we'd found and we were curled in nests of those covers, trying to convert an inadequate amount of food into an adequate amount of warmth, I said, 'So, earlier, on the stairs, Pressure Drop ...' and then just trailed off.

I suppose in a way I was expecting him to be blasé about having witnessed the out-of-body body of somebody else's experience, and an oration on the notion of being beside oneself with rage would have seemed par for the course, but when he said, 'What I don't get, Audaz, is if you saw something with your own eyes, why do you think it wasn't there?' I didn't really know what to answer.

'Audaz, women are scientists; your bodies are mad fucking laboratories, you were the creators and the guardians of the roots of all empirical knowledge: weaving, which is mathematics; pottery, which is chemistry; everything else, which is biology. That's why you and Sarah think it's fucking normal to cycle towards a place called Die, why you're able to say that the word is just a coincidence and doesn't mean anything in French, because you two are fucking scientists and women have always been scientists. Right Sarah?'

And Sarah, from her own cocoon, said, 'Well, in some ways, yes, I mean, definitely when women were burned as witches in the Middle Ages they weren't generally burned for having wild spiritual insights, they were burned for observation and deduction. Witch-hunters weren't worried about witches having strange beliefs, they were worried about them not having them – most of what doctors practised at that time was pretty strange, you know, leeches and humours and multi-coloured bile. If a woman who didn't believe in those things was able to cure people, they thought it must be because she'd had sex with the devil. Witches who cured people were supposed to be more dangerous than witches who, you know, went around souring milk and turning people into frogs.'

'There you go!' said Pressure Drop, 'So go fuck the devil then, if you're not going to be trusted either way, do you want to not be trusted for being some kind of cock-shy namby-pamby, or for being a scientist? If a scientist isn't going to believe the evidence of her own eyes then there's not much point in being one, is there?'

'That's not exactly what I meant, but he's got a point,' said Sarah, smiling.

'So what you're both saying,' I said, genuinely relatively surprised to find them singing from the same hymn sheet on this one, 'is that Pressure Drop and I can both believe that what we both saw was my spirit self pushing an utter prick down a flight of stairs?'

'No, no way,' said Pressure Drop, shaking his head emphatically, 'there's no reason I should believe it, I don't have to believe something just because I see it, I'm not a scientist, I'm a mystic.'

Sarah just laughed. I still didn't really know what to think about what I'd seen that day on the stairs — apart from that I'd seen what I saw and what I thought about it didn't seem to matter.

'I'm serious,' Pressure Drop went on, 'what it looks like is not important — it's what it means.' And he gave a long sigh, settled farther into his pile of blankets and was seemingly asleep in seconds.

It was clear that Jean-Luc was in Pressure Drop's camp, they very quickly bonded over the importance of seeing what isn't there. After *Chandeleur*, when the dust that was us had finally settled into the *Musée*, there was a whole lot of note comparing between us and Jean-Luc and Françoise, and anyone else who came by, which quite a few people did, because although the water of the river was fine the water from the spring behind the *Musée* was perfect, and sometimes you want to be sure. It's a world of minimal gains now — clean water is pretty high on the list.

Anyway, as well as the spring water, on Saturday mornings Jean-Luc and Françoise would go down into the town to the market, which wasn't a market anymore but a place to put the word out for things you needed and then swap what you had for them if and when they showed up. It was also where everything worth knowing was to be found out. We didn't have the energy to go anywhere at all for a while — I still don't — but our arrival was news that was worth slogging up the hill to the *Musée* for, and people came with all kinds of questions. I was too tired, and then also too protective of Leo, for any kind of people-facing, so I kept out of the way when there were visitors, but Sarah spoke to them.

It felt like we should've known more than they did, having started in a world capital and travelled the length of France, but actually they had a much clearer idea of what had happened to them as a group, a people. In a small town you can keep track of stuff much better. They estimated that about nine out of every ten people had died, as well as pretty much all pets and most of the livestock kept in sheds or pens or cages, like Julie's boyfriend had said. And they confirmed what we believed – the deaths were just deaths. Death is drama enough, what more do you need? There were no violent explosions of bodily fluids, no grotesque mutated faces, no zombies eating the arse-cheeks of bankers, just a cold, a fever, some difficulty breathing, then no more breathing, with everything that entails.

Jean-Luc and Françoise were certain they'd had it and survived, and you had to assume we all had by then, but maybe in an earlier form that gave us a bit of immunity or whatever. They'd had it just a few months before we found ourselves in the Arches, in the final waves where everything had come apart at the seams and getting it meant that you just gave up. Which, in fact, they had.

They got it at the same time, and when they did, Jean-Luc said he didn't want to face death frightened. By training, Jean-Luc was actually an ethno-botanist, that's what had taken him from Dakar to Oran. He didn't smoke himself, but he was wildly sympathetic to Pressure Drop's deep and meaningful relationship with a non-animal life form, and when he and Françoise got sick and didn't want to die in fear he knew what to look for. The two of them went out and wheezed themselves the length and breadth of whatever high pastures they could reach and came back with so many magic mushrooms that Françoise made mushroom soup. They shared a bottle of champagne, ate their soup, opened the bedroom windows wide, and lay down together holding hands.

And then, after a long, strange time, they got up again. Cold, because it was the middle of the night at the end of autumn in the mountains after all, but neither dead nor afraid. And what Jean-Luc reckoned was that they had survived because their lack of fear had allowed them to go through the doorway from the old world into the new without having to change their form. That whatever made them up, carbon-based life forms that they were, would have become part of the new world one way or another, but because they were unafraid they didn't have to die to pass the threshold. He said that from then on, he'd been sure that their place was woven into the new cosmology of the future, that's when he'd sent the postcard to Sarah, and not much more than a year later, here we were. Françoise said that we had all just been lucky. Pressure Drop, obviously, said that was the same thing.

Same thing or not, there were many times when we did not at all feel that lucky. When we had pulled away from Die, Pressure Drop thought that seeing the signs to death pointing in the opposite direction towards somewhere that was now behind us was a good omen, even though we were, once again, battling our way up into hills that showed no sign of not becoming mountains. A north wind came down and sliced through us. It was wild, it found any tiny chink between your outer layers and stabbed at your flesh – at one point I felt it coming in through the teeth of the closed zip on the fly of my trousers. Although the sky was clear that first day, the wind scoured every speck of warmth from it. Everything from then on was cold. You could feel it radiating from every solid object, waiting to suck the heat out of your flesh as soon as you touched it.

Nothing, not layers of clothing, not the soles of your shoes, not sleeping bags, not duvets and blankets piled on sleeping bags, nothing was enough insulation. Within a couple of days my toes and knuckles bulged with chilblains, red and shiny like fat cherries. They would suddenly split, cracks in their thin skin weeping blood and fluid uncontrollably until my socks were welded to my feet and my hands were stuck to the handlebars. I fantasised about the brained rabbit skins we'd left hanging over the chestnutters' fire, to the point that when my shivering kept me awake at night I'd mentally cut and stitch them into mittens, imagining and reimagining the pattern until they were perfect in my head.

In avoiding Die, we had come up onto a vast high plateau on roads that got worse and worse, and after erring for a time we got snowed into a tiny hamlet of half a dozen houses. There was almost no food, so little that rationing what there was seemed pointless and we ate whatever we found whenever we found it, standing up in dark kitchens, a spoon each, passing tins between us, not even bothering to cook things that could be swallowed without needing it. Pressure Drop dug through the snow to find some grass to try to bait the rabbit snare with, but the snare didn't work like that.

Two days after we'd eaten the last food – a jar of olives washed down with cornflour mixed with meltwater, not a meal you ever think you're going to feel nostalgic about, and yet – the wind shifted to the south and the sun came out. Over a couple of days the snow melted enough that we could see the contours of the roads and even at points the roads themselves. We knew we had to set off. Sarah called it '*le redoux de Noël*' and said that we had to make progress now because the cold would return before New Year's. It seemed impossible to know a thing like that, but over the next few days the weather was kind to us. We made it to the edge of the plateau, where it reared up in one last hurrah before shearing off into the below.

Looking back, we could see the way we'd come. It was all now completely free of snow except for one valley where the frost had kept hold. Everywhere else was khaki: grass and mud, leafless trees and pines stretched across the plateau, rolling up and down like a blanket, but there, in a crease, was a pocket of white. Despite its distance, the snow made everything in it look clear and precise, the road white between pale, speckled fields, a village, with bare-branched trees on the main square, the roofs of houses coated and, from the chimney of one of them, smoke was rising. It was as if everywhere around had shifted and it had stood still. Could whoever had lit that fire see up out of their valley? Did they know that all around the snow had melted? Or was it just like that always, through all seasons, an enchanted kingdom where Christmas and its softening never came, where the grip of winter never loosened, where warm coats never gave way to light jackets and eventually t-shirts, where nothing buzzed or bloomed or sang?

We were never going to find out. The road plunged off the plateau, hair-pinning towards endless-looking mountains and steep-edged shadow-filled valleys, so dark that they looked like holes in the world. The road was, once again, signposted towards Die. There was no turning off it, it lead us straight towards town. The week of hunger and exhaustion on the plateau had been a completely pointless attempt to skirt it. We stopped at a house on its edges, scavenged and ate a bastardised minestrone of tinned tomatoes, Chinese noodles and apple juice. I fell asleep wondering whether Sarah's sense of purpose or Pressure Drop's belief in the literal was more dangerous. We left early the next morning, without talking about the fact that we had nearly killed ourselves trying to avoid Die, and headed towards the next set of waiting mountains.

We were not prepared for the cold or the uncertainty or the confusion of mountains. The way the clouds would suddenly mass in huge dark piles around the peaks and then come tumbling down onto us, like a country above the country sending in its armies, burying us in rain and sleet before we could find shelter. It took so long and so much effort to dry stuff once we were wet that we became like scurrying mice at the sight of a cumulus. It is really tiring to be constantly confronted by your own tiny helplessness in the face of nature. We'd glimpse a building in the distance and, hoping that it was on our road and safe and within reach, we'd make for it as quickly as we could. Sometimes we'd make it. Sometimes we wouldn't.

We spent days wrapped in our sleeping bags trying to feed fires enough that they'd dry out our rain-soaked clothing. We spent nights in clothing that was finally dry, waiting for the heat of our bodies to drive the damp from our sleeping bags. Even if we hadn't been trying to cover ground, just staying warm and dry and fed – or whatever we'd by then come to accept as substitutes for those things – would have been a full-time job.

The days were short, and the sun was too feeble to bring any warmth into the cold, thin air. At night, even right beside a fire, we slept wearing our coats inside our sleeping bags and we were finally grateful for the coffin-like tents Adi had lumbered us with, because set up indoors they gave us an extra layer of insulation. Progress was horribly slow. The shortness of the days, the steepness of the slopes, our fear of the wolves and the weather and our total exhaustion drove our daily distance down pitilessly. Every time we gained height the squalls of rain turned to flurries of sleet and snow. None of us had the strength to scout ahead and although we knew roughly what direction we were going, the roads twisted and turned in and out through valleys and over passes in a way that too often left us freewheeling down the wrong direction, knowing that we'd have to find a way back up the other side of the mountains hemming us in. And the feeling that we had just about escaped dying of mountains once already had become something we carried with us, the weight of it adding to the cold and the wet and the wolves.

Jean-Luc told us later that we shouldn't have worried about the wolves, that the hills are so full of unguarded sheep and cattle that they have plenty of easy food. He said that what with land all over the world turning from farm and city back to wilderness, the Thames and the Venice lagoon would soon be freezing over again. So in five or six years' time when the winters bite hard and the flocks and herds have been whittled away and the cubs from the bumper years have all grown, that's when we'll have wolf problems. He also said that the wolf problems we'll have in five years will seem like nothing compared to the bear problems we'll have in ten. Even if we'd known about his theories back then, I doubt it would have made us any less scared. The sound of wolves never gets less scary as far as I can tell. I suppose it would be stupid if it did.

Every now and then we'd reach a turning point in our journey, and we'd be able to tell that the wolves had passed through before us because they shit at crossroads to make sure you know they've been there, like hikers building piles of stones. Their territory marking worked on us, and we attempted all kinds of divination on the shape and apparent directionality of their droppings to try to work out whether we were travelling towards or away from the pack. All we really decided we were sure of was that the older the turds were, the more apparent the fluffy fur of whatever they'd eaten was, which made those particular waymarkers both more reassuring and more unsettling.

What with having to stop to hide from the wolves and the weather, we were getting nowhere: less than ten, sometimes less than five kilometres in a day, not even counting those days we lost not moving at all. Our early gliding progress felt like a dream in comparison. We took warm clothing when we found it. By then there'd been a shift in what I'd consider wearing – fashion is now feral.

Françoise said that in the summer she was out in the vegetable gardens in just a straw hat, knickers and one of Jean-Luc's shirts tied around her neck by its arms like a cape, red- and blue-winged grasshoppers exploding out from under her feet like fireworks in the dry grass. I can totally imagine her, her wiry little arms and legs brown as the earth and her fried-egg tits flapping against her ribs. Though it's had to imagine it being that warm now. I spent most of January and February just wearing blankets and belts, anything that would cover up the gaps. We'll be better organised next winter – they weren't exactly expecting us.

Coming through the final stretch of mountains was so cold that I had to take my earrings out because the pain of their freezing metal through my earlobes was waking me up at night. Pressure Drop had acquired a huge pair of bright-yellow snowboarding trousers that made him look like a baggy-trousered acid casualty and Sarah's pride and joy was a hi-vis orange insulated jacket with '*Sécurité*' on the back. I took to wearing one jacket backwards and then another forwards on top of it, but I was so big by then that my belly pushed open a huge gap underneath it for the cold air to gush up through. I had no breath, my heart and lungs working overtime to push all the extra blood round and round my body. And, smaller or bigger, we were all getting worn through with the endless merry-go-round of cold, wet, hunger and tiredness and there never being enough of anything like warmth or food to get you out of the red zone.

At one point we arrived in a house with a big map pinned to the wall, a solid one, plastic, with all the peaks and valleys in relief. We could see where we were, and we were right on the edge of it. Almost everything the map showed was where we'd been. I stood there in front of it for ages, obsessively working out the path we'd taken to get there, all the wrong turns that had led us to that point, winding us up and down. We'd had no map, because it had been turned into a conceptual artwork by mice while we were stuck at the *Château*. Strange, the things you wish you'd kept. I sometimes think about what the mice did, deconstructing our road atlas and rebuilding it as a globe, the bright markings of motorways and towns made faint by having been tattered into scraps. The delicate sphere of shredded paper would never have survived the journey here, but I should've tried to keep it, it was definitely a sign. Still is a sign I suppose. But at that moment, we couldn't read it. We had been too busy shoving everything into panniers, reinflating tyres, smashing the pedals into our anklebones as we dragged the bikes out of where they'd been hidden.

It had been hard not to break down completely at leaving Adi's bike there on its own. He'd worked so hard to prepare it perfectly for the journey, ready its every bolt and bearing to lap up hundreds of kilometres, and now it was just going to sit there and seize up with dust while mice gnawed its saddle and brake cables. It seemed almost worse than having to leave his body buried on the hill.

Even though we didn't all get to leave, I couldn't shift my relief that even some of us had got away. After Leïla's baby was finally out, that was the worst waiting of all. It happened in the night, and even though I knew it was unrealistic to think that we could run as soon as the cord was cut, even though Sarah had specifically told me that we wouldn't, I just couldn't settle after. It was the beginning of autumn, but summer was leaching slowly from the land, the nights were still hot and everything seemed sticky. I fantasised about washing machines and showers.

The water situation was that there was a huge truck about three quarters full of office water-cooler bottles round the back that Charles had the keys to, and everybody was allocated a bottle every two weeks, so you had a bit less than a litre and a half per day. That's just about manageable as long as you don't have to wash or cook. Whoever was cooking, which the women took turns to do, had to use their water to cook with, so they'd end up having to drink cold pasta water supplemented with the liquid from whatever tinned foods they used to make up their ration. Which, fine, like, we also did that nearly the whole of the journey, even in the mountains where there wasn't really a need to because the one useful thing about mountains with their endless fucking crests and valleys is that they have water pouring down them all over the place, but by then drinking chickpea-water had become a habit.

But because the men never cooked – apart from barbecuing, which requires no water – they always had more water, so it just became another kind of leverage at the end of each fortnight. And it meant that the women drank whatever booze was on offer out of thirst, which just played into the whole fucking mess.

Nobody used the water for anything except drinking or cooking. All the women used wet-wipes to wash, except Sarah. She tried to teach me her minimal-water wash routine, but I never mastered it. It's technical – she can get her face and hands completely clean with just three palmfuls of water. Every once in a while they'd dump a load of chlorine into the indoor pool, and it was still pretty full so we fetched water from there for washing up, though we mostly ate off paper plates. Pretty much anything – apart from a pot or spoon or person – that got dirty enough to need washing was burnt or thrown into the pile of disgustingness in the trees.

There was something about the mixed-up-ness of their rubbish heap that made it worse, the used tampons on tin cans on shit on bed sheets on animal guts on empty bottles. The fact that it was all now irrecoverably designated as waste made it filthier. And it really stank. By August it stank badly enough that nobody even wanted to go into the trees towards it to throw new stuff onto it, so the heap started spilling outwards towards somewhere between the point where the stink got really bad and the distance the average person could hurl a turd without it hitting a tree. Which in turn meant that anyone who was trying to dump stuff properly generally ended up standing on something on their way in or out. And there were flies everywhere. It must've been a bumper year for flies, what with all kinds of stuff decomposing left, right and centre all over the world.

At the *Château* they patrolled the grounds in thick, loud swarms that, if they noticed you, formed a column above your head and then followed you everywhere like a maddening noisy shadow until you managed to trick them by slipping indoors and slamming the door behind you. Done right, you'd be left with just a few, and they'd head off disappointedly towards the windows and slowly batter themselves to death against the glass.

As summer had worn on the countryside around, which, when we arrived, had been a vivid, juicy green, had started to look worn out – the grass yellow and the leaves of the trees dusty. Several times the sky filled with bulging purple clouds in the late afternoon, but every time the lightning would strike elsewhere and the heavy veils of dark rain sweep some other bit of the countryside. Until finally it was our turn.

Even when you've been waiting for it for weeks, when a storm breaks right over your head it comes as a proper surprise all the same. We were up in our room when it happened. The first crack of thunder was so head-splitting that it felt like the place had been cracked in two and the flash of light tinged the sky pink in its intensity. As soon as the rain came battering down on the roof, Pressure Drop was up and stripping to his pants. He took a still-wrapped bar of soap and a towel from the pile that had sat untouched for months in the bathroom, like a fluffy monument to the past, pulled his boots on and strode towards the door.

As he opened it, he said, 'Either get your kits off or get some buckets, I'm going for a shower.'

Sarah and I looked at each other; she shook her head and scrabbled for her raincoat while I stripped and grabbed another towel. We followed Pressure Drop as he marched down the stairs to the front door. Handing his towel to Sarah, who tucked it under her coat, he went to the corner of the building and expertly kicked the bottom section of drainpipe out of place so the bit of the pipe spun off across the gravel, and the water now gushed out somewhere above his head. He left his boots neatly on a windowsill, then roared as he stepped in under the water – for all it being summer and all, rain is only ever as warm as the sky it falls from.

I watched Pressure Drop while I huddled under the eaves, trying not to dread the chill of it as I watched sheets of rain batter the trees at the edges of the grounds and flatten the long grasses in waves. When Pressure Drop got out to soap his body I tucked my trainers in beside his boots and braced myself. It was pretty fucking cold, and just sluicing out of the drainpipe like a never-emptying bucket pouring onto your head. I whooped, my whole body tensed up and, for the first time, I felt Leo flip inside me. It's funny, before he was born I imagined all his actions as fully voluntary, that he was doing all the things he was doing because he was reacting consciously to the world around him, to sound and light and movement. That he was choosing to respond. Then when he was born I realised that really, whatever he was doing, he was just doing it because he was a baby. Like, if he's staring intently up at the top corner of the room as if he's seen something extraordinary there, it's probably just because he can't remember how to move his head and eyes to look at something different, or if he's making all kinds of expressive faces as if he's trying to communicate something to me, he's probably just the puppet of his gas-producing gut microbes. He doesn't really have any thoughts about anything yet, just experiences.

The thing that scared me most about him being born was that once he was out he wouldn't like me. Like, he would be squeezed out through the birth canal, take his first breath, get latched on and then eye me from the tit and think, 'Oh dear.' And now here he is, so small and pink and helpless and it's not that I think he likes me, it's just that I realised it doesn't matter: even if he hated me, I'd still look after him. I'll still look after him even if I hate him. That's just how it is.

When we were at the olives, at one point a woman came over to our campfire as night was settling in. She wanted to talk to us, to me. She crouched down beside us. Sarah tried to give her something to sit on, but she stayed crouched, as if sitting down would rob what she was saying of some of its urgency. She spoke fast, first in French, telling Sarah to translate, then again in broken English, part-parroting what Sarah had said. I could understand a lot of French by then, but she wanted Sarah to translate all the same. She rocked on the balls of her feet, sometimes steadying herself with the spread fingers of a hand on the ground in front of her. Her eyes filled and emptied and filled and emptied as she spoke. She'd had three daughters, she said, seven, five and three years old, and they were dead now, and they died just after she'd discovered she loved them.

After the first was born she'd sat with friends while they talked about how much hard work little babies were, and there was always one who'd say, 'But it is amazing being a mum,' and everyone would agree. It was only after her second was born that she had the courage to ask one of them, 'Which bit? Which bit is the amazing bit?'

With the third one she said she couldn't think anymore, her whole life just became like the riddle where you have to bring a dog and a chicken and a sack of grain across the river in a boat. She was a good mum, did all the things a loving parent would – her daughters were always fed, always warm, their grazed knees always kissed, their covers always tucked in. But inside, she was sure that she was going through the motions. Faking it, when even awful people loved their children. And then one night the littlest called for her in the dark to take her to the toilet, and as they made their way down the moonlit corridor, the little warm hand and the shoulder bumping her thigh because of the stiff-legged stumble of sleep-locked knees, suddenly it happened. Love poured into her like a bottle being filled up with hot water.

'If you think you don't love your baby,' she said, 'just wait. You love him, maybe you just don't feel it yet, but you love him.'

Sarah translated it all, uneasily but she translated it, the woman repeating fragments like echoes, staring at me, desperate to transmit.

'You understand?' she asked, and I nodded. But I didn't, not then.

I understand now though. And maybe one day years from now I'll take him for a wobbly walk to the toilet and feel myself fill up with something more recognisable as love, but for now, even though he's outside me, I'm just the process by which the world is converted into food and warmth and shelter for him. And obviously that first time at the *Château* under a spout of cold rainwater he was, in a way, reacting to the world, to his world, but at the time I thought he was doing it on purpose.

I started laughing, partly because I was a bit breathless with the cold but also at the idea of him, imagining him shivering indignantly at it, and I shouted over to Sarah, 'It's moving! I felt the baby moving in the rain!'

And Pressure Drop, who at that moment was soaping his balls inside his pants, pulled his hands out, spread his arms wide and exclaimed, as soapsuds dripped from his fingers, '"Let the waters teem with living creatures!"' He grinned at us, and then went back to soaping his balls.

By that time, we had an audience, but the rain kept them in the doorway. Pressure Drop handed me the soap — fortunately I've always been able to accept the idea of soap as self-cleaning — and we swapped places so that he could rinse mountains of bubbles out of his dreads and I could attempt to wash inside my pants while ignoring the audience, keeping my back to them and then turning around to face them to wash my arse. Once we were both rinsed down, Sarah handed us the towels that she'd kept huddled under her coat, and we picked up our shoes and walked, as self-possessedly as it's possible to walk barefoot across gravel almost naked in the pouring rain, towards the waiting crowd.

When Charles opened with, 'You will have to put the pipe back you know,' I knew we'd won something important. He'd made himself sound like the host of a party who suddenly gets worried about the surface of a table and wants everybody to wipe up their drink rings. In a snap he'd gone from being king of the *Château* to its caretaker.

Pressure Drop just looked at him and smiled and nodded and said, 'Yeah, don't worry, we'll get around to it,' clearly putting it on the long finger and leaving no doubt as to which finger that was.

Charles saw what he'd done, and tried to get around it by saying, 'But, maybe we will use it first.'

Pressure Drop didn't miss a trick, and instead of taking it as an instruction, he made it sound like Charles was asking permission, and said, 'Yeah, go ahead,' and waved his arm theatrically towards it in invitation.

And that was just perfect, because normally everything, the food, the ammunition, the walls, the doors, the women, the water, everything was Charles's one way or another, but now something was Pressure Drop's and, even better, he was being magnanimous about it. Charles had no choice but to disengage from us completely, make space in the doorway so we could pass, and start a mini ruckus with the henchmen about pushing the women out into the rain.

We walked back up to our room with Pressure Drop grinning from ear to ear and when we got up there we all fell about laughing and relieved, and for the first time let out a massive collective chorus about how much we fucking hated it there and even Sarah admitted that if she'd known how awful it was going to be she'd never have made us stay and me and Pressure Drop told her that if we'd known we'd never have fucking let her and we all agreed that the sooner that Leïla and her baby got a move on out, the better it would be.

Although I'm pretty sure he'd been putting the word about already, I think it was probably at that point that Charles really doubled down on the idea that he was the cause of my pregnancy. I guess having lost ownership of one pipeline he laid claim to another.

Anyway, the day of the thunderstorm was the beginning of the end. In the weeks afterwards, the days were full of insects, the ever-present swarms of flies had been joined by punch-drunk wasps that seemed just as angry with each other as they were with us, and in the mornings the waist-high grass of the one-time lawns foamed with daddy-long-legs. We held ourselves in readiness.

Even before Sarah gave us the word to keep our rucksacks packed, I'd started to keep an eye on where all my stuff was around the room. A couple of the women warned Sarah that they'd heard that it was going to be difficult for us to leave.

I don't know if Charles had seen the long game in which Sarah's knowledge became a valuable commodity, or he didn't want us to set a precedent by walking out of there unchallenged, or he was just trying to reset the power balance after the thunderstorm, maybe all of those things. Sarah took it seriously enough to tell us anyway, which she didn't do with every bit of gossip that went around the place. Though if she heard about it before I did, she didn't pass on the rumour that Charles was spreading about me.

It is one of her super-powers, not saying stuff; she has a real talent for it. The whole lead-up to the crossing to France and the whole way across on the boat she managed to say nothing at all about my pregnancy or the deal she'd struck with Julie and Martin. At the *Château* she said nothing until the very end about how much she hated it. Coming up to Easter here, she said nothing about what she wanted from me.

There was a certain amount of discussion about when Easter would be. Easter was marked in Sarah's diary, so you'd think that would've settled it, but Jean-Luc said nobody else had one or knew how to calculate an imaginary moon into existence, and so it had to be based on a moon that people could actually see. I didn't know Easter was based on a moon, never mind an imaginary one but apparently it used to be. Our Easter, anyway, was to be the day after the next actual full moon, because if an imaginary moon waxes in the sky and nobody's mind's eye can see it, does it really light the night?

Françoise started saving eggs, putting them into a huge mixing bowl on the kitchen counter, and when it was half full Jean-Luc went into town to tell people they were invited. He had to tell most people what date it was that very day as well as what date Easter would be. Even with Sarah's diary on our side, it's hard to feel the circle of the year with so much change and chaos circling us. I can't really get my head around the fact that around a year ago I had been in the Arches listening to Joy and Trevor argue and searching the glory hole for Adi's essentials. Anyway, Jean-Luc put the word out that Easter was in a week.

A couple of days later it snowed a little in the night, a scattering, just enough to cover the ground. The sun came up over the snowy mountains like the flaming hope it is and, before it had climbed much higher than the peaks, a small group of armed men showed up at the door.

Pressure Drop and Sarah and I were scared shitless, but Françoise went straight over to let them in. They were from town and they'd come to invite Jean-Luc and, by extension, Pressure Drop, to come hunting with them, so that Easter would be a proper feast. The dusting of fresh snow meant that they'd be easily able to track something, and by now it was unlikely that any more would fall, they said. Françoise was not keen, but there was no way the invitation was going to be turned down. I remember seeing my father like that when a group of men from the town came to get him to go with them to the next town to do something, I can't remember what, set up a stage for a concert maybe, or mark the roads for a bicycle race. You could see the excitement, like a bunch of kids had called over to see if he could come out and play. Jean-Luc was just the same. Pressure Drop too. Also, he's pretty much come round to the idea of eating animals here, he's slid the scale, past the fish at Fairlight, to the *Château*, where he resisted it completely, via the blessed duck in the mountains and the chestnutters, where he became okay with catching and eating a bit of the odd rabbit, to now where he was gleefully getting ready to go out and shoot something. I'm sure he'd explain the change in more complex terms, but I think he's just doing what feels right when it feels right.

He and Jean-Luc gathered together rucksacks, food and sleeping bags and, Françoise's eyebrows notwithstanding, a bottle of hard alcohol that'd had a handful of berries and herbs sunk into it months beforehand. They all set off, the gang of them, feet crunching in the thin layer of fresh snow, trying to act serious about the business in hand, but as soon as they'd turned their backs on us in the doorway it was like they forgot we existed and they were nudging each other in the ribs and grinning. Their plan was to hike up to some shepherd's hut at the top of the valley, camp in there, and then come back the next day having shot something large and edible.

Françoise was on edge from the moment they were out of sight, anxious they'd shoot each other. The place felt very different with the two of them gone. She and Sarah threw themselves into some final bits of readying the place. It wasn't the house they were getting ready, but the *Musée*. Bit by bit we'd all been emptying out the exhibition galleries, pushing display cases out of the way, painting over wall displays of geological epochs, dismantling the mini-aquaria in a room that had held fish and aquatic insects and even two living pulsing nautiluses, the shells of which now sat on the mantlepiece in the house. All this would become Sarah's school. When the spring settled in for sure we'd go and get chairs and desks and beds and bedding from empty houses in the town. Sarah and Françoise wanted it feeling real and ready to welcome its new purpose so that the people who came would see.

Easter fell a few days after Jean-Luc, Pressure Drop and the armed men had come back down the mountain with a small sheep slung from a pole. It was a breezy sunny day that followed a night so bright you could see in colour. People started to arrive up the hill in the late morning. I was out and about with Leo in the sling, hanging up some laundry (Easter or not, good drying weather is good drying weather) and when I came back in Françoise got me at the door, saying that she'd help me with Leo while I washed up. I thought she meant dishes but she meant me – I was on the job. We went to my room, where she rewound the fabric around me and encouraged me to put on a cleaner top. She jiggled Leo while I changed and then, to my amazement, handed me a pot of Dior face cream and a tinted lip balm. Leo and I were the poster people for Sarah's project, the living, breathing proof that it was fit for purpose, and so, bright and shiny, we went to meet our public.

'They're all excited to meet you both,' said Françoise as she opened the kitchen door.

About a dozen women, maybe more, were sitting and standing around the table, which was laden with a mound of hard-boiled eggs and an even bigger mound of broad beans. Jean-Luc had just come in with a colander full of bright-pink radishes, still dripping from being rinsed outside in the spring, and while he looked for something to wipe up the water with, everyone was cooing over them and exclaiming about *salade printanière*. But Leo stole his glory. Jean-Luc didn't mind – he backed to the sidelines, perhaps knowing he'd get it back when they came outside and saw the whole sheep that he and Pressure Drop had been spit-roasting over a fire they'd built before breakfast. Obviously that's where all the men were, the world is still the world.

I was pretty freaked out to be honest, but Leo allowed himself to be passed around and have the chubbiness of his cheeks, the smallness of his hands, the softness of his skin and the alertness of his eyes marvelled over. It was really only then, in the repeating, the saying over and over of '*Leo, il s'appelle Leo*', and them all repeating it back to me, back to him, that his name finally stuck. Hearing strangers call him by it made him seem more like somebody in particular, not just a somebody.

Although I hadn't talked about it, I'd worked out before he was born that I'd call him Leo. I wanted to call him after the stars, because I knew Martin would see them too and if I honoured them by naming my child after them, maybe they'd tell him about his son. If he'd been a girl, he'd have been Cassiopeia, but Leo is really the only constellation you can name your boy after. Cancer and Virgo are obviously out, and Sagittarius or Capricorn are a bit much. I did consider both Orion and Sirius, but Leo won early. It travels well, and plus, golden and impervious are not bad baggage, may life's arrows bounce off him.

A few of the women around the table had brought little gifts for him and he came back to me wearing a pair of sheepskin booties, an amber necklace and a soft red woollen hat. It was a mark of their feelings for Jean-Luc and Françoise really, extended to Leo by virtue of us being under their roof.

Some of the women didn't want to hold him. At first I thought maybe they'd lost children themselves, but afterwards I thought, like, I was never into babies, the only reason I can stand Leo is because he's mine. Although when he finally got hungry there was a grand and unanimous chorus of '*Que c'est beau*' at the sight of him latching on.

While Leo fed, their hands reached and danced, in and across the table, peeling and podding, gathering and dumping bundles of downy pods and swishing handfuls of the translucent jade-green skins of the little broad beans and the crumpled eggshells off the edge and into a bucket for *Les Poules de la Mort*; eggshells to eggshells, dust to dust.

Every now and then one of them would let her hands go quiet and look over and smile. Seeing Leo, seeing us both in their eyes, made me wish intensely that Martin could see us too. Not even that he could be there, that was too much, just that the image of us could travel to him, arriving in his mind to fill him with joy and pride and love at our realness and aliveness. Because that's what was making the women smile at us: the simple fact that we existed.

Their chatter was like the waterfall. I could understand a lot of French by then, but even now at times it all just becomes white noise. Little early lettuce leaves were swished in a basin of water, somebody set a pot to boil, a battalion of shining knives sliced and chopped. When we were crossing to France on *Seabird*, the noises were like that, there was always something clinking or swooshing or tocking, gently and rhythmically. By the time we got to Fort Mahon it was too late to try to make other choices. We'd been gone too long, Julie was alone and would be worried sick, and although we had more food and water on the bikes, we all had it in our heads that we weren't touching it until we got to the other side, and we'd eaten all the stuff we'd packed in the boat's kitchen. So, having finally understood why Martin had been so dead against it – i.e. it was just a long stretch of sand with the tide dragging and sucking and crashing breakers, no pier, no jetty, nowhere at all to land a boat – we decided that I had to swim to the shore to reach a dinghy we could see on the beach. Martin reckoned that with the binoculars he could see that there were oars in it.

I made a brave face of it, stripped most of my clothes off and climbed down the ladder that flipped out to hang down the back of the boat. It was cold, obviously, but I played it tough. With so much resting on me I wasn't going to fail us all on something as pathetic as, 'Ooh it's a bit chilly.'

Sarah asked, 'Are you sure?'

I trod water, gave them a thumbs up and struck out. Despite the swell heading in towards the shore, the tide was still going out and the current dragged me farther and farther down the beach. I tried not to panic about it, telling myself that it was the same number of strokes even if they took me sideways, and that it would take far less energy to walk back up the beach when I was out of the water than it would to fight against the current, but as I got colder and the boat got farther away and the shore didn't seem to get any closer it got harder to believe. I started seeing things moving below me, big dark shadows in the churned-up water, which, if I'd had goggles, would surely have revealed themselves as rock or weed, but I didn't have goggles so they remained malign presences, unknown and unknowable eruptions of my unconscious, millions of years of evolution telling me I was cold and tired and should get the fuck out of the water.

Finally I twanged through an invisible barrier in the sea. The breakers rolling in towards the shore gained the upper hand over the longshore drift and, for the final fifty metres or so, dragged me two strokes forwards one stroke back until, head just about held out of the foam, I felt sand under my knees. I stood, and immediately wanted to fall back to all fours. I took a few shaky steps to get myself fully out of the reach of the water. The sand looked damp and uninviting and I fantasised about warm towels as I turned to look back at the boat. The rest of them were waving to me and I could just about hear them cheering in encouragement, and that's when I realised what had been hard to judge when looking at the empty beach from the boat – it was actually really fucking far away.

I started to jog back up the beach towards the dinghy but slowed to a plod within a few steps. My feet felt like they had been moulded in plasticine and stuck to my ankles and the soft sand sucked the last of the energy out of my legs. My lungs scratched on the shreds of saltwater they'd drawn in. The wind was cold and the grey sky showed no sign of letting a crack of sunlight through. I got to the dinghy. There was still nobody in sight and Martin had been right about the oars. It was beached well above the high-water mark. I could feel a little light-headedness beginning to seep up through me. I began to drag the dinghy to the water. It was fibreglass, but even a light dinghy is pretty heavy, and the tide was almost completely out so the distance was basically as long as it could possibly be. I got it into the water, pushed past the shallows and started trying to row it beyond the breakers.

The skin on my hands was pale and soft from being in the sea and the rowing shredded it off, leaving raw, oozing patches. It was just when I'd managed to battle beyond the white water that the cold hit me. That's what Martin had warned me about – you're okay when you're swimming, because your body draws all your blood towards your vital organs, but then once you get out of the water it sends the blood back out to your frozen extremities and every heartbeat pumps all the cold from them back into your core. And suddenly you're fucked. My teeth started chattering uncontrollably and my white and grip-less hands kept being shaken off the oars by my shivering. The edges of everything rippled and vibrated and dark-bright spots pulsed through my field of vision like jellyfish. Whenever I turned my head to see where the boat was it seemed to be the same distance from the shore but farther away from me because I was being dragged down the coast by the same longshore drift that had fucked my shit up so royally while I was swimming.

I kept rowing, the strokes becoming more ineffectual and any real progress seeming less likely. And then suddenly the water went slack, as if a kraken that had been suckered to the base of the boat and dragging it down the shore had just let go. I rowed with everything I had left. My fingers and toes were still white and lifeless, but my arms and back were lit up with pain and my ears were ringing like fire alarms. I don't remember it really, but at one point I heard Martin shouting at me and I had a rope thrown at my hands but it took me a long time to tie it to the boat because I'd forgotten how to make a knot and my hands didn't work anymore, and then they were all dragging me up the ladder.

And what Sarah had been planning on reaching when she pulled me up that ladder all those months ago was suddenly all around me at Easter. It was sleeping on my chest, was turning a spit and tending a fire surrounded by laughter, was gathered around a table to say my baby's name, was carefully assembling six huge platters of salad, quartered eggs rayed out with their yolks glowing, scattered with the pink, white and green confetti of the radishes and beans. One thing leads to another, right? I mean, I'm being flippant, but also I'm being deadly serious.

The men had set up trestle tables out on the sheltered side of the *Musée* and with Leo tucked in the sling I helped the women set out jugs of water and glasses, cutlery and plates. People pulled bottles of wine from their backpacks and clonked them with checkmate certainty among the jugs. Jean-Luc and Françoise had said that everyone who could should bring bread, and all kinds of loaves appeared like stepping stones down the length of the tables: a stack of speckled flatbreads, a lonely little golden roll, a rugged, wholemeal lump, a bubbly, white clutch of steamed buns, a huge dark round like a turtle's carapace, criss-crossed with striations and dusted with flour. Somebody, to much delight, produced a plateful of misshapen little bright-white goat's cheeses, fresh and soft and tasting of woodsmoke, which threw me straight back to the roadside yoghurt stands of my childhood.

We brought out the beautiful salads, and Jean-Luc and Pressure Drop lifted the roasted sheep onto the table, thunking it down onto the wooden board they'd prepared for it in a way that rattled glasses and sent arms reaching to steady bottles, and then suddenly everyone went still. All we wanted to do was look, because it seemed unbelievable that such a moment was possible.

You could see that some people were about to cry and nobody knew what to do or say. Jean-Luc looked at Sarah, but she shook her head, it was too much for her. And then Pressure Drop rose to the occasion.

Taking a step back from the table he looked around him, locking eyes with me for a moment, turned his palms forwards and in his most sonorous voice said: 'They shall call for the nobles of the kingdom, but no kingdom nor nobles shall there be, and all her princes shall be nothing. Thorns shall come up in the palaces, nettles and brambles in the fortresses, and it shall be a habitation of dragons, and a court for screech-owls. The wild beasts shall meet, and the wild goat shall cry to his fellow, the night creatures will lie down and find themselves a place to rest. There shall the great owl make her nest, and lay, and hatch, and gather her young under her shadow, there the vultures shall also be gathered, each one with her mate. None shall fail, and none shall want for another, for He has gathered them, He cast the lot for them, and His hand divided it between them: they shall possess it for ever, from generation to generation they shall dwell therein.'

When he'd finished, all eyes, including Pressure Drop's, turned to Jean-Luc, who was gently thumbing the blade of the carving knife as he listened.

When he saw Pressure Drop looking at him he looked around at all the faces turned towards him and, with slight secular unease, paraphrased, '*Le grand-duc a choisi cet endroit pour faire son nid, et y couvera ses oeufs. Chacun y trouvera ses semblables. Personne n'échouera. Personne ne sera abandonné. Ici sera à jamais chez nous, nous y habiterons de générations en générations.*'

He lifted the knife and began to carve the meat and there was great cheering and a rattle of cutlery and hubbub of voices and everyone began to serve themselves, echoing *bon appétits* across the table to one another as if they were night birds themselves.

After he'd helped Jean-Luc serve the meat, Pressure Drop came with his plate and sat down beside me, stretching his legs far in under the table, and I remembered him at that first meal in the Arches a year ago. It felt so far away that I couldn't believe I was there, and maybe I wasn't, not the me I am now anyway.

Maybe it's not that we were in all those places and moments, it's that all those moments and places are in us. The past is what we carry forwards with us. Maybe the future is already in there too, we just wait to bring it out into the world.

I'm not saying that we should just adopt the princess position and sit with our hands under our chins until it arrives, but waiting is part of it. Until it arrives, we wait to see what is coming. Wait for the word to spread. Wait for a woman to arrive at the foot of the hill with a swollen belly. Wait for Leo to wake, to sleep, to cry, to feed, to shit. Wait for spring, wait for summer. Wait for a tall figure in a battered oilskin, his hair still crusted with salt, to appear on the horizon.

In my mind's eye, he comes as a giant. I see him far in the distance, his head high above the tops of the trees, his hands brushing their leafy crowns as he makes his way up the valley to where we're perched on the hillside. I will have known he's coming by the flights of birds and the screeching of foxes in the night, so I'll be standing at the wall of the belvedere watching, waiting for his head to turn towards me, for his eyes to snag into me like fish hooks. He'll cross the wide river below, one leap to clear the main deep channel, the rest of it barely wetting his ankles as he steps between the braided streams from one bar of gravel to the next. He'll take the winding path up the hill to where I'm standing with Leo in my arms and the sun pouring out from behind us, me looking like the Virgin Mary and Oshun rolled into one. On the way up the hill he'll gradually become human-sized again, and then he'll be standing in front of me, speechless with the recognition of his own destiny. Or, you know, something like that.

I get that it's dangerous to have baked all these expectations of myself and Leo and the world into his coming, but I'm beyond the point where I can insert his arrival into the actuality of my life. I can't imagine it alongside the dark haloes around my eyes, the never-healing splits and sores at the corners of my mouth, the sagging, translucent skin of my stomach and the constant blinding tiredness that accompanies the slow absorption into every bit of me of the certainty that I will never belong to myself ever again.

I don't mean that in a bad way, just that it's hard. I mean, obviously a bunch of it is bad: the tiredness is bad, the aching tits is bad, the leaking blood for weeks and weeks is bad, the going another and another round long after the adrenaline has stopped carrying you through is bad. But all that isn't really hard, what's actually hard is knowing your place, re-seeing your part in the grand scheme of things as that tiny, tiny link in a long, long chain that goes all the way back to mitochondrial Eve and then just keeps going, tiny link after tiny link, right the way to the Last Universal Common Ancestor, somewhere in the Ediacara Hills in southern Australia, and then, if you knew how to imagine it, on and on beyond that through spaces too vertiginously vast to imagine until eventually you reach sub-atomic ylem. And then what?

The night after Leo was born, I had a vision. I didn't used to be one for having visions, hallucinations with the right help, but not visions. He was asleep on my chest. If I held my breath, I could feel him breathing. I was so shot-up with hormones that my mind was spinning, tired eyes pulsing colour-bursts in the infinite darkness that is the nights here. The glow of the fire had gone out, though you could still feel its warmth radiating from the stones of the fireplace. And suddenly, it came to me. There, in the blackness, I could feel myself standing in the sky, and stretching out behind me, stretching out for what seemed like forever, was a vast line of figures, outlined in specks of light as if they'd emerged from a warm sea and the phosphorescence was still clinging to their bodies. And they were the person who'd looked after their child, and that child had grown and looked after their child, and that child had grown and looked after their child, and that child had grown and looked after their child and so on and so on and so on and so on and so on hundreds of thousands of times from the dawn of humanity to where I stood in line. And in front of me was Leo.

I think that before I made a new link on the chain I wasn't joined to it, I was just floating nearby with it swirling around and filling up everything I could see. Then, when I made a new link, I latched on to the chain myself, and that's when I became aware of the pitiless void all around, so much cold darkness that it's terrifying to think about it. Those invisible forces of not existing could so easily swallow us up without it even being not the natural order of things.

One of the things that made the crossing to France complicated, and this was clear even before we left, was that there were so many invisible and incomprehensible forces at work, or, more exactly, there were forces at work that were not visible and comprehensible to everybody. Pressure Drop was the avatar of the mystical forces of words, insisting on Fort Mahon despite Martin trying several times with increasing exasperation to tell him that there was no landing place there, that the currents in the river mouth made it unpredictable and that it was much farther that we needed to sail. Pressure Drop was having none of it, he just said that there were no boats and no harbour at Fairlight and all the same in choosing there we'd found somebody to take us across. When Martin said that the fact that we'd bumped into him on a wet morning in late spring was not proof that choosing somewhere with a placename that appealed to you was a valid strategy for planning a long and complex journey, Pressure Drop countered that it was definitive proof of exactly that. In the end Martin agreed to go to Fort Mahon and see, because he was sure that we'd get there and Pressure Drop would give in and let him take us somewhere else, and Pressure Drop accepted the plan because he was sure that we'd get there and He would provide.

The forces that Martin could see, the winds and tides and currents, were equally invisible to the rest of us. He pored over navigational charts that listed tidal races and timetables of ebb and flow, but it was no good. Several times we got stuck, as motionless as if we'd run aground on a sandbank, while the wind and the sea tried to push and pull us in opposite directions. You could feel the boat straining, hear it in the ropes and the sails, the water streaming past the bows, but the land in the distance showed we were going nowhere. When it happened at night he got more and more anxious because with the dead-reckoning so out of whack he had no idea where we were. He'd be up for hours through the darkness, listening for breakers on the shore. We tried to help, or to at least be sympathetic, but we didn't even really understand what we were being sympathetic about.

But the invisible force that probably imperilled the crossing the most was love. It was invisible to me anyway – but when I think back, I'm certain that Sarah and Pressure Drop and even Adi could see it. Sarah must have already known, or at the very least strongly suspected, that I was pregnant. I haven't asked if she knew because I don't want to hear the answer. She must've been wondering all the time if I was about to suddenly realise it and, if I did, whether I'd abandon the mission and sail back with Martin to live in Fairlight instead of throwing my lot in with them. Which, I don't know, a midstream volte-face is a complex manoeuvre, but these are complex times. And how would anyone have handled it if I'd not made it to the shore or not made it back to the boat? Could she have told Martin of all this that wouldn't have been? How would Pressure Drop have lived with his push for Fort Mahon? It must have been in their minds.

When they got me back into the boat, Martin gave my back a rub and squeezed my shoulder as he went past, 'Keep up the shivering,' he said, 'it's when you come out and you're not shivering that it's dangerous.' That was the only time we ever touched in public, and the shockwaves it sent out must've nearly knocked the rest of them overboard, in fact maybe that's what did for Adi. But buffeted and battered by gusts of emotion or not, they carried on with the job in hand, loading the dinghy, living inside our love just as much as we were living inside the weather. And Martin and I didn't understand the far-reaching power of our love any more than the weather understands the effect of blowing a boat off course.

When the moment came to separate, we were in the dinghy and he was in the boat. Pressure Drop untied the knot and Martin pulled in the rope.

'Right then,' he said, 'Safe journey.'

'Safe journey,' Pressure Drop echoed.

And that was it, the goodbye moment — we were in the dinghy and he was in the boat and the rope was no longer holding us together. And what I should've done was leap out of the dinghy and scramble back up onto the boat and throw my arms around his neck and kiss him passionately while the music swelled and the world spun out of view around us. But what I actually did was inhale and nod. Like, for fuck's sake. I would love to be able to imagine that it was because I was hopped up on hypothermia or because I was being stoical about the seriousness of continuing my mission to become Sarah's right-hand woman in the life-saving work of getting small people out of bigger people, but it wasn't any of that. What it actually was, was I was trying to act cool. What fucking earthly use is that? Basically I passed up the chance, and who knows when or even whether that chance will come again, to have a real moment of truthful pain and love with the literal man of my dreams, the father of my child, because I didn't want to look too keen. Because I hadn't yet realised that everything I thought was real was fairy tales and everything I thought was fairy tales is actually what's real. Because it took living through the end of the world to realise that the end of the world is nothing compared to just the world.

Because the thing about the end of the world is that it happens all the time. Something gets lost and it's the end of the world. Something's found and it's the end of the world. Someone leaves and it's the end of the world. Someone comes back and it's the end of the world. Somebody puts their cock in you and it's the end of the world. Somebody stops putting their cock in you and it's the end of the world. You swallow something and it's the end of the world. Something swallows you and it's the end of the world. Someone wakes you and it's the end of the world. Someone lets you sleep and it's the end of the world. Somebody comes in you and it's the end of the world. Somebody comes out of you and it's the end of the world. Every second, every millisecond, the world is ending. As it always has and as it always will: it was in the beginning, is now, and ever shall be, the end of the world. For all time to come.